ALL THE
MOWGLI STORIES

ALL THE
MOWGLI STORIES

BY
RUDYARD KIPLING

MACMILLAN
ST MARTIN'S PRESS

SBN 333 01437 5

First published 1933
First issued in this format 1961
Reprinted 1962
Reprinted in Pocket Papermacs 1968, 1971, 1973, 1976, 1977

Published by
MACMILLAN LONDON LTD
London and Basingstoke
Associated companies in New York
Dublin Melbourne Johannesburg and Delhi

Printed in Great Britain by
BILLING & SONS, LIMITED
Guildford, London and Worcester

CONTENTS

HOW TO SAY THE NAMES IN THIS BOOK

Akela — A-*kay*-la.
Bagheera — Bag-eera (same as an 'era' in history).
Baloo — *Bar*-loo.
Bandar-log — Bunder-logue.
Buldeo — *Bul*-doo.
Chil — Cheel.
Dhole — Dole.
Ferao — Feer-ow.
Hathi — Huttee.
Kaa — Kar, with a sort of gasp in it.
Khanhiwara — Karny-warra.
Messua — *Mes*-war.
Mowgli — Mow rhymes with *cow*.
Mysa — *Mi*-sar.
Nathoo — *Nut*-too.
Nilghai — *Neel*-guy.
Phaona — Fay-*own*a.
Raksha — *Ruck*sher.
Rama — *Rar*-ma.
Sambhur — *Sarm*-ber.
Seeonee — See-*own*-ee.
Shere Khan — Sheer Karn.
Tabaqui — Ta-*bar*-kee.
Tha — Thar.
Waingunga — *Wine*-gunga.
Won-tolla — Woon-toller.

MOWGLI'S BROTHERS

Now Chil the Kite brings home the night
    That Mang the Bat sets free —
The herds are shut in byre and hut,
    For loosed till dawn are we.
This is the hour of pride and power,
    Talon and tush and claw.
Oh, hear the call! — Good hunting all
    That keep the Jungle Law!
              Night-Song in the Jungle.

IT was seven o'clock of a very warm evening in the Seeonee hills when Father Wolf woke up from his day's rest, scratched himself, yawned, and spread out his paws one after the other to get rid of the sleepy feeling in their tips. Mother Wolf lay with her big gray nose dropped across her four tumbling, squealing cubs, and the moon shone into the mouth of the cave where they all lived. 'Augrh!' said Father Wolf, 'it is time to hunt again'; and he was going to spring down-hill when a little shadow with a bushy tail crossed the threshold and whined: 'Good luck go with you, O Chief of the Wolves; and good luck and strong white teeth go with the noble children, that they may never forget the hungry in this world.'

It was the jackal — Tabaqui, the Dish-licker — and the wolves of India despise Tabaqui because he runs about making mischief, and telling tales, and eating rags and pieces of leather from the village rubbish-heaps. But they are afraid of him too, because Tabaqui, more than anyone else in the Jungle, is apt to to go mad, and then he forgets that he was ever afraid of any one, and runs through the forest biting everything in his way. Even the tiger runs and hides when little Tabaqui goes mad, for madness is the most disgraceful thing that can overtake a wild creature. We call it hydrophobia, but they call it *dewanee* — the madness — and run.

7

'Enter, then, and look,' said Father Wolf, stiffly; 'but there is no food here.'

'For a wolf, no,' said Tabaqui; 'but for so mean a person as myself a dry bone is a good feast. Who are we, the *Gidur-log* [the Jackal-People], to pick and choose?' He scuttled to the back of the cave, where he found the bone of a buck with some meat on it, and sat cracking the end merrily.

'All thanks for this good meal,' he said, licking his lips. 'How beautiful are the noble children! How large are their eyes! And so young too! Indeed, indeed, I might have remembered that the children of Kings are men from the beginning.'

Now, Tabaqui knew as well as any one else that there is nothing so unlucky as to compliment children to their faces; and it pleased him to see Mother and Father Wolf look uncomfortable.

Tabaqui sat still, rejoicing in the mischief that he had made: then he said spitefully:

'Shere Khan, the Big One, has shifted his hunting-grounds. He will hunt among these hills for the next moon, so he has told told me.'

Shere Khan was the tiger who lived near the Waingunga River, twenty miles away.

'He has no right!' Father Wolf began angrily — 'By the Law of the Jungle he has no right to change his quarters without due warning. He will frighten every head of game within ten miles, and I — I have to kill for two, these days.'

'His mother did not call him Lungri [the Lame One] for nothing,' said Mother Wolf, quietly. 'He has been lame in one foot from his birth. That is why he has only killed cattle. Now the villagers of the Waingunga are angry with him, and he has come here to make *our* villagers angry. They will scour the Jungle for him when he is far away, and we and our children must run when the grass is set alight. Indeed, we are very grateful to Shere Khan!'

'Shall I tell him of your gratitude?' said Tabaqui.

'Out!' snapped Father Wolf. 'Out and hunt with thy master. Thou hast done harm enough for one night.'

'I go,' said Tabaqui, quietly. 'Ye can hear Shere Khan below in the thickets. I might have saved myself the message.'

Father Wolf listened, and below in the valley that ran down to a little river, he heard the dry, angry, snarly, singsong whine of a tiger who has caught nothing and does not care if all the Jungle knows it.

'The fool!' said Father Wolf. 'To begin a night's work with that noise! Does he think that our buck are like his fat Waingunga bullocks?'

'H'sh! It is neither bullock nor buck he hunts to-night,' said Mother Wolf. 'It is Man.' The whine had changed to a sort of humming purr that seemed to come from every quarter of the compass. It was the noise that bewilders woodcutters and gipsies sleeping in the open, and makes them run sometimes into the very mouth of the tiger.

'Man!' said Father Wolf, showing all his white teeth. 'Faugh! Are there not enough beetles and frogs in the tanks that he must eat Man, and on our ground too!'

The Law of the Jungle, which never orders anything without a reason, forbids every beast to eat Man, except when he is killing to show his children how to kill, and then he must hunt outside the hunting-grounds of his pack or tribe. The real reason for this is that man-killing means, sooner or later, the arrival of white men on elephants, with guns, and hundreds of brown men with gongs and rockets and torches. Then everybody in the Jungle suffers. The reason the beasts give among themselves is that Man is the weakest and most defenceless of all living things, and it is unsportsmanlike to touch him. They say too — and it is true — that man-eaters become mangy, and lose their teeth.

The purr grew louder, and ended in the full-throated 'Aaarh!' of the tiger's charge.

Then there was a howl — an untigerish howl — from Shere Khan. 'He has missed,' said Mother Wolf. 'What is it?'

Father Wolf ran out a few paces and heard Shere Khan muttering and mumbling savagely, as he tumbled about in the scrub.

'The fool has had no more sense than to jump at a woodcutter's camp-fire, and has burned his feet,' said Father Wolf, with a grunt. 'Tabaqui is with him.'

'Something is coming up hill,' said Mother Wolf, twitching one ear. 'Get ready.'

The bushes rustled a little in the thicket, and Father Wolf dropped with his haunches under him, ready for his leap. Then, if you had been watching, you would have seen the most wonderful thing in the world — the wolf checked in mid-spring. He made his bound before he saw what it was he was jumping at, and then tried to stop himself. The result was that he shot up straight into the air for four or five feet, landing almost where he left ground.

'Man!' he snapped. 'A man's cub. Look!'

Directly in front of him, holding on by a low branch, stood a naked brown baby who could just walk — as soft and as dimpled a little atom as ever came to a wolf's cave at night. He looked up into Father Wolf's face, and laughed.

'Is that a man's cub?' said Mother Wolf. 'I have never seen one. Bring it here.'

A wolf accustomed to moving his own cubs can, if necessary, mouth an egg without breaking it, and though Father Wolf's jaws closed right on the child's back not a tooth even scratched the skin, as he laid it down among the cubs.

'How little! How naked, and — how bold!' said Mother Wolf, softly. The baby was pushing his way between the cubs to get close to the warm hide. '*Ahai!* He is taking his meal with the others. And so this is a man's cub. Now, was there ever a wolf that could boast of a man's cub among her children?'

'I have heard now and again of such a thing, but never in

our Pack or in my time,' said Father Wolf. 'He is altogether
without hair, and I could kill him with a touch of my foot. But
see, he looks up and is not afraid.'

The moonlight was blocked out of the mouth of the cave,
for Shere Khan's great square head and shoulders were thrust
into the entrance. Tabaqui, behind him, was squeaking: 'My
lord, my lord, it went in here!'

'Shere Khan does us great honour,' said Father Wolf, but
his eyes were very angry. 'What does Shere Khan need?'

'My quarry. A man's cub went this way,' said Shere Khan.
'Its parents have run off. Give it to me.'

Shere Khan had jumped at a woodcutter's camp-fire, as
Father Wolf had said, and was furious from the pain of his
burned foot. But Father Wolf knew that the mouth of the cave
was too narrow for a tiger to come in by. Even where he was,
Shere Khan's shoulders and fore-paws were cramped for want
of room, as a man's would be if he tried to fight in a barrel.

'The Wolves are a free people,' said Father Wolf. 'They take
orders from the Head of the Pack, and not from any striped
cattle-killer. The man's cub is ours — to kill if we choose.'

'Ye choose and ye do not choose! What talk is this of choos-
ing? By the bull that I killed, am I to stand nosing into your
dog's den for my fair dues? It is I, Shere Khan, who speak!'

The tiger's roar filled the cave with thunder. Mother Wolf
shook herself clear of the cubs and sprang forward, her eyes,
like two green moons in the darkness, facing the blazing eyes
of Shere Khan.

'And it is I, Raksha [The Demon], who answer. The man's
cub is mine, Lungri — mine to me! He shall not be killed. He
shall live to run with the Pack and to hunt with the Pack; and
in the end, look you, hunter of little naked cubs — frog-eater
— fish-killer — he shall hunt *thee*! Now get hence, or by the
Sambhur that I killed (*I* eat no starved cattle), back thou goest
to thy mother, burned beast of the Jungle, lamer than ever thou
camest into the world! Go!'

Father Wolf looked on amazed. He had almost forgotten the days when he won Mother Wolf in fair fight from five other wolves, when she ran in the Pack and was not called The Demon for compliment's sake. Shere Khan might have faced Father Wolf, but he could not stand up against Mother Wolf, for he knew that where he was she had all the advantage of the ground, and would fight to the death. So he backed out of the cave-mouth growling, and when he was clear he shouted:

'Each dog barks in his own yard! We will see what the Pack will say to this fostering of man-cubs. The cub is mine, and to my teeth he will come in the end, O bush-tailed thieves!'

Mother Wolf threw herself down panting among the cubs, and Father Wolf said to her gravely:

'Shere Khan speaks this much truth. The cub must be shown to the Pack. Wilt thou still keep him, Mother?'

'Keep him!' she gasped. 'He came naked, by night, alone and very hungry; yet he was not afraid! Look, he has pushed one of my babes to one side already. And that lame butcher would have killed him and would have run off to the Waingunga while the villagers here hunted through all our lairs in revenge! Keep him? Assuredly I will keep him. Lie still, little frog. O thou Mowgli — for Mowgli the Frog I will call thee — the time will come when thou wilt hunt Shere Khan as he has hunted thee.'

'But what will our Pack say?' said Father Wolf.

The Law of the Jungle lays down very clearly that any wolf may, when he marries, withdraw from the Pack he belongs to; but as soon as his cubs are old enough to stand on their feet he must bring them to the Pack Council, which is generally held once a month at full moon, in order that the other wolves may identify them. After that inspection the cubs are free to run where they please, and until they have killed their first buck no excuse is accepted if a grown wolf of the Pack kills one of them. The punishment is death where the murderer can be found; and if you think for a minute you will see that this must be so.

Father Wolf waited till his cubs could run a little, and then on the night of the Pack Meeting took them and Mowgli and Mother Wolf to the Council Rock — a hilltop covered with stones and boulders where a hundred wolves could hide. Akela, the great gray Lone Wolf, who led all the Pack by strength and cunning, lay out at full length on his rock, and below him sat forty or more wolves of every size and colour, from badger-coloured veterans who could handle a buck alone, to young black three-year-olds who thought they could. The Lone Wolf had led them for a year now. He had fallen twice into a wolf-trap in his youth, and once he had been beaten and left for dead; so he knew the manners and customs of men. There was very little talking at the Rock. The cubs tumbled over each other in the centre of the circle where their mothers and fathers sat, and now and again a senior wolf would go quietly up to a cub, look at him carefully, and return to his place on noiseless feet. Sometimes a mother would push her cub far out into the moonlight, to be sure that he had not been overlooked. Akela from his rock would cry: 'Ye know the Law — ye know the Law. Look well, O Wolves!' and the anxious mothers would take up the call: 'Look — look well, O Wolves!'

At last — and Mother Wolf's neck-bristles lifted as the time came — Father Wolf pushed 'Mowgli the Frog', as they called him, into the centre, where he sat laughing and playing with some pebbles that glistened in the moonlight.

Akela never raised his head from his paws, but went on with the monotonous cry: 'Look well!' A muffled roar came up from behind the rocks — the voice of Shere Khan crying: 'The cub is mine. Give him to me. What have the Free People to do with a man's cub?' Akela never even twitched his ears: all he said was: 'Look well, O Wolves! What have the Free People to do with the orders of any save the Free People? Look well!'

There was a chorus of deep growls, and a young wolf in his fourth year flung back Shere Khan's question to Akela: 'What

have the Free People to do with a man's cub?' Now the Law of
the Jungle lays down that if there is any dispute as to the right
of a cub to be accepted by the Pack, he must be spoken for by
at least two members of the Pack who are not his father and
mother.

'Who speaks for this cub?' said Akela. 'Among the Free
People who speaks?' There was no answer, and Mother Wolf
got ready for what she knew would be her last fight, if things
came to fighting.

Then the only other creature who is allowed at the Pack
Council—Baloo, the sleepy brown bear who teaches the wolf-
cubs the Law of the Jungle: old Baloo, who can come and go
where he pleases because he eats only nuts and roots and honey
—rose up on his hindquarters and grunted.

'The man's cub — the man's cub?' he said. '*I* speak for the
man's cub. There is no harm in a man's cub. I have no gift of
words, but I speak the truth. Let him run with the Pack, and be
entered with the others. I myself will teach him.'

'We need yet another,' said Akela. 'Baloo has spoken, and
he is our teacher for the young cubs. Who speaks besides
Baloo?'

A black shadow dropped down into the circle. It was Bagheera the Black Panther, inky black all over, but with the panther markings showing up in certain lights like the pattern of
watered silk. Everybody knew Bagheera, and nobody cared to
cross his path; for he was as cunning as Tabaqui, as bold as the
wild buffalo, and as reckless as the wounded elephant. But he
had a voice as soft as wild honey dripping from a tree, and a
skin softer than down.

'O Akela, and ye the Free People,' he purred, 'I have no
right in your assembly; but the Law of the Jungle says that if
there is a doubt which is not a killing matter in regard to a new
cub, the life of that cub may be bought at a price. And the Law
does not say who may or may not pay that price. Am I right?'

'Good! good!' said the young wolves, who are always hungry. 'Listen to Bagheera. The cub can be bought for a price. It is the Law.'

'Knowing that I have no right to speak here, I ask your leave.'

'Speak then,' cried twenty voices.

'To kill a naked cub is shame. Besides, he may make better sport for you when he is grown. Baloo has spoken in his behalf. Now to Baloo's word I will add one bull, and a fat one, newly killed, not half a mile from here, if ye will accept the man's cub according to the Law. Is it difficult?'

There was a clamour of scores of voices, saying: 'What matter? He will die in the winter rains. He will scorch in the sun. What harm can a naked frog do us? Let him run with the Pack. Where is the bull, Bagheera? Let him be accepted.' And then came Akela's deep bay, crying: 'Look well—look well, O Wolves!'

Mowgli was still deeply interested in the pebbles, and he did not notice when the wolves came and looked at him one by one. At last they all went down the hill for the dead bull, and only Akela, Bagheera, Baloo, and Mowgli's own wolves were left. Shere Khan roared still in the night, for he was very angry that Mowgli had not been handed over to him.

'Ay, roar well,' said Bagheera, under his whiskers; 'for the time comes when this naked thing will make thee roar to another tune, or I know nothing of Man.'

'It was well done,' said Akela. 'Men and their cubs are very wise. He may be a help in time.'

'Truly, a help in time of need; for none can hope to lead the Pack for ever,' said Bagheera.

Akela said nothing. He was thinking of the time that comes to every leader of every pack when his strength goes from him and he gets feebler and feebler, till at last he is killed by the wolves and a new leader comes up — to be killed in his turn.

'Take him away,' he said to Father Wolf, 'and train him as befits one of the Free People.'

And that is how Mowgli was entered into the Seeonee wolf-pack at the price of a bull and on Baloo's good word.

. . . . .

Now you must be content to skip ten or eleven whole years, and only guess at all the wonderful life that Mowgli led among the wolves, because if it were written out it would fill ever so many books. He grew up with the cubs, though they, of course, were grown wolves almost before he was a child, and Father Wolf taught him his business, and the meaning of things in the Jungle, till every rustle in the grass, every breath of the warm night air, every note of the owls above his head, every scratch of a bat's claws as it roosted for a while in a tree, and every splash of every little fish jumping in a pool, meant just as much to him as the work of his office means to a business man. When he was not learning, he sat out in the sun and slept, and ate and went to sleep again; when he felt dirty or hot he swam in the forest pools; and when he wanted honey (Baloo told him that honey and nuts were just as pleasant to eat as raw meat) he climbed up for it, and that Bagheera showed him how to do. Bagheera would lie out on a branch and call, 'Come along, Little Brother', and at first Mowgli would cling like the sloth, but afterwards he would fling himself through the branches almost as boldly as the gray ape. He took his place at the Council Rock, too, when the Pack met, and there he discovered that if he stared hard at any wolf, the wolf would be forced to drop his eyes, and so he used to stare for fun. At other times he would pick the long thorns out of the pads of his friends, for wolves suffer terribly from thorns and burrs in their coats. He would go down the hillside into the cultivated lands by night, and look very curiously at the villagers in their huts, but he had a mistrust of men because Bagheera showed him a square box with a drop-gate so cunningly hidden in the Jungle that he nearly walked into it, and told him that it was a trap. He loved better than anything else to go with Bagheera into the dark warm heart of the forest, to sleep all through the drowsy day, and at night to see how Bagheera did his killing. Bagheera killed right and left as he felt hungry, and so did Mowgli — with one exception. As soon as he was old enough to understand things, Bagheera told him that he must never touch cattle because he had been bought into the Pack at the price of a bull's life. 'All the Jungle is thine,' said Bagheera, 'and thou canst kill everything that thou art strong enough to kill; but for the sake of the bull that bought thee thou must never kill or eat any cattle, young or old. That is the Law of the Jungle.' Mowgli obeyed faithfully.

And he grew and grew strong as a boy must grow who does not know that he is learning any lessons, and who has nothing in the world to think of except things to eat.

Mother Wolf told him once or twice that Shere Khan was not a creature to be trusted, and that some day he must kill Shere Khan; but though a young wolf would have remembered that advice every hour, Mowgli forgot it because he was only a boy — though he would have called himself a wolf if he had been able to speak in any human tongue.

Shere Khan was always crossing his path in the Jungle, for as Akela grew older and feebler the lame tiger had come to be great friends with the younger wolves of the Pack, who followed him for scraps, a thing that Akela would never have allowed if he had dared to push his authority to the proper bounds. Then Shere Khan would flatter them and wonder that such fine young hunters were content to be led by a dying wolf and a man's cub. 'They tell me,' Shere Khan would say, 'that at Council ye dare not look him between the eyes'; and the young wolves would growl and bristle.

Bagheera, who had eyes and ears everywhere, knew something of this, and once or twice he told Mowgli in so many words that Shere Khan would kill him some day; and Mowgli would laugh and answer: 'I have the Pack and I have thee; and Baloo, though he is so lazy, might strike a blow or two for my sake. Why should I be afraid?'

It was one very warm day that a new notion came to Bagheera — born of something that he had heard. Perhaps Ikki the Porcupine had told him; but he said to Mowgli when they were deep in the Jungle, as the boy lay with his head on Bagheera's beautiful black skin: 'Little Brother, how often have I told thee that Shere Khan is thy enemy?'

'As many times as there are nuts on that palm,' said Mowgli, who, naturally, could not count. 'What of it? I am sleepy, Bagheera, and Shere Khan is all long tail and loud talk — like Mao, the Peacock.'

'But this is no time for sleeping. Baloo knows it; I know it; the Pack know it; and even the foolish, foolish deer know. Tabaqui has told thee, too.'

'Ho! ho!' said Mowgli. 'Tabaqui came to me not long ago with some rude talk that I was a naked man's cub and not fit to dig pig-nuts; but I caught Tabaqui by the tail and swung him twice against a palm-tree to teach him better manners.'

'That was foolishness; for though Tabaqui is a mischief-maker, he would have told thee of something that concerned thee closely. Open those eyes, Little Brother. Shere Khan dare not kill thee in the Jungle; but remember, Akela is very old, and soon the day comes when he cannot kill his buck, and then he will be leader no more. Many of the wolves that looked thee over when thou wast brought to the Council first are old too, and the young wolves believe, as Shere Khan has taught them, that a man-cub has no place with the Pack. In a little time thou wilt be a man.'

'And what is a man that he should not run with his brothers?' said Mowgli. 'I was born in the Jungle. I have obeyed the Law of the Jungle, and there is no wolf of ours from whose paws I have not pulled a thorn. Surely they are my brothers!'

Bagheera stretched himself at full length, and half shut his eyes. 'Little Brother,' said he, 'feel under my jaw.'

Mowgli put up his strong brown hand, and just under Bagheera's silky chin, where the giant rolling muscles were all hid by the glossy hair, he came upon a little bald spot.

'There is no one in the Jungle that knows that I, Bagheera, carry that mark — the mark of the collar; and yet, Little Brother, I was born among men, and it was among men that my mother died — in the cages of the King's Palace at Oodeypore. It was because of this that I paid the price for thee at the Council when thou wast a little naked cub. Yes, I too was born among men. I had never seen the Jungle. They fed me behind bars from an iron pan till one night I felt that I was Bagheera — the Panther — and no man's plaything, and I broke the silly lock with one blow of my paw and came away; and because I had learned the ways of men, I became more terrible in the Jungle than Shere Khan. Is it not so?'

'Yes,' said Mowgli; 'all the Jungle fear Bagheera — all except Mowgli.'

'Oh, *thou* art a man's cub,' said the Black Panther, very tenderly; 'and even as I returned to my Jungle, so thou must go back to men at last — to the men who are thy brothers — if thou art not killed in the Council.'

'But why — but why should any wish to kill me?' said Mowgli.

'Look at me,' said Bagheera; and Mowgli looked at him steadily between the eyes. The big panther turned his head away in half a minute.

'*That* is why,' he said, shifting his paw on the leaves. 'Not even I can look thee between the eyes, and I was born among men, and I love thee, Little Brother. The others they hate thee because their eyes cannot meet thine — because thou art wise — because thou hast pulled out thorns from their feet — because thou art a man.'

'I did not know these things,' said Mowgli, sullenly; and he frowned under his heavy black eyebrows.

'What is the Law of the Jungle? Strike first and then give tongue. By thy very carelessness they know that thou art a man. But be wise. It is in my heart that when Akela misses his next kill, — and at each hunt it costs him more to pin the buck, — the Pack will turn against him and against thee. They will hold a Jungle Council at the Rock, and then — and then — I have it!' said Bagheera, leaping up. 'Go thou down quickly to the men's huts in the valley, and take some of the Red Flower which they grow there, so that when the time comes thou mayest have even a stronger friend than I or Baloo or those of the Pack that love thee. Get the Red Flower.'

By Red Flower Bagheera meant fire, only no creature in the Jungle will call fire by its proper name. Every beast lives in deadly fear of it, and invents a hundred ways of describing it.

'The Red Flower?' said Mowgli. 'That grows outside their huts in the twilight. I will get some.'

'There speaks the man's cub,' said Bagheera, proudly. 'Remember that it grows in little pots. Get one swiftly, and keep it by thee for time of need.'

'Good!' said Mowgli. 'I go. But art thou sure, O my Bagheera' — he slipped his arm round the splendid neck, and looked deep into the big eyes — 'art thou sure that all this is Shere Khan's doing?'

'By the Broken Lock that freed me, I am sure, Little Brother.'

'Then, by the Bull that bought me, I will pay Shere Khan full tale for this, and it may be a little over,' said Mowgli; and he bounded away.

'That is a man. That is all a man,' said Bagheera to himself, lying down again. 'Oh, Shere Khan, never was a blacker hunting than that frog-hunt of thine ten years ago!'

Mowgli was far and far through the forest, running hard, and his heart was hot in him. He came to the cave as the evening mist rose, and drew breath, and looked down the valley. The cubs were out, but Mother Wolf, at the back of the cave, knew by his breathing that something was troubling her frog.

'What is it, Son?' she said.

'Some bat's chatter of Shere Khan,' he called back. 'I hunt among the ploughed fields to-night,' and he plunged downward through the bushes, to the stream at the bottom of the valley. There he checked, for he heard the yell of the Pack hunting, heard the bellow of a hunted sambhur, and the snort as the buck turned at bay. Then there were wicked, bitter howls from the young wolves: 'Akela! Akela! Let the Lone Wolf show his strength. Room for the leader of the Pack! Spring, Akela!'

The Lone Wolf must have sprung and missed his hold, for Mowgli heard the snap of his teeth and then a yelp as the sambhur knocked him over with his fore-foot.

He did not wait for anything more, but dashed on; and the yells grew fainter behind him as he ran into the crop-lands where the villagers lived.

'Bagheera spoke truth,' he panted, as he nestled down in some cattle-fodder by the window of a hut. 'To-morrow is one day both for Akela and for me.'

Then he pressed his face close to the window and watched the fire on the hearth. He saw the husbandman's wife get up and feed it in the night with black lumps; and when the morning came and the mists were all white and cold, he saw the man's child pick up a wicker pot plastered inside with earth, fill it with lumps of red-hot charcoal, put it under his blanket, and go out to tend the cows in the byre.

'Is that all?' said Mowgli. 'If a cub can do it, there is nothing to fear'; so he strode round the corner and met the boy, took the pot from his hand, and disappeared into the mist while the boy howled with fear.

'They are very like me,' said Mowgli, blowing into the pot, as he had seen the woman do. 'This thing will die if I do not give it things to eat'; and he dropped twigs and dried bark on the red stuff. Half-way up the hill he met Bagheera with the morning dew shining like moonstones on his coat.

'Akela has missed,' said the Panther. 'They would have

killed him last night, but they need thee also. They were looking for thee on the hill.'

'I was among the ploughed lands. I am ready. See!' Mowgli held up the fire-pot.

'Good! Now, I have seen men thrust a dry branch into that stuff, and presently the Red Flower blossomed at the end of it. Art thou not afraid?'

'No. Why should I fear? I remember now — if it is not a dream — how, before I was a Wolf, I lay beside the Red Flower, and it was warm and pleasant.'

All that day Mowgli sat in the cave tending his fire-pot and dipping dry branches into it to see how they looked. He found a branch that satisfied him, and in the evening when Tabaqui came to the cave and told him rudely enough that he was wanted at the Council Rock, he laughed till Tabaqui ran away. Then Mowgli went to the Council, still laughing.

Akela the Lone Wolf lay by the side of his rock as a sign that the leadership of the Pack was open, and Shere Khan with his following of scrap-fed wolves walked to and fro openly, being flattered. Bagheera lay close to Mowgli, and the fire-pot was between Mowgli's knees. When they were all gathered together, Shere Khan began to speak — a thing he would never have dared to do when Akela was in his prime.

'He has no right,' whispered Bagheera. 'Say so. He is a dog's son. He will be frightened.'

Mowgli sprang to his feet. 'Free People,' he cried, 'does Shere Khan lead the Pack? What has a tiger to do with our leadership?'

'Seeing that the leadership is yet open, and being asked to speak ——' Shere Khan began.

'By whom?' said Mowgli. 'Are we *all* jackals, to fawn on this cattle-butcher? The leadership of the Pack is with the Pack alone.'

There were yells of 'Silence, thou man's cub!' 'Let him speak. He has kept our Law'; and at last the seniors of the

Pack thundered: 'Let the Dead Wolf speak.' When a leader of the Pack has missed his kill, he is called the Dead Wolf as long as he lives, which is not long, as a rule.

Akela raised his old head wearily: —

'Free People, and ye too, jackals of Shere Khan, for many seasons I have led ye to and from the kill, and in all my time not one has been trapped or maimed. Now I have missed my kill. Ye know how that plot was made. Ye know how ye brought me up to an untried buck to make my weakness known. It was cleverly done. Your right is to kill me here on the Council Rock now. Therefore, I ask, who comes to make an end of the Lone Wolf? For it is my right, by the Law of the Jungle, that ye come one by one.'

There was a long hush, for no single wolf cared to fight Akela to the death. Then Shere Khan roared: 'Bah! what have we to do with this toothless fool? He is doomed to die! It is the Man-cub who has lived too long. Free People, he was my meat from the first. Give him to me. I am weary of this man-wolf folly. He has troubled the Jungle for ten seasons. Give me the Man-cub, or I will hunt here always, and not give you one bone. He is a man, a man's child, and from the marrow of my bones I hate him!'

Then more than half the Pack yelled: 'A man! a man! What has a man to do with us? Let him go to his own place.'

'And turn all the people of the villages against us?' clamoured Shere Khan. 'No; give him to me. He is a man, and none of us can look him between the eyes.'

Akela lifted his head again, and said: 'He has eaten our food. He has slept with us. He has driven game for us. He has broken no word of the Law of the Jungle.'

'Also, I paid for him with a bull when he was accepted. The worth of a bull is little, but Bagheera's honour is something that he will perhaps fight for,' said Bagheera, in his gentlest voice.

'A bull paid ten years ago!' the Pack snarled. 'What do we care for bones ten years old?'

'Or for a pledge?' said Bagheera, his white teeth bared under his lip. 'Well are ye called the Free People!'

'No man's cub can run with the people of the Jungle,' howled Shere Khan. 'Give him to me!'

'He is our brother in all but blood,' Akela went on; 'and ye would kill him here! In truth, I have lived too long. Some of ye are eaters of cattle, and of others I have heard that, under Shere Khan's teaching, ye go by dark night and snatch children from the villager's door-step. Therefore I know ye to be cowards, and it is to cowards I speak. It is certain that I must die, and my life is of no worth, or I would offer that in the Man-cub's place. But for the sake of the Honour of the Pack, — a little matter that by being without a leader ye have forgotten, — I promise that if ye let the Man-cub go to his own place, I will not, when my time comes to die, bare one tooth against ye. I will die without fighting. That will at least save the Pack three lives. More I cannot do; but if ye will, I can save ye the shame that comes of killing a brother against whom there is no fault, — a brother spoken for and bought into the Pack according to the Law of the Jungle.'

'He is a man — a man — a man!' snarled the Pack; and most of the wolves began to gather round Shere Khan, whose tail was beginning to switch.

'Now the business is in thy hands,' said Bagheera to Mowgli. '*We* can do no more except fight.'

Mowgli stood upright — the fire-pot in his hands. Then he stretched out his arms, and yawned in the face of the Council; but he was furious with rage and sorrow, for, wolf-like, the wolves had never told him how they hated him. 'Listen, you!' he cried. 'There is no need for this dog's jabber. Ye have told me so often to-night that I am a man (and indeed I would have been a wolf with you to my life's end), that I feel your words are true. So I do not call ye my brothers any more, but *sag* [dogs], as a man should. What ye will do, and what ye will not do, is not yours to say. That matter is with *me*; and that we may see the matter more plainly, I, the man, have brought here a little of the Red Flower, which ye, dogs, fear.'

He flung the fire-pot on the ground, and some of the red coals lit a tuft of dried moss that flared up, as all the Council drew back in terror before the leaping flames.

Mowgli thrust his dead branch into the fire till the twigs lit and crackled, and whirled it above his head among the cowering wolves.

'Thou art the master,' said Bagheera, in an undertone. 'Save Akela from the death. He was ever thy friend.'

Akela, the grim old wolf who had never asked for mercy in his life, gave one piteous look at Mowgli as the boy stood all naked, his long black hair tossing over his shoulders in the light of the blazing branch that made the shadows jump and quiver.

'Good!' said Mowgli, staring round slowly. 'I see that ye are dogs. I go from you to my own people — if they be my own people. The Jungle is shut to me, and I must forget your talk, and your companionship; but I will be more merciful than ye are. Because I was all but your brother in blood, I promise that when I am a man among men I will not betray ye to men as ye have betrayed me.' He kicked the fire with his foot, and the sparks flew up. 'There shall be no war between any of us and the Pack. But here is a debt to pay before I go.' He strode forward to where Shere Khan sat blinking stupidly at the flames, and caught him by the tuft on his chin. Bagheera followed in case of accidents. 'Up, dog!' Mowgli cried. 'Up, when a man speaks, or I will set that coat ablaze!'

Shere Khan's ears lay flat back on his head, and he shut his eyes, for the blazing branch was very near.

'This cattle-killer said he would kill me in the Council because he had not killed me when I was a cub. Thus and thus, then, do we beat dogs when we are men. Stir a whisker, Lungri, and I ram the Red Flower down thy gullet!' He beat Shere Khan over the head with the branch, and the tiger whimpered and whined in an agony of fear.

'Pah! Singed jungle-cat — go now! But remember when next I come to the Council Rock, as a man should come, it will be with Shere Khan's hide on my head. For the rest, Akela goes free to live as he pleases. Ye will *not* kill him, because that is not my will. Nor do I think ye will sit here any longer, lolling out your tongues as though ye were somebodies, instead of dogs whom I drive out — thus! Go!' The fire was burning furiously at the end of the branch, and Mowgli struck right and left round the circle, and the wolves ran howling with the sparks burning their fur. At last there were only Akela, Bagheera, and perhaps ten wolves that had taken Mowgli's part. Then something began to hurt Mowgli inside him, as he had never been hurt in his life before, and he caught his breath and sobbed, and the tears ran down his face.

'What is it? What is it?' he said. 'I do not wish to leave the Jungle, and I do not know what this is. Am I dying, Bagheera?'

'No, Little Brother. Those are only tears such as men use,' said Bagheera. 'Now I know thou art a man, and a man's cub no longer. The Jungle is shut indeed to thee henceforward. Let them fall, Mowgli. They are only tears.' So Mowgli sat and cried as though his heart would break; and he had never cried in all his life before.

'Now,' he said, 'I will go to men. But first I must say farewell to my mother'; and he went to the cave where she lived with Father Wolf, and he cried on her coat, while the four cubs howled miserably.

'Ye will not forget me?' said Mowgli.

'Never while we can follow a trail,' said the cubs. 'Come to the foot of the hill when thou art a man, and we will talk to thee; and we will come into the crop-lands to play with thee by night.'

'Come soon!' said Father Wolf. 'Oh, wise little frog, come again soon; for we be old, thy mother and I.'

'Come soon,' said Mother Wolf, 'little naked son of mine;

for, listen, child of man, I loved thee more than ever I loved my cubs.'

'I will surely come,' said Mowgli; 'and when I come it will be to lay out Shere Khan's hide upon the Council Rock. Do not forget me! Tell them in the Jungle never to forget me!'

The dawn was beginning to break when Mowgli went down the hillside alone, to meet those mysterious things that are called men.

HUNTING-SONG OF THE SEEONEE PACK

As the dawn was breaking the Sambhur belled
    Once, twice and again!
And a doe leaped up, and a doe leaped up
From the pond in the wood where the wild deer sup.
This I, scouting alone, beheld,
    Once, twice and again!

As the dawn was breaking, the Sambhur belled
    Once, twice and again!
And a wolf stole back, and a wolf stole back
To carry the word to the waiting pack,
And we sought and we found and we bayed on his track
    Once, twice and again!

As the dawn was breaking the Wolf-Pack yelled
    Once, twice and again!
Feet in the Jungle that leave no mark!
Eyes that can see in the dark — the dark!
Tongue — give tongue to it! Hark! O hark!
    Once, twice and again!

KAA'S HUNTING

His spots are the joy of the Leopard: his horns are the Buffalo's pride.
Be clean, for the strength of the hunter is known by the gloss of his hide.
If ye find that the bullock can toss you, or the heavy-browed Sambhur can
    gore,
Ye need not stop work to inform us: we knew it ten seasons before.
Oppress not the cubs of the stranger, but hail them as Sister and Brother,
For though they are little and fubsy, it may be the Bear is their mother.
'There is none like to me!' says the Cub in the pride of his earliest kill;
But the Jungle is large and the Cub he is small. Let him think and be still.

Maxims of Baloo.

ALL that is told here happened some time before Mowgli was
turned out of the Seeonee Wolf-Pack, or revenged himself on
Shere Khan the tiger. It was in the days when Baloo was teaching him the Law of the Jungle. The big, serious, old brown bear
was delighted to have so quick a pupil, for the young wolves
will only learn as much of the Law of the Jungle as applies to
their own pack and tribe, and run away as soon as they can repeat the Hunting Verse: — 'Feet that make no noise; eyes that
can see in the dark; ears that can hear the winds in their lairs,
and sharp white teeth, all these things are the marks of our
brothers except Tabaqui the Jackal and the Hyaena whom we
hate'. But Mowgli, as a Man-cub, had to learn a great deal more
than this. Sometimes Bagheera, the Black Panther, would come
lounging through the Jungle to see how his pet was getting on,
and would purr with his head against a tree while Mowgli recited the day's lesson to Baloo. The boy could climb almost as
well as he could swim, and swim almost as well as he could run;
so Baloo, the Teacher of the Law, taught him the Wood and
Water Laws: how to tell a rotten branch from a sound one;
how to speak politely to the wild bees when he came upon a
hive of them fifty feet above ground; what to say to Mang the
Bat when he disturbed him in the branches at mid-day; and

how to warn the water-snakes in the pools before he splashed down among them. None of the Jungle-People like being disturbed, and all are very ready to fly at an intruder. Then, too, Mowgli was taught the Stranger's Hunting Call, which must be repeated aloud till it is answered, whenever one of the Jungle-People hunts outside his own grounds. It means, translated: 'Give me leave to hunt here because I am hungry'; and the answer is: 'Hunt then for food, but not for pleasure'.

All this will show you how much Mowgli had to learn by heart, and he grew very tired of saying the same thing over a hundred times; but, as Baloo said to Bagheera, one day when Mowgli had been cuffed and run off in a temper: 'A Man-cub is a Man-cub, and he must learn *all* the Law of the Jungle.'

'But think how small he is,' said the Black Panther, who would have spoiled Mowgli if he had had his own way. 'How can his little head carry all thy long talk?'

'Is there anything in the Jungle too little to be killed? No. That is why I teach him these things, and that is why I hit him, very softly, when he forgets.'

'Softly! What dost thou know of softness, old Iron-feet?' Bagheera grunted. 'His face is all bruised to-day by thy — softness. Ugh!'

'Better he should be bruised from head to foot by me who love him than that he should come to harm through ignorance,' Baloo answered very earnestly. 'I am now teaching him the Master Words of the Jungle that shall protect him with the birds and the Snake-People, and all that hunt on four feet, except his own pack. He can now claim protection, if he will only remember the words, from all in the Jungle. Is not that worth a little beating?'

'Well, look to it then that thou dost not kill the Man-cub. He is no tree-trunk to sharpen thy blunt claws upon. But what are those Master Words? I am more likely to give help than to ask it' — Bagheera stretched out one paw and admired the steel-blue, ripping-chisel talons at the end of it — 'still I should like to know.'

'I will call Mowgli and he shall say them — if he will. Come, Little Brother!'

'My head is ringing like a bee-tree,' said a sullen little voice over their heads, and Mowgli slid down a tree-trunk very angry and indignant, adding as he reached the ground: 'I come for Bagheera and not for *thee*, fat old Baloo!'

'That is all one to me,' said Baloo, though he was hurt and grieved. 'Tell Bagheera, then, the Master Words of the Jungle that I have taught thee this day.'

'Master Words for which people?' said Mowgli, delighted to show off. 'The Jungle has many tongues. *I* know them all.'

'A little thou knowest, but not much. See, O Bagheera, they never thank their teacher. Not one small wolfling has ever come back to thank old Baloo for his teachings. Say the word for the Hunting-People, then — great scholar.'

'We be of one blood, ye and I,' said Mowgli, giving the words the Bear accent which all the Hunting-People use.

'Good. Now for the birds.'

Mowgli repeated, with the Kite's whistle at the end of the sentence.

'Now for the Snake-People,' said Bagheera.

The answer was a perfectly indescribable hiss, and Mowgli kicked up his feet behind, clapped his hands together to applaud himself, and jumped on to Bagheera's back, where he sat sideways, drumming with his heels on the glossy skin and making the worst faces he could think of at Baloo.

'There — there! That was worth a little bruise,' said the brown bear tenderly. 'Some day thou wilt remember me.' Then he turned aside to tell Bagheera how he had begged the Master Words from Hathi the Wild Elephant, who knows all about these things, and how Hathi had taken Mowgli down to a pool to get the Snake Word from a water-snake, because Baloo could not pronounce it, and how Mowgli was now reasonably safe against all accidents in the Jungle, because neither snake, bird, nor beast would hurt him.

'No one, then, is to be feared,' Baloo wound up, patting his big furry stomach with pride.

'Except his own tribe,' said Bagheera, under his breath; and then aloud to Mowgli: 'Have a care for my ribs, Little Brother! What is all this dancing up and down?'

Mowgli had been trying to make himself heard by pulling at Bagheera's shoulder-fur and kicking hard. When the two listened to him he was shouting at the top of his voice: 'And so I shall have a tribe of my own, and lead them through the branches all day long.'

'What is this new folly, little dreamer of dreams?' said Bagheera.

'Yes, and throw branches and dirt at old Baloo,' Mowgli went on. 'They have promised me this. Ah!'

'*Whoof!*' Baloo's big paw scooped Mowgli off Bagheera's back, and as the boy lay between the big fore-paws he could see the Bear was angry.

'Mowgli,' said Baloo, 'thou hast been talking with the *Bandar-log* — the Monkey-People.'

Mowgli looked at Bagheera to see if the Panther was angry too, and Bagheera's eyes were as hard as jade-stones.

'Thou hast been with the Monkey-People — the gray apes — the people without a Law — the eaters of everything. That is great shame.'

'When Baloo hurt my head,' said Mowgli (he was still on his back), 'I went away, and the gray apes came down from the trees and had pity on me. No one else cared.' He snuffled a little.

'The pity of the Monkey-People!' Baloo snorted. 'The stillness of the mountain stream! The cool of the summer sun! And then, Man-cub?'

'And then, and then, they gave me nuts and pleasant things to eat, and they—they carried me in their arms up to the top of the trees and said I was their blood-brother except that I had no tail, and should be their leader some day.'

'They have *no* leader,' said Bagheera. 'They lie. They have always lied.'

'They were very kind and bade me come again. Why have I never been taken among the Monkey-People? They stood on their feet as I do. They do not hit me with hard paws. They play all day. Let me get up! Bad Baloo, let me up! I will play with them again.'

'Listen, Man-cub,' said the Bear, and his voice rumbled like thunder on a hot night. 'I have taught thee all the Law of the Jungle for all the peoples of the Jungle — except the Monkey-Folk who live in the trees. They have no Law. They are out-castes. They have no speech of their own, but use the stolen words which they overhear when they listen, and peep, and wait up above in the branches. Their way is not our way. They are without leaders. They have no remembrance. They boast and chatter and pretend that they are a great people about to do great affairs in the Jungle, but the falling of a nut turns their minds to laughter and all is forgotten. We of the Jungle have no dealings with them. We do not drink where the monkeys drink; we do not go where the monkeys go; we do not hunt where they hunt; we do not die where they die. Hast thou ever heard me speak of the *Bandar-log* till to-day?'

'No,' said Mowgli in a whisper, for the forest was very still now Baloo had finished.

'The Jungle-People put them out of their mouths and out of their minds. They are very many, evil, dirty, shameless, and they desire, if they have any fixed desire, to be noticed by the Jungle-People. But we do *not* notice them even when they throw nuts and filth on our heads.'

He had hardly spoken when a shower of nuts and twigs spat-tered down through the branches; and they could hear cough-ings and howlings and angry jumpings high up in the air among the thin branches.

'The Monkey-People are forbidden,' said Baloo. 'forbidden to the Jungle-People. Remember.'

'Forbidden,' said Bagheera; 'but I still think Baloo should have warned thee against them.'

'I — I? How was I to guess he would play with such dirt? The Monkey-People! Faugh!'

A fresh shower came down on their heads and the two trotted away, taking Mowgli with them. What Baloo had said about the monkeys was perfectly true. They belonged to the tree-tops, and as beasts very seldom look up, there was no occasion for the monkeys and the Jungle-People to cross each other's path. But whenever they found a sick wolf, or a wounded tiger, or bear, the monkeys would torment him, and would throw sticks and nuts at any beast for fun and in the hope of being noticed. Then they would howl and shriek senseless songs, and invite the Jungle-People to climb up their trees and fight them, or would start furious battles over nothing among themselves, and leave the dead monkeys where the Jungle-People could see them. They were always just going to have a leader, and laws and customs of their own, but they never did, because their memories would not hold over from day to day, and so they compromised things by making up a saying: 'What the *Bandar-log* think now the Jungle will think later', and that comforted them a great deal. None of the beasts could reach them, but on the other hand none of the beasts would notice them, and that was why they were so pleased when Mowgli came to play with them, and they heard how angry Baloo was.

They never meant to do any more — the *Bandar-log* never mean anything at all; but one of them invented what seemed to him a brilliant idea, and he told all the others that Mowgli would be a useful person to keep in the tribe, because he could weave sticks together for protection from the wind; so, if they caught him, they could make him teach them. Of course Mowgli, as a woodcutter's child, inherited all sorts of instincts, and used to make little huts of fallen branches without thinking how he came to do it, and the Monkey-People, watching in the trees, considered his play most wonderful. This time, they said, they were really going to have a leader and become the wisest people in the Jungle — so wise that every one else would notice and envy them. Therefore they followed Baloo and Bagheera and Mowgli through the Jungle very quietly till it was time for the mid-day nap, and Mowgli, who was very much ashamed of himself, slept between the Panther and the Bear, resolving to have no more to do with the Monkey-People.

The next thing he remembered was feeling hands on his legs and arms — hard, strong, little hands, and then a swash of branches in his face, and then he was staring down through the swaying boughs as Baloo woke the Jungle with his deep cries and Bagheera bounded up the trunk with every tooth bared. The *Bandar-log* howled with triumph and scuffled away to the upper branches where Bagheera dared not follow, shouting: 'He has noticed us! Bagheera has noticed us. All the Jungle-People admire us for our skill and our cunning.' Then they began their flight; and the flight of the Monkey-People through tree-land is one of the things nobody can describe. They have their regular roads and cross-roads, up hills and down hills, all laid out from fifty to seventy or a hundred feet above ground, and by these they can travel even at night if necessary. Two of the strongest monkeys caught Mowgli under the arms and swung off with him through the tree-tops, twenty feet at a bound. Had they been alone they could have gone twice as fast, but the boy's weight held them back. Sick and giddy as Mowgli was he could not help enjoying the wild rush, though the glimpses of earth far down below frightened him, and the terrible check and jerk at the end of the swing over nothing but empty air brought his heart between his teeth. His escort would rush him up a tree till he felt the thinnest topmost branches crackle and bend under them, and then with a cough and a whoop would fling themselves into the air outward and downward, and bring up, hanging by their hands or their feet to the lower limbs of the next tree. Sometimes he could see for miles and miles across the still green Jungle, as a man on the top of a mast can see for miles across the sea, and then the branches and leaves would lash him across the face, and he and his two guards would be almost down to earth again. So, bounding and crashing and whooping and yelling, the whole tribe of *Bandar-log* swept along the tree-roads with Mowgli their prisoner.

For a time he was afraid of being dropped: then he grew angry but knew better than to struggle, and then he began to think. The first thing was to send back word to Baloo and Bagheera, for, at the pace the monkeys were going, he knew his friends would be left far behind. It was useless to look down, for he could only see the top-sides of the branches, so he stared upward and saw, far away in the blue, Chil the Kite balancing and wheeling as he kept watch over the Jungle waiting for things to die. Chil saw that the monkeys were carrying something, and dropped a few hundred yards to find out whether their load was good to eat. He whistled with surprise when he saw Mowgli being dragged up to a tree-top and heard him give the Kite call for — 'We be of one blood, thou and I.' The waves of the branches closed over the boy, but Chil balanced away to the next tree in time to see the little brown face come up again. 'Mark my trail,' Mowgli shouted. 'Tell Baloo of the Seeonee Pack and Bagheera of the Council Rock.'

'In whose name, Brother?' Chil had never seen Mowgli before, though of course he had heard of him.

'Mowgli, the Frog. Man-cub they call me! Mark my tra-il!'

The last words were shrieked as he was being swung through the air, but Chil nodded and rose up till he looked no bigger than a speck of dust, and there he hung, watching with his telescope eyes the swaying of the tree-tops as Mowgli's escort whirled along.

'They never go far,' he said with a chuckle. 'They never do what they set out to do. Always pecking at new things are the

Bandar-log. This time, if I have any eyesight, they have pecked
down trouble for themselves, for Baloo is no fledgling and
Bagheera can, as I know, kill more than goats.'

So he rocked on his wings, his feet gathered up under him,
and waited.

Meantime, Baloo and Bagheera were furious with rage and
grief. Bagheera climbed as he had never climbed before, but the
thin branches broke under his weight, and he slipped down, his
claws full of bark.

'Why didst thou not warn the Man-cub?' he roared to poor
Baloo, who had set off at a clumsy trot in the hope of overtaking the monkeys. 'What was the use of half slaying him with
blows if thou didst not warn him?'

'Haste! Oh, haste! We — we may catch them yet!' Baloo
panted.

'At that speed! It would not tire a wounded cow. Teacher
of the Law — cub-beater — a mile of that rolling to and fro
would burst thee open. Sit still and think! Make a plan. This is
no time for chasing. They may drop him if we follow too close.'

'*Arrula! Whoo!* They may have dropped him already, being
tired of carrying him. Who can trust the *Bandar-log*? Put dead
bats on my head! Give me black bones to eat! Roll me into the
hives of the wild bees that I may be stung to death, and bury
me with the Hyaena, for I am the most miserable of bears!
Arulala! Wahooa! Oh, Mowgli, Mowgli! why did I not warn
thee against the Monkey-Folk instead of breaking thy head?
Now perhaps I may have knocked the day's lesson out of his
mind and he will be alone in the Jungle without the Master
Words.'

Baloo clasped his paws over his ears and rolled to and fro
moaning.

'At least he gave me all the Words correctly a little time ago,'
said Bagheera, impatiently. 'Baloo, thou hast neither memory
nor respect. What would the Jungle think if I, the Black Panther, curled myself up like Ikki the Porcupine, and howled?'

'What do I care what the Jungle thinks? He may be dead by now.'

'Unless and until they drop him from the branches in sport, or kill him out of idleness, I have no fear for the Man-cub. He is wise and well-taught, and above all he has the eyes that make the Jungle-People afraid. But (and it is a great evil) he is in the power of the *Bandar-log*, and they, because they live in trees, have no fear of any of our people.' Bagheera licked one fore-paw thoughtfully.

'Fool that I am! Oh, fat, brown, root-digging fool that I am,' said Baloo, uncurling himself with a jerk, 'it is true what Hathi the Wild Elephant says: "*To each his own fear*"; and they, the *Bandar-log*, fear Kaa the Rock Snake. He can climb as well as they can. He steals the young monkeys in the night. The whisper of his name makes their wicked tails cold. Let us go to Kaa.'

'What will he do for us? He is not of our tribe, being footless — and with most evil eyes,' said Bagheera.

'He is very old and very cunning. Above all, he is always hungry,' said Baloo hopefully. 'Promise him many goats.'

'He sleeps for a full month after he has once eaten. He may be asleep now, and even were he awake what if he would rather kill his own goats?' Bagheera, who did not know much about Kaa, was naturally suspicious.

'Then in that case, thou and I together, old hunter, might make him see reason.' Here Baloo rubbed his faded brown shoulder against the Panther, and they went off to look for Kaa the Rock Python.

They found him stretched out on a warm ledge in the afternoon sun, admiring his beautiful new coat, for he had been in retirement for the last ten days, changing his skin, and now he was very splendid — darting his big blunt-nosed head along the ground, and twisting the thirty feet of his body into fantastic knots and curves, and licking his lips as he thought of his dinner to come.

'He has not eaten,' said Baloo, with a grunt of relief, as soon as he saw the beautifully mottled brown and yellow jacket. 'Be careful, Bagheera! He is always a little blind after he has changed his skin, and very quick to strike.'

Kaa was not a poison-snake — in fact he rather despised the poison-snakes as cowards — but his strength lay in his hug, and when he had once lapped his huge coils round anybody there was no more to be said. 'Good hunting!' cried Baloo, sitting up on his haunches. Like all snakes of his breed, Kaa was rather deaf, and did not hear the call at first. Then he curled up ready for any accident, his head lowered.

'Good hunting for us all!' he answered. 'Oho, Baloo, what dost thou do here? Good hunting, Bagheera! One of us at least needs food. Is there any news of game afoot? A doe now, or even a young buck? I am as empty as a dried well.'

'We are hunting,' said Baloo carelessly. He knew that you must not hurry Kaa. He is too big.

'Give me permission to come with you,' said Kaa. 'A blow more or less is nothing to thee, Bagheera or Baloo, but I — I have to wait and wait for days in a wood-path and climb half a night on the mere chance of a young ape. Pss-haw! The branches are not what they were when I was young. Rotten twigs and dry boughs are they all.'

'Maybe thy great weight has something to do with the matter,' said Baloo.

'I am a fair length — a fair length,' said Kaa, with a little pride. 'But for all that, it is the fault of this new-grown timber. I came very near to falling on my last hunt — very near indeed — and the noise of my slipping, for my tail was not tight wrapped round the tree, waked the *Bandar-log*, and they called me most evil names.'

'Footless, yellow earth-worm,' said Bagheera under his whiskers, as though he were trying to remember something.

'Sssss! Have they ever called me *that*?' said Kaa.

'Something of that kind it was that they shouted to us last moon, but we never noticed them. They will say anything —

even that thou hast lost all thy teeth, and wilt not face anything bigger than a kid, because (they are indeed shameless, these *Bandar-log*) — because thou art afraid of the he-goat's horns,' Bagheera went on sweetly.

Now a snake, especially a wary old python like Kaa, very seldom shows that he is angry, but Baloo and Bagheera could see the big swallowing-muscles on either side of Kaa's throat ripple and bulge.

'The *Bandar-log* have shifted their grounds,' he said quietly. 'When I came up into the sun to-day I heard them whooping among the tree-tops.'

'It — it is the *Bandar-log* that we follow now,' said Baloo; but the words stuck in his throat, for that was the first time in his memory that one of the Jungle-People had owned to being interested in the doings of the monkeys.

'Beyond doubt then it is no small thing that takes two such hunters — leaders in their own Jungle I am certain — on the trail of the *Bandar-log*,' Kaa replied, courteously, as he swelled with curiosity.

'Indeed,' Baloo began, 'I am no more than the old and some-times very foolish Teacher of the Law to the Seeonee wolf-cubs, and Bagheera here ——'

'Is Bagheera,' said the Black Panther, and his jaws shut with a snap, for he did not believe in being humble. 'The trouble is this, Kaa. Those nut-stealers and pickers of palm-leaves have stolen away our Man-cub, of whom thou hast perhaps heard.'

'I heard some news from Ikki (his quills make him presumptuous) of a man-thing that was entered into a wolf-pack, but I did not believe. Ikki is full of stories half heard and very badly told.'

'But it is true. He is such a Man-cub as never was,' said Baloo. 'The best and wisest and boldest of Man-cubs — my own pupil, who shall make the name of Baloo famous through all the jungles; and besides, I — we — love him, Kaa.'

'Tss! Tss!' said Kaa, shaking his head to and fro. 'I also have known what love is. There are tales I could tell that ——'

'That need a clear night when we are all well fed to praise properly,' said Bagheera, quickly. 'Our Man-cub is in the hands of the *Bandar-log* now, and we know that of all the Jungle-People they fear Kaa alone.'

'They fear me alone. They have good reason,' said Kaa. 'Chattering, foolish, vain — vain, foolish, and chattering, are the monkeys. But a man-thing in their hands is in no good luck. They grow tried of the nuts they pick, and throw them down. They carry a branch half a day, meaning to do great things with it, and then they snap it in two. That man-thing is not to be envied. They called me also — "yellow fish", was it not?'

'Worm — worm — earth-worm,' said Bagheera, 'as well as other things which I cannot now say for shame.'

'We must remind them to speak well of their master. Aaa-sssh! We must help their wandering memories. Now, whither went they with the cub?'

'The Jungle alone knows. Toward the sunset, I believe,' said Baloo. 'We had thought that thou wouldst know, Kaa.'

'I? How? I take them when they come in my way, but I do not hunt the *Bandar-log*, or frogs — or green scum on a water-hole for that matter.'

'Up, Up! Up, Up! Hillo! Illo! Illo! Look up, Baloo of the Seeonee Wolf-Pack!'

Baloo looked up to see where the voice came from, and there was Chil the Kite, sweeping down with the sun shining on the upturned flanges of his wings. It was near Chil's bed-time, but he had ranged all over the Jungle looking for the Bear and had missed him in the thick foliage.

'What is it?' said Baloo.

'I have seen Mowgli among the *Bandar-log*. He bade me tell you. I watched. The *Bandar-log* have taken him beyond the river to the monkey city — to the Cold Lairs. They may stay there for a night, or ten nights, or an hour. I have told the bats to watch through the dark time. That is my message. Good hunting, all you below!'

'Full gorge and a deep sleep to you, Chil,' cried Bagheera. 'I will remember thee in my next kill, and put aside the head for thee alone, O best of kites!'

'It is nothing. It is nothing. The boy held the Master Word. I could have done no less,' and Chil circled up again to his roost.

'He has not forgotten to use his tongue,' said Baloo, with a chuckle of pride. 'To think of one so young remembering the Master Word for the birds too while he was being pulled across-trees!'

'It was most firmly driven into him,' said Bagheera. 'But I am proud of him, and now we must go to the Cold Lairs.'

They all knew where that place was, but few of the Jungle-People ever went there, because what they called the Cold Lairs was an old deserted city, lost and buried in the Jungle, and beasts seldom use a place that men have once used. The wild boar will, but the hunting-tribes do not. Besides, the monkeys lived there as much as they could be said to live anywhere, and no self-respecting animal would come within eye-shot of it except in times of drouth, when the half-ruined tanks and reservoirs held a little water.

'It is half a night's journey — at full speed,' said Bagheera, and Baloo looked very serious. 'I will go as fast as I can,' he said, anxiously.

'We dare not wait for thee. Follow, Baloo. We must go on the quick-foot — Kaa and I."

'Feet or no feet, I can keep abreast of all thy four,' said Kaa, shortly. Baloo made one effort to hurry, but had to sit down panting, and so they left him to come on later, while Bagheera hurried forward, at the quick panther-canter. Kaa said nothing, but, strive as Bagheera might, the huge Rock Python held level with him. When they came to a hill-stream, Bagheera gained, because he bounded across while Kaa swam, his head and two feet of his neck clearing the water, but on level ground Kaa made up the distance.

'By the Broken Lock that freed me,' said Bagheera, when twilight had fallen, 'thou art no slow goer!'

'I am hungry,' said Kaa. 'Besides, they called me speckled frog.'

'Worm — earth-worm, and yellow to boot.'

'All one. Let us go on,' and Kaa seemed to pour himself along the ground, finding the shortest road with his steady eyes, and keeping to it.

In the Cold Lairs the Monkey-People were not thinking of Mowgli's friends at all. They had brought the boy to the Lost City, and were very pleased with themselves for the time. Mowgli had never seen an Indian city before, and though this was almost a heap of ruins it seemed very wonderful and splendid. Some king had built it long ago on a little hill. You could still trace the stone causeways that led up to the ruined gates where the last splinters of wood hung to the worn, rusted hinges. Tree had grown into and out of the walls; the battlements were tumbled down and decayed, and wild creepers hung out of the windows of the towers on the walls in bushy hanging clumps.

A great roofless palace crowned the hill, and the marble of the courtyards and the fountains was split, and stained with red and green, and the very cobble-stones in the courtyard where the king's elephants used to live had been thrust up and apart by grasses and young trees. From the palace you could see the rows and rows of roofless houses that made up the city looking like empty honeycombs filled with blackness; the shapeless block of stone that had been an idol, in the square where four roads met; the pits and dimples at street corners where the public wells once stood, and the shattered domes of temples with wild figs sprouting on their sides. The monkeys called the place their city, and pretended to despise the Jungle-People because they lived in the forest. And yet they never knew what the buildings were made for nor how to use them. They would sit in circles on the hall of the king's council chamber, and scratch for fleas and pretend to be men; or they would run in and out of the roofless houses and collect pieces of plaster and old bricks in a corner, and forget where they had hidden them, and fight and cry in scuffling crowds, and then break off to play up and down the terraces of the king's garden, where they would shake the rose-trees and the oranges in sport to see the fruit and flowers fall. They explored all the passages and dark tunnels in the palace and the hundreds of little dark rooms, but they never remembered what they had seen and what they had not; and so drifted about in ones and twos or crowds telling each other that they were doing as men did. They drank at the tanks and made the water all muddy, and then they fought over it, and then they would all rush together in mobs and shout: 'There is no one in the Jungle so wise and good and clever and strong and gentle as the *Bandar-log*.' Then all would begin again till they grew tired of the city and went back to the tree-tops, hoping the Jungle-People would notice them.

Mowgli, who had been trained under the Law of the Jungle, did not like or understand this kind of life. The monkeys dragged him into the Cold Lairs late in the afternoon, and instead of going to sleep, as Mowgli would have done after a long journey, they joined hands and danced about and sang their foolish songs. One of the monkeys made a speech and told his companions that Mowgli's capture marked a new thing in the history of the *Bandar-log*, for Mowgli was going to show them how to weave sticks and canes together as a protection against rain and cold. Mowgli picked up some creepers and began to work them in and out, and the monkeys tried to imitate; but in a very few minutes they lost interest and began to pull their friends' tails or jump up and down on all fours, coughing.

'I wish to eat,' said Mowgli. 'I am a stranger in this part of the Jungle. Bring me food, or give me leave to hunt here.'

Twenty or thirty monkeys bounded away to bring him nuts

and wild pawpaws; but they fell to fighting on the road, and it was too much trouble to go back with what was left of the fruit. Mowgli was sore and angry as well as hungry, and he roamed through the empty city giving the Stranger's Hunting Call from time to time, but no one answered him, and Mowgli felt that he had reached a very bad place indeed. 'All that Baloo has said about the *Bandar-log* is true,' he thought to himself. 'They have no Law, no Hunting Call, and no leaders — nothing but foolish words and little picking thievish hands. So if I am starved or killed here, it will be all my own fault. But I must try to return to my own Jungle. Baloo will surely beat me, but that is better than chasing silly rose-leaves with the *Bandar-log*.'

No sooner had he walked to the city wall than the monkeys pulled him back, telling him that he did not know how happy he was, and pinching him to make him grateful. He set his teeth and said nothing, but went with the shouting monkeys to a terrace above the red sandstone reservoirs that were half-full of rain-water. There was a ruined summer-house of white marble in the centre of the terrace, built for queens dead a hundred years ago. The domed roof had half fallen in and blocked up the underground passage from the palace by which the queens used to enter; but the walls were made of screens of marble tracery — beautiful milk-white fretwork, set with agates and cornelians and jasper and lapis lazuli, and as the moon came up behind the hill it shone through the open-work, casting shadows on the ground like black velvet embroidery. Sore, sleepy, and hungry as he was, Mowgli could not help laughing when the *Bandar-log* began, twenty at a time, to tell him how great and wise and strong and gentle they were, and how foolish he was to wish to leave them. 'We are great. We are free. We are wonderful. We are the most wonderful people in all the Jungle! We all say so, and so it must be true,' they shouted. 'Now, as you are a new listener and can carry our words back to the Jungle-People so that they may notice us in future, we will tell you all about our most excellent selves.'

Mowgli made no objection, and the monkeys gathered by hundreds and hundreds on the terrace to listen to their own speakers singing the praises of the *Bandar-log*, and whenever a speaker stopped for want of breath they would all shout together: 'This is true; we all say so.' Mowgli nodded and blinked, and said 'Yes' when they asked him a question, and his head spun with the noise. 'Tabaqui, the Jackal, must have bitten all these people,' he said to himself, 'and now they have the madness. Certainly this is *dewanee*, the madness. Do they never go to sleep? Now there is a cloud coming to cover that moon. If it were only a big enough cloud I might try to run away in the darkness. But I am tired.'

That same cloud was being watched by two good friends in the ruined ditch below the city wall, for Bagheera and Kaa, knowing well how dangerous the Monkey-People were in large numbers, did not wish to run any risks. The monkeys never fight unless they are a hundred to one, and few in the Jungle care for those odds.

'I will go to the west wall,' Kaa whispered, 'and come down swiftly with the slope of the ground in my favour. They will not throw themselves upon *my* back in their hundreds, but ——'

'I know it,' said Bagheera. 'Would that Baloo were here; but we must do what we can. When that cloud covers the moon I shall go to the terrace. They hold some sort of council there over the boy.'

'Good hunting!' said Kaa, grimly, and glided away to the west wall. That happened to be the least ruined of any, and the big snake was delayed a while before he could find a way up the stones. The cloud hid the moon, and as Mowgli wondered what would come next he heard Bagheera's light feet on the terrace. The Black Panther had raced up the slope almost without a sound and was striking — he knew better than to waste time in biting — right and left among the monkeys, who were seated round Mowgli in circles fifty and sixty deep. There was a howl of fright and rage, and then as Bagheera tripped on the rolling kicking bodies beneath him, a monkey shouted: 'There is only one here! Kill him! Kill!' A scuffling mass of monkeys, biting, scratching, tearing, and pulling, closed over Bagheera, while five or six laid hold of Mowgli, dragged him up the wall of the summer-house and pushed him through the hole of the broken dome. A man-trained boy would have been badly bruised, for the fall was a good fifteen feet, but Mowgli fell as Baloo had taught him to fall, and landed on his feet.

'Stay there,' shouted the monkeys, 'till we have killed thy friends, and later we will play with thee — if the Poison-People leave thee alive.'

'We be of one blood, ye and I,' said Mowgli, quickly giving the Snake's Call. He could hear rustling and hissing in the rubbish all round him and gave the Call a second time, to make sure.

'Even ssso! Down hoods all!' said half a dozen low voices (every ruin in India becomes sooner or later a dwelling-place of snakes, and the old summer-house was alive with cobras). 'Stand still, Little Brother, for thy feet may do us harm.'

Mowgli stood as quietly as he could, peering through the open-work and listening to the furious din of the fight round the Black Panther — the yells and chatterings and scufflings, and Bagheera's deep, hoarse cough as he backed and bucked and twisted and plunged under the heaps of his enemies. For the first time since he was born, Bagheera was fighting for his life.

'Baloo must be at hand; Bagheera would not have come alone,' Mowgli thought; and then he called aloud: 'To the tank, Bagheera. Roll to the water-tanks. Roll and plunge! Get to the water!'

Bagheera heard, and the cry that told him Mowgli was safe gave him new courage. He worked his way desperately, inch by inch, straight for the reservoirs, hitting in silence. Then from the ruined wall nearest the Jungle rose up the rumbling war-shout of Baloo. The old Bear had done his best, but he could not come before. 'Bagheera,' he shouted, 'I am here. I climb!

I haste! *Ahuwora!* The stones slip under my feet! Wait my coming, O most infamous *Bandar-log*!' He panted up the terrace
only to disappear to the head in a wave of monkeys, but he
threw himself squarely on his haunches, and, spreading out his
fore-paws, hugged as many as he could hold, and then began
to hit with a regular *bat-bat-bat*, like the flipping strokes of a
paddle-wheel. A crash and a splash told Mowgli that Bagheera
had fought his way to the tank where the monkeys could not
follow. The Panther lay gasping for breath, his head just out of
water, while the monkeys stood three deep on the red steps,
dancing up and down with rage, ready to spring upon him from
all sides if he came out to help Baloo. It was then that Bagheera
lifted up his dripping chin, and in despair gave the Snake's Call
for protection — 'We be of one blood, ye and I' — for he believed that Kaa had turned tail at the last minute. Even Baloo,
half smothered under the monkeys on the edge of the terrace,
could not help chuckling as he heard the Black Panther asking
for help.

Kaa had only just worked his way over the west wall, landing with a wrench that dislodged a coping-stone into the ditch.
He had no intention of losing any advantage of the ground, and
coiled and uncoiled himself once or twice, to be sure that every
foot of his long body was in working order. All that while the
fight with Baloo went on, and the monkeys yelled in the tank
round Bagheera, and Mang the Bat, flying to and fro, carried
the news of the great battle over the Jungle, till even Hathi the
Wild Elephant trumpeted, and, far away, scattered bands of
the Monkey-Folk woke and came leaping along the tree-roads
to help their comrades in the Cold Lairs, and the noise of the
fight roused all the day-birds for miles round. Then Kaa came
straight, quickly, and anxious to kill. The fighting-strength of a
python is in the driving blow of his head backed by all the
strength and weight of his body. If you can imagine a lance, or
a battering-ram, or a hammer weighing nearly half a ton driven
by a cool, quiet mind living in the handle of it, you can roughly

imagine what Kaa was like when he fought. A python four or five feet long can knock a man down·if he hits him fairly in the chest, and Kaa was thirty feet long, as you know. His first stroke was delivered into the heart of the crowd round Baloo — was sent home with shut mouth in silence, and there was no need of a second. The monkeys scattered with cries of — 'Kaa! It is Kaa! Run! Run!'

Generations of monkeys had been scared into good behaviour by the stories their elders told them of Kaa, the night-thief, who could slip along the branches as quietly as moss grows, and steal away the strongest monkey that ever lived; of old Kaa, who could make himself look so like a dead branch or a rotten stump that the wisest were deceived, till the branch caught them. Kaa was everything that the monkeys feared in the Jungle, for none of them knew the limits of his power, none of them could look him in the face, and none had ever come alive out of his hug. And so they ran, stammering with terror, to the walls and the roofs of the houses, and Baloo drew a deep breath of relief. His fur was much thicker than Bagheera's, but he had suffered sorely in the fight. Then Kaa opened his mouth for the first time and spoke one long hissing word, and the far-away monkeys, hurrying to the defence of the Cold Lairs, stayed where they were, cowering, till the loaded branches bent and crackled under them. The monkeys on the walls and the empty houses stopped their cries, and in the stillness that fell upon the city Mowgli heard Bagheera shaking his wet sides as he came up from the tank. Then the clamour broke out again. The monkeys leaped higher up the walls; they clung round the necks of the big stone idols and shrieked as they skipped along the battlements, while Mowgli, dancing in the summer-house, put his eye to the screen-work and hooted owl-fashion between his front teeth, to show his derision and contempt.

'Get the Man-cub out of that trap; I can do no more,' Bagheera gasped. 'Let us take the Man-cub and go. They may attack again.'

'They will not move till I order them. Stay you sssso!' Kaa hissed, and the city was silent once more. 'I could not come before, Brother, but I *think* I heard thee call' — this was to Bagheera.

'I — I may have cried out in the battle,' Bagheera answered. 'Baloo, art thou hurt?'

'I am not sure that they have not pulled me into a hundred little bearlings,' said Baloo gravely, shaking one leg after the other. 'Wow! I am sore. Kaa, we owe thee, I think, our lives — Bagheera and I.'

'No matter. Where is the Manling?'

'Here, in a trap. I cannot climb out,' cried Mowgli. The curve of the broken dome was above his head.

'Take him away. He dances like Mao the Peacock. He will crush our young,' said the cobras inside.

'Hah!' said Kaa, with a chuckle, 'he has friends everywhere, this Manling. Stand back, Manling; and hide you, O Poison-People. I break down the wall.'

Kaa looked carefully till he found a discoloured crack in the marble tracery showing a weak spot, made two or three light taps with his head to get the distance, and then lifting up six feet of his body clear of the ground, sent home half a dozen full-power, smashing blows, nose-first. The screen-work broke and fell away in a cloud of dust and rubbish, and Mowgli leaped through the opening and flung himself between Baloo and Bagheera — an arm round each big neck.

'Art thou hurt?' said Baloo, hugging him softly.

'I am sore, hungry, and not a little bruised; but, oh, they have handled ye grievously, my Brothers! Ye bleed.'

'Others also,' said Bagheera, licking his lips, and looking at the monkey-dead on the terrace and round the tank.

'It is nothing, it is nothing, if thou art safe, O my pride of all little frogs!' whimpered Baloo.

'Of that we shall judge later,' said Bagheera, in a dry voice that Mowgli did not at all like. 'But here is Kaa, to whom we owe the battle and thou owest thy life. Thank him according to our customs, Mowgli.'

Mowgli turned and saw the great python's head swaying a foot above his own.

'So this is the Manling,' said Kaa. 'Very soft is his skin, and he is not so unlike the *Bandar-log*. Have a care, Manling, that I do not mistake thee for a monkey some twilight when I have newly changed my coat.'

'We be of one blood, thou and I,' Mowgli answered. 'I take my life from thee, to-night. My kill shall be thy kill if ever thou art hungry, O Kaa.'

'All thanks, Little Brother,' said Kaa, though his eyes twinkled. 'And what may so bold a hunter kill? I ask that I may follow when next he goes abroad.'

'I kill nothing, — I am too little, — but I drive goats toward such as can use them. When thou art empty come to me and see if I speak the truth. I have some skill in these' — he held out his hands — 'and if ever thou art in a trap, I may pay the debt which I owe to thee, to Bagheera, and to Baloo, here. Good hunting to ye all, my masters.'

'Well said,' growled Baloo, for Mowgli had returned thanks very prettily. The python dropped his head lightly for a minute on Mowgli's shoulder. 'A brave heart and a courteous tongue,' said he. 'They shall carry thee far through the Jungle, Manling. But now go hence quickly with thy friends. Go and sleep, for the moon sets, and what follows it is not well that thou shouldst see.'

The moon was sinking behind the hills, and the lines of trembling monkeys huddled together on the walls and battlements looked like ragged, shaky fringes of things. Baloo went down to the tank for a drink, and Bagheera began to put his fur in order, as Kaa glided out into the centre of the terrace and brought his jaws together with a ringing snap that drew all the monkeys' eyes upon him.

'The moon sets,' he said. 'Is there yet light to see?'

From the walls came a moan like the wind in the tree-tops: 'We see, O Kaa.'

'Good. Begins now the Dance — the Dance of the Hunger of Kaa. Sit still and watch.'

He turned twice or thrice in a big circle, weaving his head from right to left. Then he began making loops and figures of eight with his body, and soft, oozy triangles that melted into squares and five-sided figures, and coiled mounds, never resting, never hurrying, and never stopping his low, humming song. It grew darker and darker, till at last the dragging, shifting coils disappeared, but they could hear the rustle of the scales.

Baloo and Bagheera stood still as stone, growling in their throats, their neck-hair bristling, and Mowgli watched and wondered.

'*Bandar-log*,' said the voice of Kaa at last, 'can ye stir foot or hand without my order? Speak!'

'Without thy order we cannot stir foot or hand, O Kaa!'

'Good! Come all one pace closer to me.'

The lines of the monkeys swayed forward helplessly, and Baloo and Bagheera took one stiff step forward with them.

'Closer!' hissed Kaa, and they all moved again.

Mowgli laid his hands on Baloo and Bagheera to get them away, and the two great beasts started as though they had been waked from a dream.

'Keep thy hand on my shoulder,' Bagheera whispered. 'Keep it there, or I must go back — must go back to Kaa. *Aah!*'

'It is only old Kaa making circles on the dust,' said Mowgli; 'let us go'; and the three slipped off through a gap in the walls to the Jungle.

'*Whoof!*' said Baloo, when he stood under the still trees again. 'Never more will I make an ally of Kaa,' and he shook himself all over.

'He knows more than we,' said Bagheera, trembling. 'In a

little time, had I stayed, I should have walked down his throat.'

'Many will walk by that road before the moon rises again,' said Baloo. 'He will have good hunting — after his own fashion.'

'But what was the meaning of it all?' said Mowgli, who did not know anything of a python's powers of fascination. 'I saw no more than a big snake making foolish circles till the dark came. And his nose was all sore. Ho! Ho!'

'Mowgli,' said Bagheera angrily, 'his nose was sore on *thy* account; as my ears and sides and paws and Baloo's neck and shoulders are bitten on *thy* account. Neither Baloo nor Bagheera will be able to hunt with pleasure for many days.'

'It is nothing,' said Baloo; 'we have the Man-cub again.'

'True; but he has cost us heavily in time which might have been spent in good hunting, in wounds, in hair — I am half plucked along my back, — and last of all, in honour. For, remember, Mowgli, I, who am the Black Panther, was forced to call upon Kaa for protection, and Baloo and I were both made stupid as little birds by the Hunger-Dance. All this, Man-cub, came of thy playing with the *Bandar-log*.'

'True; it is true,' said Mowgli, sorrowfully. 'I am an evil Man-cub, and my stomach is sad in me.'

'*Mf!* What says the Law of the Jungle, Baloo?'

Baloo did not wish to bring Mowgli into any more trouble, but he could not tamper with the Law, so he mumbled: 'Sorrow never stays punishment. But remember, Bagheera, he is very little.'

'I will remember; but he has done mischief, and blows must be dealt now. Mowgli, hast thou anything to say?'

'Nothing. I did wrong. Baloo and thou are wounded. It is just.'

Bagheera gave him half a dozen love-taps; from a panther's point of view they would hardly have waked one of his own cubs, but for a seven-year-old boy they amounted to as severe a beating as you could wish to avoid. When it was all over Mowgli sneezed, and picked himself up without a word.

'Now,' said Bagheera, 'jump on my back, Little Brother, and we will go home.'

One of the beauties of Jungle Law is that punishment settles all scores. There is no nagging afterward.

Mowgli laid his head down on Bagheera's back and slept so deeply that he never waked when he was put down by Mother Wolf's side in the home-cave.

ROAD-SONG OF THE BANDAR-LOG

Here we go in a flung festoon,
Half-way up to the jealous moon!
Don't you envy our pranceful bands?
Don't you wish you had extra hands?
Wouldn't you like if your tails were — *so* —
Curved in the shape of a Cupid's bow?
　Now you're angry, but — never mind,
　Brother, thy tail hangs down behind!

Here we sit in a branchy row,
Thinking of beautiful things we know;
Dreaming of deeds that we mean to do,
All complete, in a minute or two —
Something noble and grand and good,
Won by merely wishing we could.
　Now we're going to — never mind,
　Brother, thy tail hangs down behind!

All the talk we ever have heard
Uttered by bat or beast or bird —
Hide or fin or scale or feather —
Jabber it quickly and all together!
Excellent! Wonderful! Once again!
Now we are talking just like men.
　Let's pretend we are . . . never mind,
　Brother, thy tail hangs down behind!
　This is the way of the Monkey-kind.

Then join our leaping lines that scumfish through the pines,
That rocket by where, light and high, the wild-grape swings.
By the rubbish in our wake, and the noble noise we make,
Be sure, be sure, we're going to do some splendid things!

HOW FEAR CAME

The stream is shrunk — the pool is dry,
And we be comrades, thou and I;
With fevered jowl and dusty flank
Each jostling each along the bank;
And by one drouthy fear made still,
Forgoing thought of quest or kill.
Now 'neath his dam the fawn may see
The lean Pack-wolf as cowed as he,
And the tall buck, unflinching, note
The fangs that tore his father's throat.
The pools are shrunk — the streams are dry
And we be playmates, thou and I,
Till yonder cloud — Good Hunting! — loose
The rain that breaks our Water Truce.

The Law of the Jungle — which is by far the oldest law in the world — has arranged for almost every kind of accident that may befall the Jungle-People, till now its code is as perfect as time and custom can make it. You will remember that Mowgli spent a great part of his life in the Seeonee Wolf-Pack, learning the Law from Baloo, the Brown Bear; and it was Baloo who told him, when the boy grew impatient at the constant orders, that the Law was like the Giant Creeper, because it dropped across every one's back and no one could escape. 'When thou hast lived as long as I have, Little Brother, thou wilt see how all the Jungle obeys at least one Law. And that will be no pleasant sight,' said Baloo.

This talk went in at one ear and out at the other, for a boy who spends his life eating and sleeping does not worry about anything till it actually stares him in the face. But, one year, Baloo's words came true, and Mowgli saw all the Jungle working under the Law.

It began when the winter Rains failed almost entirely, and Ikki, the Porcupine, meeting Mowgli in a bamboo-thicket, told him that the wild yams were drying up. Now everybody knows that Ikki is ridiculously fastidious in his choice of food, and will eat nothing but the very best and ripest. So Mowgli laughed and said, 'What is that to me?'

'Not much *now*,' said Ikki, rattling his quills in a stiff, uncomfortable way, 'but later we shall see. Is there any more diving into the deep rock-pool below the Bee-Rocks, Little Brother?'

'No. The foolish water is going all away, and I do not wish to break my head,' said Mowgli, who, in those days, was quite sure that he knew as much as any five of the Jungle-People put together.

'That is thy loss. A small crack might let in some wisdom.' Ikki ducked quickly to prevent Mowgli from pulling his nose-bristles, and Mowgli told Baloo what Ikki had said. Baloo looked very grave, and mumbled half to himself: 'If I were alone I would change my hunting-grounds now, before the others began to think. And yet — hunting among strangers ends in fighting; and they might hurt the Man-cub. We must wait and see how the *mohwa* blooms.'

That spring the *mohwa* tree, that Baloo was so fond of, never flowered. The greeny, cream-coloured, waxy blossoms were heat-killed before they were born, and only a few bad-smelling petals came down when he stood on his hind legs and shook the tree. Then, inch by inch, the untempered heat crept into the heart of the Jungle, turning it yellow, brown, and at last black. The green growths in the sides of the ravines burned up to broken wires and curled films of dead stuff; the hidden pools sank down and caked over, keeping the last least footmark on their edges as if it had been cast in iron; the juicy-stemmed creepers fell away from the trees they clung to and died at their feet; the bamboos withered, clanking when the hot winds blew, and the moss peeled off the rocks deep in the Jungle, till they were as bare and as hot as the quivering blue boulders in the bed of the stream.

The birds and the Monkey-People went north early in the

year, for they knew what was coming; and the deer and the
wild pig broke far away to the perished fields of the villages
dying sometimes before the eyes of men too weak to kill them
Chil, the Kite, stayed and grew fat, for there was a great deal of
carrion, and evening after evening he brought the news to the
beasts, too weak to force their way to fresh hunting-grounds
that the sun was killing the Jungle for three days' flight in every
direction.

Mowgli, who had never known what real hunger meant, fell
back on stale honey, three years old, scraped out of deserted
rock-hives — honey black as a sloe, and dusty with dried sugar
He hunted, too, for deep-boring grubs under the bark of the
trees, and robbed the wasps of their new broods. All the game
in the Jungle was no more than skin and bone, and Bagheera
could kill thrice in a night, and hardly get a full meal. But the
want of water was the worst, for though the Jungle-People
drink seldom they must drink deep.

And the heat went on and on, and sucked up all the moisture,
till at last the main channel of the Waingunga was the only
stream that carried a trickle of water between its dead banks;
and when Hathi, the Wild Elephant, who lives for a hundred
years and more, saw a long, lean blue ridge of rock show dry in
the very centre of the stream, he knew that he was looking at
the Peace Rock, and then and there he lifted up his trunk and
proclaimed the Water Truce, as his father before him had proclaimed it fifty years ago. The deer, wild pig, and buffalo took
up the cry hoarsely; and Chil, the Kite, flew in great circles far
and wide, whistling and shrieking the warning.

By the Law of the Jungle it is death to kill at the drinking-
places when once the Water Truce has been declared. The
reason of this is that drinking comes before eating. Every one
in the Jungle can scramble along somehow when only game is
scarce; but water is water, and when there is but one source of
supply, all hunting stops while the Jungle-People go there for
their needs. In good seasons, when water was plentiful, those

who came down to drink at the Waingunga — or anywhere else, for that matter — did so at the risk of their lives, and that risk made no small part of the fascination of the night's doings. To move down so cunningly that never a leaf stirred; to wade knee-deep in the roaring shallows that drown all noise from behind; to drink, looking backward over one shoulder, every muscle ready for the first desperate bound of keen terror; to roll on the sandy margin, and return, wet-muzzled and well plumped out, to the admiring herd, was a thing that all tall-antlered young bucks took a delight in, precisely because they knew that at any moment Bagheera or Shere Khan might leap upon them and bear them down. But now all that life-and-death fun was ended, and the Jungle-People came up, starved and weary, to the shrunken river, — tiger, bear, deer, buffalo, and pig, all together, — drank the fouled waters, and hung above them, too exhausted to move off.

The deer and the pig had tramped all day in search of something better than dried bark and withered leaves. The buffaloes had found no wallows to be cool in, and no green crops to steal. The snakes had left the Jungle and come down to the river in the hope of finding a stray frog. They curled round wet stones, and never offered to strike when the nose of a rooting pig dislodged them. The river-turtles had long ago been killed by Bagheera, cleverest of hunters, and the fish had buried themselves deep in the dry mud. Only the Peace Rock lay across the shallows like a long snake, and the little tired ripples hissed as they dried on its hot side.

It was here that Mowgli came nightly for the cool and the companionship. The most hungry of his enemies would hardly have cared for the boy then. His naked hide made him seem more lean and wretched than any of his fellows. His hair was bleached to tow colour by the sun; his ribs stood out like the ribs of a basket, and the lumps on his knees and elbows, where he was used to track on all fours, gave his shrunken limbs the look of knotted grass-stems. But his eye, under his matted forelock, was cool and quiet, for Bagheera was his adviser in this time of trouble, and told him to go quietly, hunt slowly, and never, on any account, to lose his temper.

'It is an evil time,' said the Black Panther, one furnace-hot evening, 'but it will go if we can live till the end. Is thy stomach full, Man-cub?'

'There is stuff in my stomach, but I get no good of it. Think you, Bagheera, the Rains have forgotten us and will never come again?'

'Not I! We shall see the *mohwa* in blossom yet, and the little fawns all fat with new grass. Come down to the Peace Rock and hear the news. On my back, Little Brother.'

'This is no time to carry weight. I can still stand alone, but — indeed we be no fatted bullocks, we two.'

Bagheera looked along his ragged, dusty flank and whispered: 'Last night I killed a bullock under the yoke. So low was I brought that I think I should not have dared to spring if he had been loose. *Wou!*'

Mowgli laughed. 'Yes, we be great hunters now,' said he. 'I am very bold — to eat grubs,' and the two came down together through the crackling undergrowth to the river-bank and the lacework of shoals that ran out from it in every direction.

'The water cannot live long,' said Baloo, joining them. 'Look across. Yonder are trails like the roads of Man.'

On the level plain of the farther bank the stiff jungle-grass had died standing, and, dying, had mummied. The beaten tracks of the deer and the pig, all heading toward the river, had striped that colourless plain with dusty gullies driven through the ten-foot grass, and, early as it was, each long avenue was full of first-comers hastening to the water. You could hear the does and fawns coughing in the snuff-like dust.

Up-stream, at the bend of the sluggish pool round the Peace Rock, and Warden of the Water Truce, stood Hathi, the Wild Elephant, with his sons, gaunt and gray in the moonlight, rocking to and fro — always rocking. Below him a little were the vanguard of the deer; below these, again, the pig and the wild buffalo; and on the opposite bank, where the tall trees came down to the water's edge, was the place set apart for the Eaters of Flesh — the tiger, the wolves, the panther, the bear, and the others.

'We are under one Law, indeed,' said Bagheera, wading into the water and looking across at the lines of clicking horns and starting eyes where the deer and the pig pushed each other to and fro. 'Good hunting, all you of my blood,' he added, lying down at full length, one flank thrust out of the shallows; and then, between his teeth, 'But for that which is the Law it would be *very* good hunting.'

The quick-spread ears of the deer caught the last sentence, and a frightened whisper ran along the ranks. 'The Truce! Remember the Truce!'

'Peace there, peace!' gurgled Hathi, the Wild Elephant. 'The Truce holds, Bagheera. This is no time to talk of hunting.'

'Who should know better than I?' Bagheera answered, rolling his yellow eyes up-stream. 'I am an eater of turtles — a fisher of frogs. *Ngaayah!* Would I could get good from chewing branches!'

'*We* wish so, very greatly,' bleated a young fawn, who had only been born that spring, and did not at all like it. Wretched as the Jungle-People were, even Hathi could not help chuckling; while Mowgli, lying on his elbows in the warm water, laughed aloud, and beat up the scum with his feet.

'Well spoken, little bud-horn,' Bagheera purred. 'When the Truce ends that shall be remembered in thy favour,' and he looked keenly through the darkness to make sure of recognising the fawn again.

Gradually the talking spread up and down the drinking-places. One could hear the scuffling, snorting pig asking for more room; the buffaloes grunting among themselves as they lurched out across the sand-bars, and the deer telling pitiful stories of their long footsore wanderings in quest of food. Now and again they asked some question of the Eaters of Flesh across the river, but all the news was bad, and the roaring hot wind of the Jungle came and went between the rocks and the rattling branches, and scattered twigs and dust on the water.

'The men-folk, too, they die beside their ploughs,' said a young sambhur. 'I passed three between sunset and night. They lay still, and their bullocks with them. We also shall lie still in a little.'

'The river has fallen since last night,' said Baloo. 'O Hathi, hast thou ever seen the like of this drought?'

'It will pass, it will pass,' said Hathi, squirting water along his back and sides.

'We have one here that cannot endure long,' said Baloo; and he looked towards the boy he loved.

'I?' said Mowgli indignantly, sitting up in the water. 'I have no long fur to cover my bones, but — but if *thy* hide were taken off, Baloo ——'

Hathi shook all over at the idea, and Baloo said severely:

'Man-Cub, that is not seemly to tell a Teacher of the Law. *Never* have I been seen without my hide.'

'Nay, I meant no harm, Baloo; but only that thou art, as it were, like the coconut in the husk, and I am the same coconut all naked. Now that brown husk of thine ——' Mowgli was sitting cross-legged, and explaining things with his forefinger in his usual way, when Bagheera put out a paddy paw and pulled him over backward into the water.

'Worse and worse,' said the Black Panther, as the boy rose spluttering. 'First Baloo is to be skinned, and now he is a coco-nut. Be careful that he does not do what the ripe coconuts do.'

'And what is that?' said Mowgli, off his guard for the min-ute, though that is one of the oldest catches in the Jungle.

'Break thy head,' said Bagheera quietly, pulling him under again.

'It is not good to make a jest of thy teacher,' said the bear, when Mowgli had been ducked for the third time.

'Not good! What would ye have? That naked thing running to and fro makes a monkey-jest of those who have once been good hunters, and pulls the best of us by the whiskers for sport.' This was Shere Khan, the Lame Tiger, limping down to the water. He waited a little to enjoy the sensation he made among the deer on the opposite bank; then he dropped his square, frilled head and began to lap, growling: 'The Jungle has become a whelping-ground for naked cubs, now. Look at me, Man-cub!'

Mowgli looked — stared, rather — as insolently as he knew how, and in a minute Shere Khan turned away uneasily. 'Man-cub this, and Man-cub that,' he rumbled, going on with his drink, 'the cub is neither man nor cub, or he would have been afraid. Next season I shall have to beg his leave for a drink. *Augrh!*'

'That may come, too,' said Bagheera, looking him steadily between the eyes. 'That may come, too — Faugh, Shere Khan! — what new shame hast thou brought here?'

The Lame Tiger had dipped his chin and jowl in the water, and dark, oily streaks were floating from it down-stream.

'Man!' said Shere Khan coolly. 'I killed an hour since.' He went on purring and growling to himself.

The line of beasts shook and wavered to and fro, and a whisper went up that grew to a cry: 'Man! Man! He has killed Man!' Then all looked towards Hathi, the Wild Elephant, but he seemed not to hear. Hathi never does anything till the time comes, and that is one of the reasons why he lives so long.

'At such a season as this to kill Man! Was no other game afoot?' said Bagheera scornfully, drawing himself out of the tainted water, and shaking each paw, cat-fashion, as he did so.

'I killed for choice — not for food.' The horrified whisper began again, and Hathi's watchful little white eye cocked itself in Shere Khan's direction. 'For choice,' Shere Khan drawled. 'Now come I to drink and make me clean again. Is there any to forbid?'

Bagheera's back began to curve like a bamboo in a high wind, but Hathi lifted up his trunk and spoke quietly.

'Thy kill was from choice?' he asked; and when Hathi asks a question it is best to answer.

'Even so. It was my right and my Night. Thou knowest, O Hathi.' Shere Khan spoke almost courteously.

'Yes, I know,' Hathi answered; and, after a little silence, 'Hast thou drunk thy fill?'

'For to-night, yes.'

'Go, then. The river is to drink, and not to defile. None but the Lame Tiger would so have boasted of his right at this season when — when we suffer together — Man and Jungle-People alike. Clean or unclean, get to thy lair, Shere Khan!'

The last words rang out like silver trumpets, and Hathi's three sons rolled forward half a pace, though there was no need. Shere Khan slunk away, not daring to growl, for he knew — what every one else knows — that when the last comes to the last, Hathi is the Master of the Jungle.

'What is this right Shere Khan speaks of?' Mowgli whispered in Bagheera's ear. 'To kill Man is *always* shameful. The Law says so. And yet Hathi says ——'

'Ask him. I do not know, Little Brother. Right or no right, if Hathi had not spoken I would have taught that lame butcher his lesson. To come to the Peace Rock fresh from a kill of Man — and to boast of it — is a jackal's trick. Besides, he tainted the good water.'

Mowgli waited for a minute to pick up his courage, because no one cared to address Hathi directly, and then he cried: 'What is Shere Khan's right, O Hathi?' Both banks echoed his words, for all the People of the Jungle are intensely curious, and they had just seen something that none, except Baloo, who looked very thoughtful, seemed to understand.

'It is an old tale,' said Hathi; 'a tale older than the Jungle. Keep silence along the banks, and I will tell that tale.'

There was a minute or two of pushing and shouldering

among the pig and the buffalo, and then the leaders of the herds grunted, one after another, 'We wait,' and Hathi strode forward till he was nearly knee-deep in the pool by the Peace Rock. Lean and wrinkled and yellow-tusked though he was, he looked what the Jungle knew him to be — their master.

'Ye know, children,' he began, 'that of all things ye most fear Man'; and there was a mutter of agreement.

'This tale touches thee, Little Brother,' said Bagheera to Mowgli.

'I? I am of the Pack — a hunter of the Free People,' Mowgli answered. 'What have I to do with Man?'

'And ye do not know why ye fear Man?' Hathi went on. 'This is the reason. In the beginning of the Jungle, and none know when that was, we of the Jungle walked together, having no fear of one another. In those days there was no drought, and leaves and flowers and fruit grew on the same tree, and we ate nothing at all except leaves and flowers and grass and fruit and bark.'

'I am glad I was not born in those days,' said Bagheera. 'Bark is only good to sharpen claws.'

'And the Lord of the Jungle was Tha, the First of the Elephants. He drew the Jungle out of deep waters with his trunk; and where he made furrows in the ground with his tusks, there the rivers ran; and where he struck with his foot, there rose ponds of good water; and when he blew through his trunk, — thus, — the trees fell. That was the manner in which the Jungle was made by Tha; and so the tale was told to me.'

'It has not lost fat in the telling,' Bagheera whispered, and Mowgli laughed behind his hand.

'In those days there was no corn or melons or pepper or sugar-cane, nor were there any little huts such as ye have all seen; and the Jungle-People knew nothing of Man, but lived in the Jungle together, making one people. But presently they began to dispute over their food, though there was grazing enough for all. They were lazy. Each wished to eat where he lay, as sometimes we can do now when the spring Rains are good. Tha, the First of the Elephants, was busy making new jungles and leading the rivers in their beds. He could not walk in all places; therefore he made the First of the Tigers the master and the judge of the Jungle, to whom the Jungle-People should bring their disputes. In those days the First of the Tigers ate fruit and grass with the others. He was as large as I am, and he was very beautiful, in colour all over like the blossom of the yellow creeper. There was never stripe nor bar upon his hide in those good days when this the Jungle was new. All the Jungle-People came before him without fear, and his word was the Law of all the Jungle. We were then, remember ye, one people.

'Yet upon a night there was a dispute between two bucks — a grazing-quarrel such as ye now settle with the horns and the fore-feet — and it is said that as the two spoke together before the First of the Tigers lying among the flowers, a buck pushed him with his horns, and the First of the Tigers forgot that he was the master and judge of the Jungle, and, leaping upon that buck, broke his neck.

'Till that night never one of us had died, and the First of the Tigers, seeing what he had done, and being made foolish by the scent of the blood, ran away into the Marshes of the North, and we of the Jungle, left without a judge, fell to fighting among ourselves; and Tha heard the noise of it and came back. Then some of us said this and some of us said that, but he saw the dead buck among the flowers, and asked who had killed, and we of the Jungle would not tell because the smell of the blood made us foolish. We ran to and fro in circles, capering and crying out and shaking our heads. Then Tha gave an order to the trees that hang low, and to the trailing creepers of the Jungle, that they should mark the killer of the buck so that he should know him again, and he said, "Who will now be master of the Jungle-People?" Then up leaped the Gray Ape who lives in the branches, and said, "I will now be master of the Jungle." At this Tha laughed, and said, "So be it," and went away very angry.

'Children, ye know the Gray Ape. He was then as he is now. At the first he made a wise face for himself, but in a little while he began to scratch and to leap up and down, and when Tha came back he found the Gray Ape hanging, head down, from a bough, mocking those who stood below; and they mocked him again. And so there was no Law in the Jungle — only foolish talk and senseless words.

'Then Tha called us all together and said: "The first of your masters has brought Death into the Jungle, and the second Shame. Now it is time there was a Law, and a Law that ye must not break. Now ye shall know Fear, and when ye have found him ye shall know that he is your master, and the rest shall follow." Then we of the Jungle said, "What is Fear?" And Tha said, "Seek till ye find." So we went up and down the Jungle seeking for Fear, and presently the buffaloes ——'

'Ugh!' said Mysa, the leader of the buffaloes, from their sand-bank.

'Yes, Mysa, it was the buffaloes. They came back with the news that in a cave in the Jungle sat Fear, and that he had no hair, and went upon his hind legs. Then we of the Jungle followed the herd till we came to that cave, and Fear stood at the mouth of it, and he was, as the buffaloes had said, hairless, and he walked upon his hinder legs. When he saw us he cried out, and his voice filled us with the fear that we have now of that voice when we hear it, and we ran away, tramping upon and tearing each other because we were afraid. That night, so it was told to me, we of the Jungle did not lie down together as used to be our custom, but each tribe drew off by itself — the pig with the pig, the deer with the deer; horn to horn, hoof to hoof, — like keeping to like, and so lay shaking in the Jungle.

'Only the First of the Tigers was not with us, for he was still hidden in the Marshes of the North, and when word was brought to him of the Thing we had seen in the cave, he said:

"I will go to this Thing and break his neck." So he ran all the night till he came to the cave; but the trees and the creepers on his path, remembering the order that Tha had given, let down their branches and marked him as he ran, drawing their fingers across his back, his flank, his forehead, and his jowl. Wherever they touched him there was a mark and a stripe upon his yellow hide. *And those stripes do his children wear to this day!* When he came to the cave, Fear, the Hairless One, put out his hand and called him "The Striped One that comes by night," and the First of the Tigers was afraid of the Hairless One, and ran back to the swamps howling.'

Mowgli chuckled quietly here, his chin in the water.

'So loud did he howl that Tha heard him and said, "What is the sorrow?" And the First of the Tigers, lifting up his muzzle to the new-made sky, which is now so old, said: "Give me back my power, O Tha. I am made ashamed before all the Jungle, and I have run away from a Hairless One, and he has called me a shameful name." "And why?" said Tha. "Because I am smeared with the mud of the marshes," said the First of the Tigers. "Swim, then, and roll on the wet grass, and if it be mud it will wash away," said Tha; and the First of the Tigers swam, and rolled and rolled upon the grass, till the Jungle ran round and round before his eyes, but not one little bar upon all his hide was changed, and Tha, watching him, laughed. Then the First of the Tigers said, "What have I done that this comes to me?" Tha said, "Thou hast killed the buck, and thou hast let Death loose in the Jungle, and with Death has come Fear, so that the People of the Jungle are afraid one of the other, as thou art afraid of the Hairless One." The First of the Tigers said, "They will never fear me, for I knew them since the beginning." Tha said, "Go and see." And the First of the Tigers ran to and fro, calling aloud to the deer and the pig and the sambhur and the porcupine and all the Jungle Peoples, and they all ran away from him who had been their judge, because they were afraid.

'Then the First of the Tigers came back, and his pride was

broken in him, and, beating his head upon the ground, he tore
up the earth with all his feet and said: "Remember that I was
once the Master of the Jungle. Do not forget me, O Tha! Let
my children remember that I was once without shame or fear!"
And Tha said: "This much I will do, because thou and I together saw the Jungle made. For one night in each year it shall
be as it was before the buck was killed — for thee and for thy
children. In that one night, if ye meet the Hairless One — and
his name is Man — ye shall not be afraid of him, but he shall
be afraid of you, as though ye were judges of the Jungle and
masters of all things. Show him mercy in that night of his fear,
for thou hast known what Fear is."

'Then the First of the Tigers answered, "I am content"; but
when next he drank he saw the black stripes upon his flank and
his side, and he remembered the name that the Hairless One
had given him, and he was angry. For a year he lived in the
marshes, waiting till Tha should keep his promise. And upon a
night when the Jackal of the Moon [the Evening Star] stood
clear of the Jungle, he felt that his Night was upon him, and he
went to that cave to meet the Hairless One. Then it happened as
Tha promised, for the Hairless One fell down before him and
lay along the ground, and the First of the Tigers struck him
and broke his back, for he thought that there was but one such
Thing in the Jungle, and that he had killed Fear. Then, nosing
above the kill, he heard Tha coming down from the woods of
the North, and presently the voice of the First of the Elephants,
which is the voice that we hear now ——'

The thunder was rolling up and down the dry, scarred hills,
but it brought no rain — only heat-lightning that flickered
along the ridges — and Hathi went on: '*That* was the voice he
heard, and it said: "Is this thy mercy?" The First of the Tigers
licked his lips and said: "What matter? I have killed Fear."
And Tha said: "O blind and foolish! Thou hast untied the feet
of Death, and he will follow thy trail till thou diest. Thou hast
taught Man to kill!"'

'The First of the Tigers, standing stiffly to his kill, said: "He is as the buck was. There is no Fear. Now I will judge the Jungle Peoples once more."

'And Tha said: "Never again shall the Jungle Peoples come to thee. They shall never cross thy trail, nor sleep near thee, nor follow after thee, nor browse by thy lair. Only Fear shall follow thee, and with a blow that thou canst not see he shall bid thee wait his pleasure. He shall make the ground to open under thy feet, and the creepers to twist about thy neck, and the tree-trunks to grow together about thee higher than thou canst leap, and at the last he shall take thy hide to wrap his cubs when they are cold. Thou hast shown him no mercy, and none will he show thee."

'The First of the Tigers was very bold, for his Night was still on him, and he said: "The Promise of Tha is the Promise of Tha. He will not take away my Night?" And Tha said: "The one Night is thine, as I have said, but there is a price to pay. Thou hast taught Man to kill, and he is no slow learner."

'The First of the Tigers said: "He is here under my foot, and his back is broken. Let the Jungle know I have killed Fear."

'Then Tha laughed, and said: "Thou hast killed one of many, but thou thyself shalt tell the Jungle — for thy Night is ended."

'So the day came; and from the mouth of the cave went out another Hairless One, and he saw the kill in the path, and the First of the Tigers above it, and he took a pointed stick ——'

'They throw a thing that cuts now,' said Ikki, rustling down the bank; for Ikki was considered uncommonly good eating by the Gonds — they called him Ho-Igoo — and he knew something of the wicked little Gondee axe that whirls across a clearing like a dragon-fly.

'It was a pointed stick, such as they put in the foot of a pit-trap,' said Hathi, 'and throwing it, he struck the First of the Tigers deep in the flank. Thus it happened as Tha said, for the First of the Tigers ran howling up and down the Jungle till he tore out the stick, and all the Jungle knew that the Hairless One could strike from far off, and they feared more than before. So it came about that the First of the Tigers taught the Hairless One to kill — and ye know what harm that has since done to all our peoples — through the noose, and the pitfall, and the hidden trap, and the flying stick, and the stinging fly that comes out of white smoke [Hathi meant the rifle], and the Red Flower that drives us into the open. Yet for one night in the year the Hairless One fears the Tiger, as Tha promised, and never has the Tiger given him cause to be less afraid. Where he finds him, there he kills him, remembering how the First of the Tigers was made ashamed. For the rest, Fear walks up and down the Jungle by day and by night.'

'*Ahi! Aoo!*' said the deer, thinking of what it all meant to them.

'And only when there is one great Fear over all, as there is now, can we of the Jungle lay aside our little fears, and meet together in one place as we do now.'

'For one night only does Man fear the Tiger?' said Mowgli.

'For one night only,' said Hathi.

'But I — but we — but all the Jungle knows that Shere Khan kills Man twice and thrice in a moon.'

'Even so. *Then* he springs from behind and turns his head aside as he strikes, for he is full of fear. If Man looked at him he would run. But on his one Night he goes openly down to the village. He walks between the houses and thrusts his head into the doorway, and the men fall on their faces, and there he does his kill. One kill in that Night.'

'Oh!' said Mowgli to himself, rolling over in the water. '*Now* I see why it was Shere Khan bade me look at him! He got no good of it, for he could not hold his eyes steady, and — and I certainly did not fall down at his feet. But then I am not a man, being of the Free People.'

'Umm!' said Bagheera deep in his furry throat. 'Does the Tiger know his Night?'

'Never till the Jackal of the Moon stands clear of the evening mist. Sometimes it falls in the dry summer and sometimes in the wet rains — this one Night of the Tiger. But for the First of the Tigers, this would never have been, nor would any of us have known fear.'

The deer grunted sorrowfully, and Bagheera's lips curled in a wicked smile. 'Do men know this — tale?' said he.

'None know it except the tigers, and we, the elephants — the children of Tha. Now ye by the pools have heard it, and I have spoken.'

Hathi dipped his trunk into the water as a sign that he did not wish to talk.

'But — but — but,' said Mowgli, turning to Baloo, 'why did not the First of the Tigers continue to eat grass and leaves and trees? He did but break the buck's neck. He did not *eat*. What led him to the hot meat?'

'The trees and the creepers marked him, Little Brother, and made him the striped thing that we see. Never again would he eat their fruit; but from that day he revenged himself upon the deer, and the others, the Eaters of Grass,' said Baloo.

'Then *thou* knowest the tale. Heh? Why have I never heard?'

'Because the Jungle is full of such tales. If I made a beginning there would never be an end to them. Let go my ear, Little Brother.'

THE LAW OF THE JUNGLE

Just to give you an idea of the immense variety of the Jungle Law, I have translated into verse (Baloo always recited them in a sort of sing-song) a few of the laws that apply to the wolves. There are, of course, hundreds and hundreds more, but these will do for specimens of the simpler rulings.

Now this is the Law of the Jungle — as old and as true as the sky;
And the Wolf that shall keep it may prosper, but the Wolf that shall break it
*   must die.*

As the creeper that girdles the tree-trunk, the Law runneth forward and
*   back —*
For the strength of the Pack is the Wolf, and the strength of the Wolf is the
*   Pack.*

Wash daily from nose-tip to tail-tip; drink deeply, but never too deep;
And remember the night is for hunting, and forget not the day is for sleep.

The Jackal may follow the Tiger, but, Cub, when thy whiskers are grown,
Remember the Wolf is a hunter — go forth and get food of thine own.

Keep peace with the Lords of the Jungle — the Tiger, the Panther, the
    Bear;
And trouble not Hathi the Silent, and mock not the Boar in his lair.

When Pack meets with Pack in the Jungle, and neither will go from the
    trail,
Lie down till the leaders have spoken — it may be fair words shall prevail.

When ye fight with a Wolf of the Pack, ye must fight him alone and afar,
Lest others take part in the quarrel, and the Pack be diminished by war.

The Lair of the Wolf is his refuge, and where he has made him his home,
Not even the Head Wolf may enter, not even the Council may come.

The Lair of the Wolf is his refuge, but where he has digged it too plain,
The Council shall send him a message, and so he shall change it again.

If ye kill before midnight, be silent, and wake not the woods with your
    bay,
Lest ye frighten the deer from the crops, and the brothers go empty away.

Ye may kill for yourselves, and your mates, and your cubs as they need,
    and ye can;
But kill not for pleasure of killing, and *seven times never kill Man.*

If ye plunder his Kill from a weaker, devour not all in thy pride;
Pack-Right is the right of the meanest; so leave him the head and the hide.

The Kill of the Pack is the meat of the Pack. Ye must eat where it lies;
And no one may carry away of that meat to his lair, or he dies.

The Kill of the Wolf is the meat of the Wolf. He may do what he will,
But, till he has given permission, the Pack may not eat of that Kill.

Cub-Right is the right of the Yearling. From all of his Pack he may claim
Full-gorge when the killer has eaten; and none may refuse him the same.

Lair-Right is the right of the Mother. From all of her year she may claim
One haunch of each kill for her litter, and none may deny her the same.

Cave-Right is the right of the Father — to hunt by himself for his own:
He is freed of all calls to the Pack; he is judged by the Council alone.

Because of his age and his cunning, because of his gripe and his paw,
In all that the Law leaveth open, the word of the Head Wolf is Law.

Now these are the Laws of the Jungle, and many and mighty are they;
But the head and the hoof of the Law and the haunch and the hump is —
    Obey!

'TIGER! TIGER!'

What of the hunting, hunter bold?
  Brother, the watch was long and cold.
What of the quarry ye went to kill?
  Brother, he crops in the jungle still.
Where is the power that made your pride?
  Brother, it ebbs from my flank and side.
Where is the haste that ye hurry by?
  Brother, I go to my lair — to die!

Now we must go back to the first tale. When Mowgli left the wolf's cave after the fight with the Pack at the Council Rock, he went down to the ploughed lands where the villagers lived, but he would not stop there because it was too near to the Jungle, and he knew that he had made at least one bad enemy at the Council. So he hurried on, keeping to the rough road that ran down the valley, and followed it at a steady jog-trot for nearly twenty miles, till he came to a country that he did not know. The valley opened out into a great plain dotted over with rocks and cut up by ravines. At one end stood a little village, and at the other the thick Jungle came down in a sweep to the grazing-grounds, and stopped there as though it had been cut off with a hoe. All over the plain, cattle and buffaloes were grazing, and when the little boys in charge of the herds saw Mowgli they shouted and ran away, and the yellow pariah dogs that hang about every Indian village barked. Mowgli walked on, for he was feeling hungry, and when he came to the village gate he saw the big thorn-bush that was drawn up before the gate at twilight pushed to one side.

'Umph!' he said, for he had come across more than one such barricade in his night rambles after things to eat. 'So men are afraid of the People of the Jungle here also.' He sat down by the gate, and when a man came out he stood up, opened his mouth, and pointed down it to show that he wanted food. The man stared, and ran back up the one street of the village shouting for the priest, who was a big, fat man dressed in white, with a red and yellow mark on his forehead. The priest came to the gate, and with him at least a hundred people, who stared and talked and shouted and pointed at Mowgli.

'They have no manners, these Men-Folk,' said Mowgli to himself. 'Only the gray ape would behave as they do.' So he threw back his long hair and frowned at the crowd.

'What is there to be afraid of?' said the priest. 'Look at the marks on his arms and legs. They are the bites of wolves. He is but a wolf-child run away from the Jungle.'

Of course, in playing together, the cubs had often nipped Mowgli harder than they intended, and there were white scars all over his arms and legs. But he would have been the last person in the world to call these bites, for he knew what real biting meant.

'*Arré! Arré!*' said two or three women together. 'To be bitten by wolves, poor child! He is a handsome boy. He has eyes like red fire. By my honour, Messua, he is not unlike thy boy that was taken by the tiger.'

'Let me look,' said a woman with heavy copper rings on her wrists and ankles, and she peered at Mowgli under the palm of her hand. 'Indeed he is not. He is thinner, but he has the very look of my boy.'

The priest was a clever man, and he knew that Messua was wife to the richest villager in the place. So he looked up at the sky for a minute, and said solemnly: 'What the Jungle has taken the Jungle has restored. Take the boy into thy house, my sister, and forget not to honour the priest who sees so far into the lives of men.'

'By the Bull that bought me,' said Mowgli to himself, 'but all this talking is like another looking-over by the Pack! Well, if I am a man, a man I must become.'

The crowd parted as the woman beckoned Mowgli to her hut, where there was a red-lacquered bedstead, a great earthen grain-chest with curious raised patterns on it, half a dozen copper cooking-pots, an image of a Hindu god in a little alcove, and on the wall a real looking-glass, such as they sell at the country fairs.

She gave him a long drink of milk and some bread, and then she laid her hand on his head and looked into his eyes; for she thought that perhaps he might be her real son come back from the Jungle where the tiger had taken him. So she said: 'Nathoo, O Nathoo!' Mowgli did not show that he knew the name. 'Dost thou not remember the day when I gave thee thy new shoes?' She touched his foot, and it was almost as hard as horn. 'No,' she said, sorrowfully; 'those feet have never worn shoes, but thou art very like my Nathoo, and thou shalt be my son.'

Mowgli was uneasy, because he had never been under a roof before; but as he looked at the thatch, he saw that he could tear it out any time if he wanted to get away, and that the window had no fastenings. 'What is the good of a man,' he said to himself at last, 'if he does not understand man's talk? Now I am as silly and dumb as a man would be with us in the Jungle. I must learn their talk.'

It was not for fun that he had learned while he was with the wolves to imitate the challenge of bucks in the Jungle and the grunt of the little wild pig. So as soon as Messua pronounced a word Mowgli would imitate it almost perfectly, and before dark he had learned the names of many things in the hut.

There was a difficulty at bedtime, because Mowgli would not sleep under anything that looked so like a panther-trap as that hut, and when they shut the door he went through the window. 'Give him his will,' said Messua's husband. 'Remember he can never till now have slept on a bed. If he is indeed sent in the place of our son he will not run away.'

So Mowgli stretched himself in some long, clean grass at the edge of the field, but before he had closed his eyes a soft gray nose poked him under the chin.

'Phew!' said Gray Brother (he was the eldest of Mother Wolf's cubs). 'This is a poor reward for following thee twenty miles. Thou smellest of wood-smoke and cattle — altogether like a man already. Wake, Little Brother; I bring news.'

'Are all well in the Jungle?' said Mowgli, hugging him.

'All except the wolves that were burned with the Red Flower. Now, listen. Shere Khan has gone away to hunt far off till his coat grows again, for he is badly singed. When he returns he swears that he will lay thy bones in the Waingunga.'

'There are two words to that. I also have made a little promise. But news is always good. I am tired to-night, — very tired with new things, Gray Brother, — but bring me the news always.'

'Thou wilt not forget that thou art a wolf? Men will not make thee forget?' said Gray Brother anxiously.

'Never. I will always remember that I love thee and all in our cave; but also I will always remember that I have been cast out of the Pack.'

'And that thou mayest be cast out of another pack. Men are only men, Little Brother, and their talk is like the talk of frogs in a pond. When I come down here again, I will wait for thee in the bamboos at the edge of the grazing-ground.'

For three months after that night Mowgli hardly ever left the village gate, he was so busy learning the ways and customs of men. First he had to wear a cloth round him, which annoyed him horribly; and then he had to learn about money, which he did not in the least understand, and about ploughing, of which he did not see the use. Then the little children in the village made him very angry. Luckily, the Law of the Jungle had taught him to keep his temper, for in the Jungle life and food depend on keeping your temper; but when they made fun of him because he would not play games or fly kites, or because he mispronounced some word, only the knowledge that it was unsportsmanlike to kill little naked cubs kept him from picking them up and breaking them in two.

He did not know his own strength in the least. In the Jungle he knew he was weak compared with the beasts, but in the village people said that he was as strong as a bull.

And Mowgli had not the faintest idea of the difference that caste makes between man and man. When the potter's donkey slipped in the clay-pit, Mowgli hauled it out by the tail, and helped to stack the pots for their journey to the market at Khanhiwara. That was very shocking, too, for the potter is a low-caste man, and his donkey is worse. When the priest scolded him, Mowgli threatened to put him on the donkey, too, and the priest told Messua's husband that Mowgli had better be set to work as soon as possible; and the village head-man told Mowgli that he would have to go out with the buffaloes next day, and herd them while they grazed. No one was more pleased than Mowgli; and that night, because he had been appointed, as it were, a servant of the village, he went off to a circle that met every evening on a masonry platform under a great fig-tree. It was the village club, and the head-man and the watch-man and the barber (who knew all the gossip of the village), and old Buldeo, the village hunter, who owned a Tower musket, met and smoked. The monkeys sat and talked in the upper branches, and there was a hole under the platform where a cobra lived, and he had his little platter of milk every night because he was sacred; and the old men sat around the tree and talked, and pulled at the big hookahs [water-pipes], till far into the night. They told wonderful tales of gods and men and ghosts; and Buldeo told even more wonderful ones of the ways of beasts in the Jungle, till the eyes of the children sitting outside the circle bulged out of their heads. Most of the tales were about animals, for the Jungle was always at their door. The deer and the wild pig grubbed up their crops, and now and again the tiger carried off a man at twilight, within sight of the village gates.

Mowgli, who, naturally, knew something about what they were talking of, had to cover his face not to show that he was laughing, while Buldeo, the Tower musket across his knees, climbed on from one wonderful story to another, and Mowgli's shoulders shook.

Buldeo was explaining how the tiger that had carried away Messua's son was a ghost-tiger, and his body was inhabited by the ghost of a wicked old money-lender, who had died some years ago. 'And I know that this is true,' he said, 'because Purun Dass always limped from the blow that he got in a riot when his account-books were burned, and the tiger that I speak of, *he* limps, too, for the tracks of his pads are unequal.'

'True, true; that must be the truth,' said the graybeards, nodding together.

'Are all these tales such cobwebs and moon-talk?' said Mowgli. 'That tiger limps because he was born lame, as every one knows. To talk of the soul of a money-lender in a beast that never had the courage of a jackal is child's talk.'

Buldeo was speechless with surprise for a moment, and the head-man stared.

'Oho! It is the jungle brat, is it?' said Buldeo. 'If thou art so wise, better bring his hide to Khanhiwara, for the Government has set a hundred rupees on his life. Better still, do not talk when thy elders speak.'

Mowgli rose to go. 'All the evening I have lain here listening,' he called back over his shoulder, 'and, except once or twice, Buldeo has not said one word of truth concerning the Jungle, which is at his very doors. How, then, shall I believe the tales of ghosts and gods and goblins which he says he has seen?'

'It is full time that boy went to herding,' said the head-man, while Buldeo puffed and snorted at Mowgli's impertinence.

The custom of most Indian villages is for a few boys to take the cattle and buffaloes out to graze in the early morning, and bring them back at night; and the very cattle that would trample a white man to death allow themselves to be banged and bullied and shouted at by children that hardly come up to their noses. So long as the boys keep with the herds they are safe, for not even the tiger will charge a mob of cattle. But if they straggle to pick flowers or hunt lizards, they are sometimes carried off. Mowgli went through the village street in the dawn, sitting on the back of Rama, the great herd bull; and the slaty-blue buffaloes, with their long, backward-sweeping horns and savage eyes, rose out of their byres, one by one, and followed him, and Mowgli made it very clear to the children with him that he was the master. He beat the buffaloes with a long, polished bamboo, and told Kamya, one of the boys, to graze the cattle by themselves, while he went on with the buffaloes, and to be very careful not to stray away from the herd.

An Indian grazing-ground is all rock and scrubs and tussocks and little ravines, among which the herds scatter and disappear. The buffaloes generally keep to the pools and muddy places, where they lie wallowing or basking in the warm mud for hours. Mowgli drove them on to the edge of the plain where the Wain-gunga River came out of the Jungle; then he dropped from Rama's neck, trotted off to a bamboo clump, and found Gray Brother. 'Ah!' said Gray Brother. 'I have waited here very many days. What is the meaning of this cattle-herding work?'

'It is an order,' said Mowgli. 'I am a village herd for a while. What news of Shere Khan?'

'He has come back to this country, and has waited here a long time for thee. Now he has gone off again, for the game is scarce. But he means to kill thee.'

'Very good,' said Mowgli. 'So long as he is away do thou or one of the four brothers sit on that rock, so that I can see thee as I come out of the village. When he comes back wait for me in the ravine by the *dhâk*-tree in the centre of the plain. We need not walk into Shere Khan's mouth.'

Then Mowgli picked out a shady place, and lay down and slept while the buffaloes grazed round him. Herding in India is one of the laziest things in the world. The cattle move and crunch, and lie down, and move on again, and they do not even low. They only grunt, and the buffaloes very seldom say anything, but get down into the muddy pools one after another, and work their way into the mud till only their noses and staring china-blue eyes show above the surface, and there they lie like logs. The sun makes the rocks dance in the heat, and the herd-children hear one kite (never any more) whistling almost out of sight overhead, and they know that if they died, or a cow died, that kite would sweep down, and the next kite miles away would see him drop and would follow, and the next, and the next, and almost before they were dead there would be a score of hungry kites come out of nowhere. Then they sleep and wake and sleep again, and weave little baskets of dried grass and put grasshoppers in them; or catch two praying-mantises and make them fight; or string a necklace of red and black Jungle-nuts; or watch a lizard basking on a rock, or a snake hunting a frog near the wallows. Then they sing long, long songs with odd native quavers at the end of them, and the day seems longer than most people's whole lives, and perhaps they make a mud castle with mud figures of men and horses and buffaloes, and put reeds into the men's hands, and pretend that they are kings and the figures are their armies, or that they are gods to be worshipped. Then evening comes, and the children call, and the buffaloes lumber up out of the sticky mud with noises like gunshots going off one after the other, and they all string across the gray plain back to the twinkling village lights.

Day after day Mowgli would lead the buffaloes out to their wallows, and day after day he would see Gray Brother's back a mile and a half away across the plain (so he knew that Shere Khan had not come back), and day after day he would lie on the grass listening to the noises round him, and dreaming of old days in the Jungle. If Shere Khan had made a false step with his lame paw up in the jungles by the Waingunga, Mowgli would have heard him in those long, still mornings.

At last a day came when he did not see Gray Brother at the signal-place, and he laughed and headed the buffaloes for the ravine by the *dhâk*-tree, which was all covered with golden-red flowers. There sat Gray Brother, every bristle on his back lifted.

'He has hidden for a month to throw thee off thy guard. He crossed the ranges last night with Tabaqui, hot-foot on thy trail,' said the wolf, panting.

Mowgli frowned. 'I am not afraid of Shere Khan, but Tabaqui is very cunning.'

'Have no fear,' said Gray Brother, licking his lips a little. 'I met Tabaqui in the dawn. Now he is telling all his wisdom to the kites, but he told *me* everything before I broke his back. Shere Khan's plan is to wait for thee at the village gate this evening — for thee and for no one else. He is lying up now in the big dry ravine of the Waingunga.'

'Has he eaten to-day, or does he hunt empty?' said Mowgli, for the answer meant life or death to him.

'He killed at dawn, — a pig, — and he has drunk too. Remember, Shere Khan could never fast, even for the sake of revenge.'

'Oh! Fool, fool! What a cub's cub it is! Eaten and drunk too, and he thinks that I shall wait till he has slept! Now, where does he lie up? If there were but ten of us we might pull him down as he lies. These buffaloes will not charge unless they wind him, and I cannot speak their language. Can we get behind his track so that they may smell it?'

'He swam far down the Waingunga to cut that off,' said Gray Brother.

'Tabaqui told him that, I know. He would never have thought of it alone.' Mowgli stood with his finger in his mouth, thinking. 'The big ravine of the Waingunga. That opens out on the plain not half a mile from here. I can take the herd round through the Jungle to the head of the ravine and then sweep down — but he would slink out at the foot. We must block that end. Gray Brother, canst thou cut the herd in two for me?'

'Not I, perhaps — but I have brought a wise helper.' Gray Brother trotted off and dropped into a hole. Then there lifted up a huge gray head that Mowgli knew well, and the hot air was filled with the most desperate cry of all the Jungle — the hunting-howl of a wolf at mid-day.

'Akela! Akela!' said Mowgli, clapping his hands. 'I might have known that thou wouldst not forget me. We have a big work in hand. Cut the herd in two, Akela. Keep the cows and calves together, and the bulls and the plough-buffaloes by themselves.'

The two wolves ran, ladies'-chain fashion, in and out of the herd, which snorted and threw up its head, and separated into two clumps. In one the cow-buffaloes stood, with their calves in the centre, and glared and pawed, ready, if a wolf would only stay still, to charge down and trample the life out of him. In the other the bulls and the young bulls snorted and stamped; but, though they looked more imposing, they were much less dangerous, for they had no calves to protect. No six men could have divided the herd so neatly.

'What orders?' panted Akela. 'They are trying to join again.'

Mowgli slipped on to Rama's back. 'Drive the bulls away to the left, Akela. Gray Brother, when we are gone, hold the cows together, and drive them into the foot of the ravine.'

'How far?' said Gray Brother, panting and snapping.

'Till the sides are higher than Shere Khan can jump,' shouted Mowgli. 'Keep them there till we come down.' The bulls swept off as Akela bayed, and Gray Brother stopped in front of the cows. They charged down on him, and he ran just before them to the foot of the ravine, as Akela drove the bulls far to the left.

'Well done! Another charge and they are fairly started. Careful, now — careful, Akela. A snap too much, and the bulls will charge. *Huyah!* This is wilder work than driving black-buck. Didst thou think these creatures could move so swiftly?' Mowgli called.

'I have — have hunted these too in my time,' gasped Akela in the dust. 'Shall I turn them into the Jungle?'

'Ay, turn! Swiftly turn them! Rama is mad with rage. Oh, if I could only tell him what I need of him to-day!'

The bulls were turned to the right this time, and crashed into the standing thicket. The other herd-children, watching with the cattle half a mile away, hurried to the village as fast as their legs could carry them, crying that the buffaloes had gone mad and run away.

But Mowgli's plan was simple enough. All he wanted to do was to make a big circle uphill and get at the head of the ravine, and then take the bulls down it and catch Shere Khan between the bulls and the cows; for he knew that after a meal and a full drink Shere Khan would not be in any condition to fight or to clamber up the sides of the ravine. He was soothing the buffaloes now by voice, and Akela had dropped far to the rear, only whimpering once or twice to hurry the rear-guard. It was a long, long circle, for they did not wish to get too near the ravine and give Shere Khan warning. At last Mowgli rounded up the bewildered herd at the head of the ravine on a grassy patch that sloped steeply down to the ravine itself. From that height you could see across the tops of the trees down to the plain below; but what Mowgli looked at was the sides of the ravine, and he saw with a great deal of satisfaction that they ran nearly straight up and down, while the vines and creepers that hung over them would give no foothold to a tiger who wanted to get out.

'Let them breathe, Akela,' he said, holding up his hand. 'They have not winded him yet. Let them breathe. I must tell Shere Khan who comes. We have him in the trap.'

He put his hands to his mouth and shouted down the ravine, — it was almost like shouting down a tunnel, — and the echoes jumped from rock to rock.

After a long time there came back the drawling, sleepy snarl of a full-fed tiger just wakened.

'Who calls?' said Shere Khan, and a splendid peacock fluttered up out of the ravine screeching.

'I, Mowgli. Cattle thief, it is time to come to the Council

Rock! Down — hurry them down, Akela! Down, Rama, down!'

The herd paused for an instant at the edge of the slope, but Akela gave tongue in the full hunting-yell, and they pitched over one after the other, just as steamers shoot rapids, the sand and stones spurting up round them. Once started, there was no chance of stopping, and before they were fairly in the bed of the ravine Rama winded Shere Khan and bellowed.

'Ha! Ha!' said Mowgli, on his back. 'Now thou knowest!' and the torrent of black horns, foaming muzzles, and staring eyes whirled down the ravine like boulders in flood-time; the weaker buffaloes being shouldered out to the sides of the ravine, where they tore through the creepers. They knew what the business was before them — the terrible charge of the buffalo-herd, against which no tiger can hope to stand. Shere Khan heard the thunder of their hoofs, picked himself up, and lumbered down the ravine, looking from side to side for some way of escape; but the walls of the ravine were straight, and he had to keep on, heavy with his dinner and his drink, willing to do anything rather than fight. The herd splashed through the pool he had just left, bellowing till the narrow cut rang. Mowgli heard an answering bellow from the foot of the ravine, saw Shere Khan turn (the tiger knew if the worst came to the worst it was better to meet the bulls than the cows with their calves), and then Rama tripped, stumbled, and went on again over something soft, and, with the bulls at his heels, crashed full into the other herd, while the weaker buffaloes were lifted clean off their feet by the shock of the meeting. That charge carried both herds out into the plain, goring and stamping and snorting. Mowgli watched his time, and slipped off Rama's neck, laying about him right and left with his stick.

'Quick, Akela! Break them up. Scatter them, or they will be fighting one another. Drive them away, Akela. *Hai*, Rama! *Hai! hai! hai!* my children. Softly now, softly! It is all over.'

Akela and Gray Brother ran to and fro nipping the buffaloes' legs, and though the herd wheeled once to charge up the ravine again, Mowgli managed to turn Rama, and the others followed him to the wallows.

Shere Khan needed no more trampling. He was dead, and the kites were coming for him already.

'Brothers, that was a dog's death,' said Mowgli, feeling for the knife he always carried in a sheath round his neck now that he lived with men. 'But he would never have shown fight. His hide will look well on the Council Rock. We must get to work swiftly.'

A boy trained among men would never have dreamed of skinning a ten-foot tiger alone, but Mowgli knew better than any one else how an animal's skin is fitted on, and how it can be taken off. But it was hard work, and Mowgli slashed and tore and grunted for an hour, while the wolves lolled out their tongues, or came forward and tugged as he ordered them.

Presently a hand fell on his shoulder, and looking up he saw Buldeo with the Tower musket. The children had told the village about the buffalo stampede, and Buldeo went out angrily, only too anxious to correct Mowgli for not taking better care of the herd. The wolves dropped out of sight as soon as they saw the man coming.

'What is this folly?' said Buldeo angrily. 'To think that thou canst skin a tiger! Where did the buffaloes kill him? It is the Lame Tiger, too, and there is a hundred rupees on his head. Well, well, we will overlook thy letting the herd run off, and perhaps I will give thee one of the rupees of the reward when I have taken the skin to Khanhiwara.' He fumbled in his waist-cloth for flint and steel, and stooped down to singe Shere Khan's whiskers. Most native hunters singe a tiger's whiskers to prevent his ghost haunting them.

'Hum!' said Mowgli, half to himself as he ripped back the skin of a fore-paw. 'So thou wilt take the hide to Khanhiwara for the reward, and perhaps give me one rupee? Now it is in my mind that I need the skin for my own use. Heh! old man, take away that fire!'

'What talk is this to the chief hunter of the village? Thy luck and the stupidity of the buffaloes have helped thee to this kill. The tiger has just fed, or he would have gone twenty miles by this time. Thou canst not even skin him properly, little beggar-brat, and forsooth I, Buldeo, must be told not to singe his whiskers. Mowgli, I will not give thee one anna of the reward, but only a very big beating. Leave the carcass!'

'By the Bull that bought me,' said Mowgli, who was trying to get at the shoulder, 'must I stay babbling to an old ape all noon? Here, Akela, this man plagues me.'

Buldeo, who was still stooping over Shere Khan's head, found himself sprawling on the grass, with a gray wolf standing over him, while Mowgli went on skinning as though he were alone in all India.

'Ye-es,' he said, between his teeth. 'Thou art altogether right, Buldeo. Thou wilt never give me one anna of the reward. There is an old war between this lame tiger and myself — a very old war, and — I have won.'

To do Buldeo justice, if he had been ten years younger he would have taken his chance with Akela had he met the wolf in the woods; but a wolf who obeyed the orders of this boy who had private wars with man-eating tigers was not a common animal. It was sorcery, magic of the worst kind, thought Buldeo, and he wondered whether the amulet round his neck would protect him. He lay as still as still, expecting every minute to see Mowgli turn into a tiger, too.

'Maharaj! Great King,' he said at last, in a husky whisper.

'Yes,' said Mowgli, without turning his head, chuckling a little.

'I am an old man. I did not know that thou wast anything more than a herd-boy. May I rise up and go away, or will thy servant tear me to pieces?'

'Go, and peace go with thee. Only, another time do not meddle with my game. Let him go, Akela.'

Buldeo hobbled away to the village as fast as he could, looking back over his shoulder in case Mowgli should change into something terrible. When he got to the village he told a tale of magic and enchantment and sorcery that made the priest look very grave.

Mowgli went on with his work, but it was nearly twilight before he and the wolves had drawn the great gay skin clear of the body.

'Now we must hide this and take the buffaloes home! Help me to herd them, Akela.'

The herd rounded up in the misty twilight, and when they got near the village Mowgli saw lights, and heard the conches and bells in the temple blowing and banging. Half the village seemed to be waiting for him by the gate. 'That is because I have killed Shere Khan,' he said to himself; but a shower of stones whistled about his ears, and the villagers shouted: 'Sorcerer! Wolf's brat! Jungle-demon! Go away! Get hence quickly, or the priest will turn thee into a wolf again. Shoot, Buldeo, shoot!'

The old Tower musket went off with a bang, and a young buffalo bellowed in pain.

'More sorcery!' shouted the villagers. 'He can turn bullets. Buldeo, that was *thy* buffalo.'

'Now what is this?' said Mowgli, bewildered, as the stones flew thicker.

'They are not unlike the Pack, these brothers of thine,' said Akela, sitting down composedly. 'It is in my head that, if bullets mean anything, they would cast thee out.'

'Wolf! Wolf's cub! Go away!' shouted the priest, waving a sprig of the sacred *tulsi* plant.

'Again? Last time it was because I was a man. This time it is because I am a wolf. Let us go, Akela.'

A woman — it was Messua — ran across to the herd, and cried: 'Oh, my son, my son! They say thou art a sorcerer who can turn himself into a beast at will. I do not believe, but go away or they will kill thee. Buldeo says thou art a wizard, but I know thou hast avenged Nathoo's death.'

'Come back, Messua!' shouted the crowd. 'Come back, or we will stone thee.'

Mowgli laughed a little short ugly laugh, for a stone had hit him in the mouth. 'Run back, Messua. This is one of the foolish tales they tell under the big tree at dusk. I have at least paid for thy son's life. Farewell; and run quickly, for I shall send the herd in more swiftly than their brickbats. I am no wizard, Messua. Farewell!'

'Now, once more, Akela,' he cried. 'Bring the herd in.'

The buffaloes were anxious enough to get to the village. They hardly needed Akela's yell, but charged through the gate like a whirlwind, scattering the crowd right and left.

'Keep count!' shouted Mowgli scornfully. 'It may be that I have stolen one of them. Keep count, for I will do your herding no more. Fare you well, children of men, and thank Messua that I do not come in with my wolves and hunt you up and down your street.'

He turned on his heel and walked away with the Lone Wolf; and as he looked up at the stars he felt happy. 'No more sleeping in traps for me, Akela. Let us get Shere Khan's skin and go away. No; we will not hurt the village, for Messua was kind to me.'

When the moon rose over the plain, making it look all milky, the horrified villagers saw Mowgli, with two wolves at his heels and a bundle on his head, trotting across at the steady wolf's trot that eats up the long miles like fire. Then they banged the temple bells and blew the conches louder than ever; and Messua cried and Buldeo embroidered the story of his adventures in the Jungle, till he ended by saying that Akela stood up on his hind legs and talked like a man.

The moon was just going down when Mowgli and the two wolves came to the hill of the Council Rock, and they stopped at Mother Wolf's cave.

'They have cast me out from the Man-Pack, Mother,' shouted Mowgli, 'but I come with the hide of Shere Khan to keep my word.' Mother Wolf walked stiffly from the cave with the cubs behind her, and her eyes glowed as she saw the skin.

'I told him on that day, when he crammed his head and shoulders into this cave, hunting for thy life, Little Frog — I told him that the hunter would be the hunted. It is well done.'

'Little Brother, it is well done,' said a deep voice in the thicket. 'We were lonely in the Jungle without thee,' and Bagheera came running to Mowgli's bare feet. They clambered up the Council Rock together, and Mowgli spread the skin out on the flat stone where Akela used to sit, and pegged it down with four slivers of bamboo, and Akela lay down upon it, and called the old call to the Council, 'Look — look well, O Wolves!' exactly as he had called when Mowgli was first brought there.

Ever since Akela had been deposed, the Pack had been without a leader, hunting and fighting at their own pleasure. But they answered the call from habit, and some of them were lame from the traps they had fallen into, and some limped from shot-wounds, and some were mangy from eating bad food, and many were missing; but they came to the Council Rock, all that were left of them, and saw Shere Khan's striped hide on the rock, and the huge claws dangling at the end of the empty, dangling feet. It was then that Mowgli made up a song without any rhymes, a song that came up into his throat all by itself, and he shouted it aloud, leaping up and down on the rattling skin, and beating time with his heels till he had no more breath left, while Gray Brother and Akela howled between the verses.

'Look well, O Wolves. Have I kept my word?' said Mowgli when he had finished; and the wolves bayed, 'Yes', and one tattered wolf howled:

'Lead us again, O Akela. Lead us again, O Man-Cub, for we be sick of this lawlessness, and we would be the Free People once more.'

'Nay,' purred Bagheera 'that may not be. When ye are full fed, the madness may come upon ye again. Not for nothing are ye called the Free People. Ye fought for freedom, and it is yours. Eat it, O Wolves.'

'Man-Pack and Wolf-Pack have cast me out,' said Mowgli. 'Now I will hunt alone in the Jungle.'

'And we will hunt with thee,' said the four cubs.

So Mowgli went away and hunted with the four cubs in the Jungle from that day on. But he was not always alone, because years afterwards he became a man and married.

MOWGLI'S SONG

THE Song of Mowgli — I, Mowgli, am singing. Let the Jungle listen to the things I have done.

Shere Khan said he would kill — would kill! At the gates in the twilight he would kill Mowgli, the Frog!

He ate and he drank. Drink deep, Shere Khan, for when wilt thou drink again? Sleep and dream of the kill.

I am alone on the grazing-grounds. Gray Brother, come to me! Come to me, Lone Wolf, for there is big game afoot.

Bring up the great bull-buffaloes, the blue-skinned herd-bulls with the angry eyes. Drive them to and fro as I order.

Sleepest thou still, Shere Khan? Wake, oh, wake! Here come I, and the bulls are behind.

Rama, the King of the Buffaloes, stamped with his foot. Waters of the Waingunga, whither went Shere Khan?

He is not Ikki to dig holes, nor Mao, the Peacock, that he should fly. He is not Mang, the Bat, to hang in the branches. Little bamboos that creak together, tell me where he ran?

Ow! He is there. *Ahoo!* He is there. Under the feet of Rama lies the Lame One! Up, Shere Khan! Up and kill! Here is meat; break the necks of the bulls!

Hsh! He is asleep. We will not wake him, for his strength is very great. The kites have come down to see it. The black ants have come up to know it. There is a great assembly in his honour.

Alala! I have no cloth to wrap me. The kites will see that I am naked. I am ashamed to meet all these people.

Lend me thy coat, Shere Khan. Lend me thy gay striped coat that I may go to the Council Rock.

By the Bull that bought me, I have made a promise — a little promise. Only thy coat is lacking before I keep my word.

With the knife — with the knife that men use — with the knife of the hunter, the man, I will stoop down for my gift.

Waters of the Waingunga, bear witness that Shere Khan gives me his coat for the love that he bears me. Pull, Gray Brother! Pull, Akela! Heavy is the hide of Shere Khan.

The Man-Pack are angry. They throw stones and talk child's talk. My mouth is bleeding. Let us run away.

Through the night, through the hot night, run swiftly with me, my brothers.
We will leave the lights of the village and go to the low moon.

Waters of the Waingunga, the Man-Pack have cast me out. I did them no
harm, but they were afraid of me. Why?

Wolf-Pack, ye have cast me out too. The Jungle is shut to me and the village gates are shut. Why?

As Mang flies between the beasts and the birds, so fly I between the village
and the Jungle. Why?

I dance on the hide of Shere Khan, but my heart is very heavy. My mouth
is cut and wounded with the stones from the village, but my heart is
very light because I have come back to the Jungle. Why?

These two things fight together in me as the snakes fight in the spring.

The water comes out of my eyes; yet I laugh while it falls. Why?

I am two Mowglis, but the hide of Shere Khan is under my feet.

All the Jungle knows that I have killed Shere Khan. Look — look well, O
Wolves!

Ahae! My heart is heavy with the things that I do not understand.

LETTING IN THE JUNGLE

Veil them, cover them, wall them round —
  Blossom, and creeper, and weed —
Let us forget the sight and the sound,
  The smell and the touch of the breed!

Fat black ash by the altar-stone,
  Here is the white-foot rain,
And the does bring forth in the fields unsown,
  And none shall affright them again;
And the blind walls crumble, unknown, o'erthrown,
  And none shall inhabit again!

YOU will remember that after Mowgli had pinned Shere Khan's hide to the Council Rock, he told as many as were left of the Seeonee Pack that henceforward he would hunt in the Jungle alone; and the four children of Mother and Father Wolf said that they would hunt with him. But it is not easy to change one's life all in a minute — particularly in the Jungle. The first thing Mowgli did, when the disorderly Pack had slunk off, was to go to the home-cave, and sleep for a day and a night. Then he told Mother Wolf and Father Wolf as much as they could understand of his adventures among men; and when he made the morning sun flicker up and down the blade of his skinning-knife, — the same he had skinned Shere Khan with, — they said he had learned something. Then Akela and Gray Brother had to explain their share of the great buffalo-drive in the ravine, and Baloo toiled up the hill to hear all about it, and Bagheera scratched himself all over with pure delight at the way in which Mowgli had managed his war.

It was long after sunrise, but no one dreamed of going to sleep, and from time to time, during the talk, Mother Wolf would throw up her head, and sniff a deep snuff of satisfaction as the wind brought her the smell of the tiger-skin on the Council Rock.

'But for Akela and Gray Brother here,' Mowgli said, at the end, 'I could have done nothing. Oh, mother, mother! if thou hadst seen the black herd-bulls pour down the ravine, or hurry through the gates when the Man-Pack flung stones at me!'

'I am glad I did not see that last,' said Mother Wolf stiffly. 'It is not *my* custom to suffer my cubs to be driven to and fro like jackals. *I* would have taken a price from the Man-Pack; but I would have spared the woman who gave thee the milk. Yes, I would have spared her alone.'

'Peace, peace, Raksha!' said Father Wolf, lazily. 'Our Frog has come back again — so wise that his own father must lick his feet; and what is a cut, more or less, on the head? Leave Men alone.' Baloo and Bagheera both echoed: 'Leave Men alone.'

Mowgli, his head on Mother Wolf's side, smiled contentedly, and said that, for his own part, he never wished to see, or hear, or smell Man again.

'But what,' said Akela, cocking one ear — 'but what if men do not leave thee alone, Little Brother?'

'We be *five*,' said Gray Brother, looking round at the company, and snapping his jaws on the last word.

'We also might attend to that hunting,' said Bagheera, with a little *switch-switch* of his tail, looking at Baloo. 'But why think of men now, Akela?'

'For this reason,' the Lone Wolf answered: 'when that yellow thief's hide was hung up on the rock, I went back along our trail to the village, stepping in my tracks, turning aside, and lying down, to make a mixed trail in case one should follow us. But when I had fouled the trail so that I myself hardly knew it again, Mang, the Bat, came hawking between the trees, and hung up above me. Said Mang, "The village of the Man-Pack, where they cast out the Man-cub, hums like a hornets' nest."'

'It was a big stone that I threw,' chuckled Mowgli, who had often amused himself by throwing ripe pawpaws into a hornets' nest, and racing off to the nearest pool before the hornets caught him.

'I asked of Mang what he had seen. He said that the Red Flower blossomed at the gate of the village, and men sat about it carrying guns. Now *I* know, for I have good cause,' — Akela looked down at the old dry scars on his flank and side, —'that men do not carry guns for pleasure. Presently, Little Brother, a man with a gun follows our trail — if, indeed, he be not already on it.'

'But why should he? Men have cast me out. What more do they need?' said Mowgli angrily.

'Thou art a man, Little Brother,' Akela returned. 'It is not for *us*, the Free Hunters, to tell thee what thy brethren do, or why.'

He had just time to snatch up his paw as the skinning-knife cut deep into the ground below. Mowgli struck quicker than an average human eye could follow, but Akela was a wolf; and even a dog, who is very far removed from the wild wolf, his ancestor, can be waked out of deep sleep by a cart-wheel touching his flank, and can spring away unharmed before that wheel comes on.

'Another time,' Mowgli said quietly, returning the knife to its sheath, 'speak of the Man-Pack and of Mowgli in *two* breaths — not one.'

'Phff! That is a sharp tooth,' said Akela, snuffing at the blade's cut in the earth, 'but living with the Man-Pack has spoiled thine eye, Little Brother. I could have killed a buck while thou wast striking.'

Bagheera sprang to his feet, thrust up his head as far as he could, sniffed, and stiffened through every curve in his body. Gray Brother followed his example quickly, keeping a little to his left to get the wind that was blowing from the right, while Akela bounded fifty yards up wind, and, half-crouching, stiffened too. Mowgli looked on enviously. He could smell things as very few human beings could, but he had never reached the

hair-trigger-like sensitiveness of a Jungle nose; and his three
months in the smoky village had set him back sadly. However,
he dampened his finger, rubbed it on his nose, and stood erect
to catch the upper scent, which, though it is the faintest, is the
truest.

'Man!' Akela growled, dropping on his haunches.

'Buldeo!' said Mowgli, sitting down. 'He follows our trail,
and yonder is the sunlight on his gun. Look!'

It was no more than a splash of sunlight, for a fraction of a
second, on the brass clamps of the old Tower musket, but
nothing in the Jungle winks with just that flash, except when the
clouds race over the sky. Then a piece of mica, or a little pool,
or even a highly-polished leaf will flash like a heliograph. But
that day was cloudless and still.

'I knew men would follow,' said Akela triumphantly. 'Not
for nothing have I led the Pack.'

The four cubs said nothing, but ran down hill on their bellies,
melting into the thorn and under-brush as a mole melts into a
lawn.

'Where go ye, and without word?' Mowgli called.

'H'sh! We roll his skull here before mid-day!' Gray Brother
answered.

'Back! Back and wait! Man does not eat Man!' Mowgli
shrieked.

'Who was a wolf but now? Who drove the knife at me for
thinking he might be Man?' said Akela, as the four wolves
turned back sullenly and dropped to heel.

'Am I to give reason for all I choose to do?' said Mowgli
furiously.

'That is Man! There speaks Man!' Bagheera muttered under
his whiskers. 'Even so did men talk round the King's cages at
Oodeypore. We of the Jungle know that Man is wisest of all. If
we trusted our ears we should know that of all things he is most
foolish.' Raising his voice, he added, 'The Man-cub is right in
this. Men hunt in packs. To kill one, unless we know what the

others will do, is bad hunting. Come, let us see what this Man means toward us.'

'We will not come,' Gray Brother growled. 'Hunt alone, Little Brother. *We* know our own minds. The skull would have been ready to bring by now.'

Mowgli had been looking from one to the other of his friends, his chest heaving and his eyes full of tears. He strode forward to the wolves, and, dropping on one knee, said: 'Do I not know my mind? Look at me!'

They looked uneasily, and when their eyes wandered, he called them back again and again, till their hair stood up all over their bodies, and they trembled in every limb, while Mowgli stared and stared.

'Now,' said he, 'of us five, which is leader?'

'Thou art leader, Little Brother,' said Gray Brother, and he licked Mowgli's foot.

'Follow, then,' said Mowgli, and the four followed at his heels with their tails between their legs.

'This comes of living with the Man-Pack,' said Bagheera, slipping down after them.'There is more in the Jungle now than Jungle Law, Baloo.'

The old bear said nothing, but he thought many things.

Mowgli cut across noiselessly through the Jungle, at right angles to Buldeo's path, till, parting the undergrowth, he saw the old man, his musket on his shoulder, running up the trail of overnight at a dog-trot.

You will remember that Mowgli had left the village with the heavy weight of Shere Khan's raw hide on his shoulders, while Akela and Gray Brother trotted behind, so that the triple trail was very clearly marked. Presently Buldeo came to where Akela, as you know, had gone back and mixed it all up. Then he sat down, and coughed and grunted, and made little casts round and about into the Jungle to pick it up again, and all the time he could have thrown a stone over those who were watching him. No one can be so silent as a wolf when he does not care to be heard; and Mowgli, though the wolves thought he moved very clumsily, could come and go like a shadow. They ringed the old man as a school of porpoises ring a steamer at full speed, and as they ringed him they talked unconcernedly, for their speech began below the lowest end of the scale that untrained human beings can hear. [The other end is bounded by the high squeak of Mang, the Bat, which very many people cannot catch at all. From that note all the bird and bat and in-sect talk takes on.]

'This is better than any kill,' said Gray Brother, as Buldeo stooped and peered and puffed. 'He looks like a lost pig in the Jungles by the river. What does he say?' Buldeo was muttering savagely.

Mowgli translated. 'He says that packs of wolves must have danced round me. He says that he never saw such a trail in his life. He says he is tired.'

'He will be rested before he picks it up again,' said Bagheera coolly, as he slipped round a tree-trunk, in the game of blind-man's-buff that they were playing. '*Now*, what does the lean thing do?'

'Eat or blow smoke out of his mouth. Men always play with their mouths,' said Mowgli; and the silent trailers saw the old man fill and light and puff at a water-pipe, and they took good note of the smell of the tobacco, so as to be sure of Buldeo in the darkest night, if necessary.

Then a little knot of charcoal-burners came down the path, and naturally halted to speak to Buldeo, whose fame as a hun-ter reached for at least twenty miles round. They all sat down and smoked, and Bagheera and the others came up and watched while Buldeo began to tell the story of Mowgli, the Devil-child, from one end to another, with additions and inventions. How he himself had really killed Shere Khan; and how Mowgli had turned himself into a wolf, and fought with him all the after-noon, and changed into a boy again and bewitched Buldeo's rifle, so that the bullet turned the corner, when he pointed it at

Mowgli, and killed one of Buldeo's own buffaloes; and how the village, knowing him to be the bravest hunter in Seeonee, had sent him out to kill this Devil-child. But meantime the village had got hold of Messua and her husband, who were undoubtedly the father and mother of this Devil-child, and had barricaded them in their own hut, and presently would torture them to make them confess they were witch and wizard, and then they would be burned to death.

'When?' said the charcoal-burners, because they would very much like to be present at the ceremony.

Buldeo said that nothing would be done till he returned, because the village wished him to kill the Jungle Boy first. After that they would dispose of Messua and her husband, and divide their lands and buffaloes among the village. Messua's husband had some remarkably fine buffaloes, too. It was an excellent thing to destroy wizards. Buldeo thought; and people who entertained Wolf-children out of the Jungle were clearly the worst kind of witches.

But, said the charcoal-burners, what would happen if the English heard of it? The English, they had heard, were a perfectly mad people, who would not let honest farmers kill witches in peace.

Why, said Buldeo, the head-man of the village would report that Messua and her husband had died of snake-bite. *That* was all arranged, and the only thing now was to kill the Wolf-child. They did not happen to have seen anything of such a creature?

The charcoal-burners looked round cautiously, and thanked their stars they had not; but they had no doubt that so brave a man as Buldeo would find him if any one could. The sun was getting rather low, and they had an idea that they would push on to Buldeo's village and see that wicked witch. Buldeo said that, though it was his duty to kill the Devil-child, he could not think of letting a party of unarmed men go through the Jungle, which might produce the Wolf-demon at any minute, without his escort. He, therefore, would accompany them, and if the sorcerer's child appeared — well, he would show them how the best hunter in Seeonee dealt with such things. The Brahmin, he said, had given him a charm against the creature that made everything perfectly safe.

'What says he? What says he? What says he?' the wolves repeated every few minutes; and Mowgli translated until he came to the witch part of the story, which was a little beyond him, and then he said that the man and woman who had been so kind to him were trapped.

'Does Man trap Man?' said Bagheera.

'So he says. I cannot understand the talk. They are all mad together. What have Messua and her man to do with me that they should be put in a trap; and what is all this talk about the Red Flower? I must look to this. Whatever they would do to Messua they will not do till Buldeo returns. And so ——' Mowgli thought hard, with his fingers playing round the haft of the skinning-knife, while Buldeo and the charcoal-burners went off very valiantly in single file.

'I go hot-foot back to the Man-Pack,' Mowgli said at last.

'And those?' said Gray Brother, looking hungrily after the brown backs of the charcoal-burners.

'Sing them home,' said Mowgli, with a grin; 'I do not wish them to be at the village gates till it is dark. Can ye hold them?'

Gray Brother bared his white teeth in contempt. 'We can head them round and round in circles like tethered goats — if I know Man.'

'That I do not need. Sing to them a little, lest they be lonely on the road, and, Gray Brother, the song need not be of the sweetest. Go with them, Bagheera, and help make that song. When night is shut down, meet me by the village — Gray Brother knows the place.'

'It is no light hunting to work for a Man-cub. When shall I sleep?' said Bagheera, yawning, though his eyes showed that he was delighted with the amusement. 'Me to sing to naked men! But let us try.'

He lowered his head so that the sound would travel, and cried a long, long, 'Good hunting!' — a midnight call in the afternoon, which was quite awful enough to begin with. Mowgli heard it rumble, and rise, and fall, and die off in a creepy sort of whine behind him, and laughed to himself as he ran through the Jungle. He could see the charcoal-burners huddled in a knot; old Buldeo's gun-barrel waving, like a banana-leaf, to every point of the compass at once. Then Gray Brother gave the *Ya-la-hi! Yalahi!* call for the buck-driving, when the Pack drives the nilghai, the big blue cow, before them, and it seemed to come from the very ends of the earth, nearer, and nearer, and nearer, till it ended in a shriek snapped off short. The other three answered, till even Mowgli could have vowed that the full Pack was in full cry, and then they all broke into the magnificent Morning-song in the Jungle, with every turn, and flourish, and grace-note that a deep-mouthed wolf of the Pack knows. This is a rough rendering of the song, but you must imagine what it sounds like when it breaks the afternoon hush of the Jungle: —

> One moment past our bodies cast
>   · No shadow on the plain;
> Now clear and black they stride our track,
>   And we run home again.
> In morning hush, each rock and bush
>   Stands hard, and high, and raw:
> Then give the Call: '*Good rest to all
>   That keep the Jungle Law!*'
>
> Now horn and pelt our peoples melt
>   In covert to abide;
> Now, crouched and still, to cave and hill
>   Our Jungle Barons glide.
> Now, stark and plain, Man's oxen strain,
>   That draw the new-yoked plough;
> Now, stripped and dread, the dawn is red
>   Above the lit *talao*.

Ho! Get to lair! The sun's aflare
  Behind the breathing grass:
And creaking through the young bamboo
  The warning whispers pass.
By day made strange, the woods we range
  With blinking eyes we scan;
While down the skies the wild duck cries,
  '*The Day — the Day to Man!*'

The dew is dried that drenched our hide
  Or washed about our way;
And where we drank, the puddled bank
  Is crisping into clay.
The traitor Dark gives up each mark
  Of stretched or hooded claw;
Then hear the Call: '*God rest to all
  That keep the Jungle Law!*'

But no translation can give the effect of it, or the yelping scorn the Four threw into every word of it, as they heard the trees crash when the men hastily climbed up into the branches, and Buldeo began repeating incantations and charms. Then they lay down and slept, for, like all who live by their own exertions, they were of a methodical cast of mind; and no one can work well without sleep.

Meantime, Mowgli was putting the miles behind him, nine to the hour, swinging on, delighted to find himself so fit after all his cramped months among men. The one idea in his head was to get Messua and her husband out of the trap, whatever it was; for he had a natural mistrust of traps. Later on, he promised himself, he would pay his debts to the village at large.

It was at twilight when he saw the well-remembered grazing-grounds, and the *dhâk*-tree where Gray Brother had waited for him on the morning that he killed Shere Khan. Angry as he was at the whole breed and community of Man, something jumped up in his throat and made him catch his breath when he looked at the village roofs. He noticed that every one had come in from the fields unusually early, and that, instead of getting to their evening cooking, they gathered in a crowd under the village tree, and chattered, and shouted.

'Men must always be making traps for men, or they are not content,' said Mowgli. 'Last night it was Mowgli — but that night seems many Rains ago. To-night it is Messua and her man. To-morrow, and for very many nights after, it will be Mowgli's turn again.'

He crept along outside the wall till he came to Messua's hut, and looked through the window into the room. There lay Messua, gagged, and bound hand and foot, breathing hard, and groaning: her husband was tied to the gaily-painted bed-stead. The door of the hut that opened into the street was shut fast, and three or four people were sitting with their backs to it.

Mowgli knew the manners and customs of the villagers very fairly. He argued that so long as they could eat, and talk, and smoke, they would not do anything else; but as soon as they had fed they would begin to be dangerous. Buldeo would be coming in before long, and if his escort had done its duty, Buldeo would have a very interesting tale to tell. So he went in through the window, and, stooping over the man and the woman, cut their thongs, pulling out the gags, and looked round the hut for some milk.

Messua was half wild with pain and fear (she had been beaten and stoned all the morning), and Mowgli put his hand over her mouth just in time to stop a scream. Her husband was only bewildered and angry, and sat picking dust and things out of his torn beard.

'I knew — I knew he would come,' Messua sobbed at last. 'Now do I *know* that he is my son!' and she hugged Mowgli to her heart. Up to that time Mowgli had been perfectly steady, but now he began to tremble all over, and that surprised him immensely.

'Why are these thongs? Why have they tied thee?' he asked, after a pause.

'To be put to the death for making a son of thee — what else?' said the man sullenly. 'Look! I bleed.'

Messua said nothing, but it was at *her* wounds that Mowgli looked, and they heard him grit his teeth when he saw the blood.

'Whose work is this?' said he. 'There is a price to pay.'

'The work of all the village. I was too rich. I had too many cattle. *Therefore* she and I are witches, because we gave thee shelter.'

'I do not understand. Let Messua tell the tale.'

'I gave thee milk, Nathoo; dost thou remember?' Messua said timidly. 'Because thou wast my son, whom the tiger took, and because I loved thee very dearly. They said that I was thy mother, the mother of a devil, and therefore worthy of death.'

'And what is a devil?' said Mowgli. 'Death I have seen.'

The man looked up gloomily, but Messua laughed. 'See!' she said to her husband, 'I knew — I said that he was no sorcerer. He is my son — my son!'

'Son or sorcerer, what good will that do us?' the man answered. 'We be as dead already.'

'Yonder is the road to the Jungle' — Mowgli pointed through the window. 'Your hands and feet are free. Go now.'

'We do not know the Jungle, my son, as — as thou knowest,' Messua began. 'I do not think that I could walk far.'

'And the men and women would be upon our backs and drag us here again,' said the husband.

'H'm!' said Mowgli, and he tickled the palm of his hand with the tip of his skinning-knife; 'I have no wish to do harm to any one of this village— *yet*. But I do not think they will stay thee. In a little while they will have much else to think upon. Ah!' he lifted his head and listened to shouting and trampling outside. 'So they have let Buldeo come home at last?'

'He was sent out this morning to kill thee,' Messua cried. 'Didst thou meet him?'

'Yes — we — I met him. He has a tale to tell; and while he is telling it there is time to do much. But first I will learn what they mean. Think where ye would go, and tell me when I come back.'

He bounded through the window and ran along again outside the wall of the village till he came within ear-shot of the crowd round the peepul-tree. Buldeo was lying on the ground, coughing and groaning, and every one was asking him questions. His hair had fallen about his shoulders; his hands and legs were skinned from climbing up trees, and he could hardly speak, but he felt the importance of his position keenly. From time to time he said something about devils and singing devils, and magic enchantment, just to give the crowd a taste of what was coming. Then he called for water.

'Bah!' said Mowgli. 'Chatter — chatter! Talk, talk! Men are blood-brothers of the *Bandar-log*. Now he must wash his mouth with water; now he must blow smoke; and when all that is done he has still his story to tell. They are very wise people — men. They will leave no one to guard Messua till their ears are stuffed with Buldeo's tales. And — I grow as lazy as they!'

He shook himself and glided back to the hut. Just as he was at the window he felt a touch on his foot.

'Mother,' said he, for he knew that tongue well, 'what dost *thou* here?'

'I heard my children singing through the woods, and I followed the one I loved best. Little Frog, I have a desire to see that woman who gave thee milk,' said Mother Wolf, all wet with the dew.

'They have bound and mean to kill her. I have cut those ties, and she goes with her man through the Jungle.'

'I also will follow. I am old, but not yet toothless.' Mother Wolf reared herself up on end, and looked through the window into the dark of the hut.

In a minute she dropped noiselessly, and all she said was: 'I gave thee thy first milk; but Bagheera speaks truth; Man goes to Man at the last.'

'Maybe,' said Mowgli, with a very unpleasant look on his face; 'but to-night I am very far from that trail. Wait here, but do not let her see.'

'*Thou* wast never afraid of *me*, Little Frog,' said Mother Wolf, backing into the high grass, and blotting herself out, as she knew how.

'And now,' said Mowgli cheerfully, as he swung into the hut again, 'they are all sitting round Buldeo, who is saying that which did not happen. When his talk is finished, they say they will assuredly come here with the Red — with fire and burn you both. And then?'

'I have spoken to my man,' said Messua. 'Khanhiwara is thirty miles from here, but at Khanhiwara we may find the English ——'

'And what Pack are they?' said Mowgli.

'I do not know. They be white, and it is said that they govern all the land, and do not suffer people to burn or beat each other without witnesses. If we can get thither to-night, we live. Otherwise we die.'

'Live, then. No man passes the gates to-night. But what does *he* do?' Messua's husband was on his hands and knees digging up the earth in one corner of the hut.

'It is his little money,' said Messus. 'We can take nothing else.'

'Ah, yes. The stuff that passes from hand to hand and never grows warmer. Do they need it outside this place also?' said Mowgli.

The man stared angrily. 'He is a fool, and no devil,' he muttered. 'With the money I can buy a horse. We are too bruised to walk far, and the village will follow us in an hour.'

'I say they will *not* follow till I choose; but a horse is well thought of, for Messua is tired.' Her husband stood up and knotted the last of the rupees into his waist-cloth. Mowgli helped Messua through the window, and the cool night air revived her, but the Jungle in the starlight looked very dark and terrible.

'Ye know the trail to Khanhiwara?' Mowgli whispered. They nodded.

'Good. Remember, now, not to be afraid. And there is no need to go quickly. Only — only there may be some small singing in the Jungle behind you and before.'

'Think you we would have risked a night in the Jungle through anything less than the fear of burning? It is better to be killed by beasts than by men,' said Messua's husband; but Messua looked at Mowgli and smiled.

'I say,' Mowgli went on, just as though he were Baloo repeating an old Jungle Law for the hundredth time to a foolish cub — 'I say that not a tooth in the Jungle is bared against you; not a foot in the Jungle is lifted against you. Neither man nor beast shall stay you till you come within eye-shot of Khanhiwara. There will be a watch about you.' He turned quickly to Messua, saying, '*He* does not believe, but thou wilt believe?'

'Ay, surely, my son. Man, ghost, or wolf of the Jungle, I believe.'

'*He* will be afraid when he hears my people singing. Thou wilt know and understand. Go now, and slowly, for there is no need of any haste. The gates are shut.'

Messua flung herself sobbing at Mowgli's feet, but he lifted her very quickly with a shiver. Then she hung about his neck and called him every name of blessing she could think of, but her husband looked enviously across his fields, and said: '*If* we reach Khanhiwara, and I get the ear of the English, I will bring such a lawsuit against the Brahmin and old Buldeo and the others as shall eat the village to the bone. They shall pay me twice over for my crops untilled and my buffaloes unfed. I will have a great justice.'

Mowgli laughed. 'I do not know what justice is, but — come next Rains and see what is left.'

They went off toward the Jungle, and Mother Wolf leaped from her place of hiding.

'Follow!' said Mowgli; 'and look to it that all the Jungle knows these two are safe. Give tongue a little. I would call Bagheera.'

The long, low howl rose and fell, and Mowgli saw Messua's husband flinch and turn, half minded to run back to the hut.

'Go on,' Mowgli called cheerfully. 'I said there might be singing. That call will follow up to Khanhiwara. It is Favour of the Jungle.'

Messua urged her husband forward, and the darkness shut down on them and Mother Wolf as Bagheera rose up almost under Mowgli's feet, trembling with delight of the night that drives the Jungle-People wild.

'I am ashamed of thy brethren,' he said, purring.

'What? Did they not sing sweetly to Buldeo?' said Mowgli.

'Too well! Too well! They made even *me* forget my pride, and, by the Broken Lock that freed me, I went singing through the Jungle as though I were out wooing in the spring! Didst thou not hear us?'

'I had other game afoot. Ask Buldeo if he liked the song. But where are the Four? I do not wish one of the Man-Pack to leave the gates to-night.'

'What need of the Four, then?' said Bagheera, shifting from foot to foot, his eyes ablaze, and purring louder than ever. 'I can hold them, Little Brother. Is it killing at last? The singing and the sight of the men climbing up the trees have made me very ready. Who is Man that we should care for him — the naked brown digger, the hairless and toothless, the eater of earth? I have followed him all day — at noon — in the white sunlight. I herded him as the wolves herd buck. I am Bagheera! Bagheera! Bagheera! As I dance with my shadow, so danced I with those men. Look!' The great panther leaped as a kitten leaps at a dead leaf whirling overhead, struck left and right into the empty air, that sang under the strokes, landed noiselessly, and leaped again and again, while the half purr, half growl gathered head as steam rumbles in a boiler. 'I am Bagheera — in the Jungle — in the night, and my strength is in me. Who shall stay my stroke? Man-cub, with one blow of my paw I could beat thy head flat as a dead frog in the summer!'

'Strike, then!' said Mowgli, in the dialect of the village, *not* the talk of the Jungle, and the human words brought Bagheera to a full stop, flung back on haunches that quivered under him, his head just at the level of Mowgli's. Once more Mowgli stared, as he had stared at the rebellious cubs, full into the beryl-green eyes till the red glare behind their green went out like the light of a lighthouse shut off twenty miles across the sea; till the eyes dropped, and the big head with them — dropped lower and lower, and the red rasp of a tongue grated on Mowgli's instep.

'Brother — Brother — Brother!' the boy whispered, stroking steadily and lightly from the neck along the heaving back: 'Be still, be still! It is the fault of the night, and no fault of thine.'

'It was the smells of the night,' said Bagheera penitently. 'This air cries aloud to me. But how dost *thou* know?'

Of course the air round an Indian village is full of all kinds of smells, and to any creature who does nearly all his thinking through his nose, smells are as maddening as music and drugs are to human beings. Mowgli gentled the panther for a few minutes longer, and he lay down like a cat before a fire, his paws tucked under his breast, and his eyes half shut.

'Thou art of the Jungle, and *not* of the Jungle,' he said at last. 'And I am only a black panther. But I love thee, Little Brother.'

'They are very long at their talk under the tree,' Mowgli said, without noticing the last sentence. 'Buldeo must have told many tales. They should come soon to drag the woman and her man out of the trap and put them into the Red Flower. They will find that trap sprung. Ho! ho!'

'Nay, listen,' said Bagheera. 'The fever is out of my blood

now. Let them find *me* there! Few would leave their houses after meeting me. It is not the first time I have been in a cage; and I do not think they will tie *me* with cords.'

'Be wise, then,' said Mowgli, laughing; for he was beginning to feel as reckless as the panther, who had glided into the hut.

'Pah!' Bagheera grunted. 'This place is rank with Man, but here is just such a bed as they gave me to lie upon in the King's cages at Oodeypore. Now I lie down.' Mowgli heard the strings of the cot crack under the great brute's weight. 'By the Broken Lock that freed me, they will think they have caught big game! Come and sit beside me, Little Brother; we will give them "good hunting" together!'

'No; I have another thought in my stomach. The Man-Pack shall not know what share I have in the sport. Make thine own hunt. I do not wish to see them.'

'Be it so,' said Bagheera. 'Ah, now they come!'

The conference under the peepul-tree had been growing noisier and noisier, at the far end of the village. It broke in wild yells, and a rush up the street of men and women, waving clubs and bamboos and sickles and knives. Buldeo and the Brahmin were at the head of it, but the mob was close at their heels, and they cried, 'The witch and the wizard! Let us see if hot coins will make them confess! Burn the hut over their heads! We will teach them to shelter wolf-devils! Nay, beat them first! Torches! More torches! Buldeo, heat the gun-barrels!'

Here was some little difficulty with the catch of the door. It had been very firmly fastened, but the crowd tore it away bodily, and the light of the torches streamed into the room where, stretched at full length on the bed, his paws crossed and lightly hung down over one end, black as the Pit, and terrible as a demon, was Bagheera. There was one half-minute of desperate silence, as the front ranks of the crowd clawed and tore their way back from the threshold, and in that minute Bagheera raised his head and yawned — elaborately, carefully, and osten- tatiously — as he would yawn when he wished to insult an equal. The fringed lips drew back and up; the red tongue curled; the lower jaw dropped and dropped till you could see half-way down the hot gullet; and the gigantic dog-teeth stood clear to the pit of the gums till they rang together, upper and under, with the snick of steel-faced wards shooting home round the edges of a safe. Next instant the street was empty; Bagheera had leaped back through the window, and stood at Mowgli's side, while a yelling, screaming torrent scrambled and tumbled one over another in their panic haste to get to their own huts.

'They will not stir till day comes,' said Bagheera quietly. 'And now?'

The silence of the afternoon sleep seemed to have overtaken the village; but, as they listened, they could hear the sound of heavy grain-boxes being dragged over earthen floors and set down against doors. Bagheera was quite right; the village would not stir till daylight. Mowgli sat still, and thought, and his face grew darker and darker.

'What have I done?' said Bagheera, at last, coming to his feet, fawning.

'Nothing but great good. Watch them now till the day. I sleep.' Mowgli ran off into the Jungle, and dropped like a dead man across a rock, and slept and slept the day round, and the night back again.

When he waked, Bagheera was at his side, and there was a newly-killed buck at his feet. Bagheera watched curiously while Mowgli went to work with his skinning-knife, ate and drank, and turned over with his chin in his hands.

'The man and the woman are come safe within eye-shot of Khanhiwara,' Bagheera said. 'Thy lair-mother sent the word back by Chil, the Kite. They found a horse before midnight of the night they were freed, and went very quickly. Is not that well?'

'That is well,' said Mowgli.

'And thy Man-Pack in the village did not stir till the sun was high this morning. Then they ate their food and ran back quickly to their houses.'

'Did they, by chance, see thee?'

'It may have been. I was rolling in the dust before the gate at dawn, and I may have made also some small song to myself. Now, Little Brother, there is nothing more to do. Come hunting with me and Baloo. He has new hives that he wishes to show, and we all desire thee back again as of old. Take off that look which makes even me afraid! The man and woman will not be put into the Red Flower, and all goes well in the Jungle. Is it not true? Let us forget the Man-Pack.'

'They shall be forgotten in a little while. Where does Hathi feed to-night?'

'Where he chooses. Who can answer for the Silent One? But why? What is there Hathi can do which we cannot?'

'Bid him and his three sons come here to me.'

'But, indeed, and truly, Little Brother, it is not — it is not seemly to say "Come", and "Go", to Hathi. Remember, he is the Master of the Jungle, and before the Man-Pack changed the look on thy face, he taught thee the Master Words of the Jungle.'

'That is all one. I have a Master Word for him now. Bid him come to Mowgli, the Frog; and if he does not hear at first, bid him come because of the Sack of the Fields of Bhurtpore.'

'The Sack of the Fields of Bhurtpore,' Bagheera repeated two or three times to make sure. 'I go. Hathi can but be angry at the worst, and I would give a moon's hunting to hear a Master Word that compels the Silent One.'

He went away, leaving Mowgli stabbing furiously with his skinning-knife into the earth. Mowgli had never seen human blood in his life before till he had seen, and — what meant much more to him — smelled Messua's blood on the thongs that bound her. And Messua had been kind to him, and, so far as he knew anything about love, he loved Messua as completely as he hated the rest of mankind. But deeply as he loathed them, their talk, their cruelty, and their cowardice, not for anything the Jungle had to offer could he bring himself to take a human life, and have that terrible scent of blood back again in his nostrils. His plan was simpler, but much more thorough; and he laughed to himself when he thought that it was one of old Buldeo's tales told under the peepul-tree in the evening that had put the idea into his head.

'It *was* a Master Word,' Bagheera whispered in his ear. 'They were feeding by the river, and they obeyed as though they were bullocks. Look, where they come now!'

Haiti and his three sons had arrived in their usual way, without a sound. The mud of the river was still fresh on their flanks, and Hathi was thoughtfully chewing the green stem of a young plantain-tree that he had gouged up with his tusks. But every line in his vast body showed to Bagheera, who could see things when he came across them, that it was not the Master of the Jungle speaking to a Man-cub, but one who was afraid coming before one who was not. His three sons rolled side by side, behind their father.

Mowgli hardly lifted his head as Hathi gave him 'Good hunting.' He kept him swinging and rocking, and shifting from one foot to another, for a long time before he spoke; and when he opened his mouth it was to Bagheera, not to the elephants.

'I will tell a tale that was told to me by the hunter ye hunted to-day,' said Mowgli. 'It concerns an elephant, old and wise, who fell into a trap, and the sharpened stake in the pit scarred him from a little above his heel to the crest of his shoulder, leaving a white mark.' Mowgli threw out his hand, and as Hathi wheeled the moonlight showed a long white scar on his slaty side, as though he had been struck with a red-hot whip. 'Men came to take him from the trap,' Mowgli continued, 'but he broke his ropes, for he was strong, and went away till his wound was healed. Then came he, angry, by night to the fields of those hunters. And I remember now that he had three sons. These things happened many, many Rains ago, and very far away — among the fields of Bhurtpore. What came to those fields at the next reaping, Hathi?'

'They were reaped by me and by my three sons,' said Hathi.

'And to the ploughing that follows the reaping?' said Mowgli.

'There was no ploughing,' said Hathi.

'And to the men that live by the green crops on the ground?' said Mowgli.

'They went away.'

'And to the huts in which the men slept?' said Mowgli.

'We tore the roofs to pieces, and the Jungle swallowed up the walls,' said Hathi.

'And what more?' said Mowgli.

'As much good ground as I can walk over in two nights from the east to the west, and from the north to the south as much as I can walk over in three nights, the Jungle took. We let in the Jungle upon five villages; and in those villages, and in their lands, the grazing-ground and the soft crop-grounds, there is not one man to-day who takes his food from the ground. That was the Sack of the Fields of Bhurtpore, which I and my three sons did; and now I ask, Man-cub, how the news of it came to thee?' said Hathi.

'A man told me, and now I see even Buldeo can speak truth. It was well done, Hathi with the white mark; but the second time it shall be done better, for the reason that there is a man to direct. Thou knowest the village of the Man-Pack that cast me out? They are idle, senseless, and cruel; they play with their mouths, and they do not kill the weaker for food, but for sport. When they are full-fed they would throw their own breed into the Red Flower. This I have seen. It is not well that they should live here any more. I hate them!'

'Kill, then,' said the youngest of Hathi's three sons, picking up a tuft of grass, dusting it against his fore-legs, and throwing it away, while his little red eyes glanced furtively from side to side.

'What good are white bones to me?' Mowgli answered angrily. 'Am I the cub of a wolf to play in the sun with a raw head? I have killed Shere Khan, and his hide rots on the Council Rock; but — but I do not know whither Shere Khan is gone, and my stomach is still empty. Now I will take that which I can see and touch. Let in the Jungle upon that village, Hathi!'

Bagheera shivered, and cowered down. He could understand, if the worst came to the worst, a quick rush down the village street, and a right and left blow into a crowd, or a crafty killing of men as they ploughed in the twilight; but this scheme for deliberately blotting out an entire village from the eyes of man and beast frightened him. Now he saw why Mowgli had sent for Hathi. No one but the long-lived elephant could plan and carry through such a war.

'Let them run as the men ran from the fields of Bhurtpore, till we have the rain-water for the only plough, and the noise of the rain on the thick leaves for the pattering of their spindles — till Bagheera and I lair in the house of the Brahmin, and the buck drink at the tank behind the temple! Let in the Jungle, Hathi!'

'But I — but we have no quarrel with them, and it needs the red rage of great pain ere we tear down the places where men sleep,' said Hathi doubtfully.

'Are ye the only eaters of grass in the Jungle? Drive in your peoples. Let the deer and the pig and the nilghai look to it. Ye need never show a hand's-breadth of hide till the fields are naked. Let in the Jungle, Hathi!'

'There will be no killing? My tusks were red at the Sack of the Fields of Bhurtpore, and I would not wake that smell again.'

'Nor I. I do not wish even their bones to lie on the clean earth. Let them go and find a fresh lair. They cannot stay here. I have seen and smelled the blood of the woman that gave me food — the woman whom they would have killed but for me.

Only the smell of the new grass on their door-steps can take away that smell. It burns in my mouth. Let in the Jungle, Hathi!'

'Ah!' said Hathi. 'So did the scar of the stake burn on my hide till we watched the villages die under in the spring growth. Now I see. Thy war shall be our war. We will let in the Jungle!'

Mowgli had hardly time to catch his breath — he was shaking all over with rage and hate — before the place where the elephants had stood was empty, and Bagheera was looking at him with terror.

'By the Broken Lock that freed me!' said the Black Panther at last. 'Art *thou* the naked thing I spoke for in the Pack when all was young? Master of the Jungle, when my strength goes, speak for me — speak for Baloo — speak for us all! We are cubs before thee! Snapped twigs under foot! Fawns that have lost their doe!'

The idea of Bagheera being a stray fawn upset Mowgli altogether, and he laughed and caught his breath, and sobbed and laughed again, till he had to jump into a pool to make himself stop. Then he swam round and round, ducking in and out of the bars of the moonlight like the frog, his namesake.

By this time Hathi and his three sons had turned, each to one point of the compass, and were striding silently down the valleys a mile away. They went on and on for two days' march — that is to say, a long sixty miles — through the Jungle; and every step they took, and every wave of their trunks, was known and noted and talked over by Mang and Chil and the Monkey-People and all the birds. Then they began to feed, and fed quietly for a week or so. Hathi and his sons are like Kaa, the Rock Python. They never hurry till they have to.

At the end of that time — and none knew who had started it — a rumour went through the Jungle that there was better food and water to be found in such and such a valley. The pig — who, of course, will go to the ends of the earth for a full meal — moved first by companies, scuffling over the rocks, and the deer followed, with the small wild foxes that live on the dead and dying of the herds; and the heavy-shouldered nilghai moved parallel with the deer, and the wild buffaloes of the swamps came after the nilghai. The least little thing would have turned the scattered, straggling droves that grazed and sauntered and drank and grazed again; but whenever there was an alarm some one would rise up and soothe them. At one time it would be Ikki the Porcupine, full of news of good feed just a little farther on; at another Mang would cry cheerily and flap down a glade to show it was all empty; or Baloo, his mouth full of roots, would shamble alongside a wavering line and half frighten, half romp it clumsily back to the proper road. Very many creatures broke back or ran away or lost interest, but very many were left to go forward. At the end of another ten days or so the situation was this. The deer and the pig and the nilghai were milling round and round in a circle of eight or ten miles radius, while the Eaters of Flesh skirmished round its edge. And the centre of that circle was the village, and round the village the crops were ripening, and in the crops sat men on what they call *machans* — platforms like pigeon-perches, made of sticks at the top of four poles — to scare away birds and other stealers. Then the deer were coaxed no more. The Eaters of Flesh were close behind them, and forced them forward and inward.

It was a dark night when Hathi and his three sons slipped down from the Jungle, and broke off the poles of the *machans* with their trunks; they fell as a snapped stalk of hemlock in bloom falls, and the men that tumbled from them heard the deep gurgling of the elephants in their ears. Then the vanguard of the bewildered armies of the deer broke down and flooded into the village grazing-grounds and the ploughed fields; and the sharp-hoofed, rooting wild pig came with them, and what the deer left the pig spoiled, and from time to time an alarm of wolves would shake the herds, and they would rush to and fro desperately, treading down the young barley, and cutting flat the banks of the irrigating channels. Before the dawn broke the pressure on the outside of the circle gave way at one point. The Eaters of Flesh had fallen back and left an open path to the south, and drove upon drove of buck fled along it. Others, who were bolder, lay up in the thickets to finish their meal next night.

But the work was practically done. When the villagers looked in the morning they saw their crops were lost. And that meant death if they did not get away, for they lived year in and year out as near to starvation as the Jungle was near to them. When the buffaloes were sent to graze the hungry brutes found that the deer had cleared the grazing-grounds, and so wandered into the Jungle and drifted off with their wild mates; and when twilight fell the three or four ponies that belonged to the village lay in their stables with their heads beaten in. Only Bagheera could have given those strokes, and only Bagheera would have thought of insolently dragging the last carcass to the open street.

The villagers had no heart to make fires in the fields that night, so Hathi and his three sons went gleaning among what was left; and where Hathi gleans there is no need to follow. The men decided to live on their stored seed-corn until the Rains had fallen, and then to take work as servants till they could catch up with the lost year; but as the grain-dealer was thinking of his well-filled crates of corn, and the prices he would levy at the sale of it, Hathi's sharp tusks were picking out the corner of his mud-house, and smashing open the big wicker chest, leeped with cow-dung, where the precious stuff lay.

When that last loss was discovered, it was the Brahmin's turn to speak. He had prayed to his own Gods without answer. It might be, he said, that, unconsciously, the village had offended some one of the Gods of the Jungle, for, beyond doubt, the Jungle was against them. So they sent for the head-man of the nearest tribe of wandering Gonds — little, wise, and very black hunters, living in the deep Jungle, whose fathers came of the

oldest race in India — the aboriginal owners of the land. They
made the Gond welcome with what they had, and he stood on
one leg, his bow in his hand, and two or three poisoned arrows
stuck through his top-knot, looking half afraid and half contemptuously at the anxious villagers and their ruined fields.
They wished to know whether his Gods — the Old Gods —
were angry with them, and what sacrifices should be offered.
The Gond said nothing, but picked up a trail of the *Karela*, the
vine that bears the bitter wild gourd, and laced it to and fro
across the temple door in the face of the staring red Hindu
image. Then he pushed with his hand in the open air along the
road to Khanhiwara, and went back to his Jungle, and watched
the Jungle-People drifting through it. He knew that when the
Jungle moves only white men can hope to turn it aside.

There was no need to ask his meaning. The wild gourd would
grow where they had worshipped their God, and the sooner
they saved themselves the better.

But it is hard to tear a village from its moorings. They stayed
on as long as any summer food was left to them, and they tried
to gather nuts in the Jungle, but shadows with glaring eyes
watched them, and rolled before them even at mid-day; and
when they ran back afraid to their walls, on the tree-trunks
they had passed not five minutes before the bark would be
stripped and chiselled with the stroke of some great taloned
paw. The more they kept to their village, the bolder grew the
wild things that gambolled and bellowed on the grazing-
grounds by the Waingunga. They had no time to patch and
plaster the rear walls of the empty byres that backed on to the
Jungle; the wild pig trampled them down, and the knotty-
rooted vines hurried after and threw their elbows over the new-
won ground, and the coarse grass bristled behind the vines like
the lances of a goblin army following a retreat. The unmarried
men ran away first, and carried the news far and near that the
village was doomed. Who could fight, they said, against the
Jungle, or the Gods of the Jungle, when the very village cobra

had left his hole in the platform under the peepul-tree? So their little commerce with the outside world shrunk as the trodden paths across the open grew fewer and fainter. At last the nightly trumpetings of Hathi and his three sons ceased to trouble them; for they had no more to be robbed of. The crop on the ground and the seed in the ground had been taken. The outlying fields were already losing their shape, and it was time to throw themselves on the charity of the English at Khanhiwara.

Native fashion, they delayed their departure from one day to another till the first Rains caught them and the unmended roofs let in a flood, and the grazing-ground stood ankle-deep, and all life came on with a rush after the heat of the summer. Then they waded out — men, women, and children — through the blinding hot rain of the morning, but turned naturally for one farewell look at their homes.

They heard, as the last burdened family filed through the gate, a crash of falling beams and thatch behind the walls. They saw a shiny, snaky black trunk lifted for an instant, scattering sodden thatch. It disappeared, and there was another crash, followed by a squeal. Hathi had been plucking off the roofs of the huts as you pluck water-lilies, and a rebounding beam had pricked him. He needed only this to unchain his full strength, for of all things in the Jungle the wild elephant enraged is the most wantonly destructive. He kicked backward at a mud wall that crumbled at the stroke, and, crumbling, melted to yellow mud under the torrent of rain. Then he wheeled and squealed, and tore through the narrow streets, leaning against the huts right and left, shivering the crazy doors, and crumpling up the eaves; while his three sons raged behind as they had raged at the Sack of the Fields of Bhurtpore.

'The Jungle will swallow these shells,' said a quiet voice in the wreckage. 'It is the outer wall that must lie down,' and Mowgli, with the rain sluicing over his bare shoulders and arms, leaped back from a wall that was settling like a tired buffalo.

'All in good time,' panted Hathi. 'Oh, but my tusks were red at Bhurtpore! To the outer wall, children! With the head! To-gether! Now!'

The four pushed side by side; the outer wall bulged, split, and fell, and the villagers, dumb with horror, saw the savage, clay-streaked heads of the wreckers in the ragged gap. Then they fled, houseless and foodless, down the valley, as their village, shredded and tossed and trampled, melted behind them.

A month later the place was a dimpled mound, covered with soft, green young stuff; and by the end of the Rains there was the roaring Jungle in full blast on the spot that had been under plough not six months before.

MOWGLI'S SONG AGAINST PEOPLE

I will let loose against you the fleet-footed vines —
I will call in the Jungle to stamp out your lines!
    The roofs shall fade before it,
      The house-beams shall fall,
    And the *Karela*, the bitter *Karela*,
      Shall cover it all!

In the gates of these your councils my people shall sing,
In the doors of these your garners the Bat-folk shall cling;
    And the snake shall be your watchman
      By a hearthstone unswept;
    For the *Karela*, the bitter *Karela*,
      Shall fruit where ye slept!

Ye shall not see my strikers; ye shall hear them and guess;
By night, before the moon-rise, I will send for my cess,
    And the wolf shall be your herdsman
      By a landmark removed,
    For the *Karela*, the bitter *Karela*,
      Shall seed where ye loved!

I will reap your fields before you at the hands of a host;
Ye shall glean behind my reapers, for the bread that is lost;
    And the deer shall be your oxen
      By a headland untilled,
    For the *Karela*, the bitter *Karela*,
      Shall leaf where ye build!

I have untied against you the club-footed vines,
I have sent in the Jungle to swamp out your lines!
    The trees — the trees are on you!
      The house-beams shall fall,
    And the *Karela*, the bitter *Karela*,
      Shall cover you all!

THE KING'S ANKUS

These are the Four that are never content, that have never been filled since
   the Dews began —
Jacala's mouth, and the glut of the Kite, and the hands of the Ape, and
   the Eyes of Man.

Jungle Saying.

KAA, the big Rock Python, had changed his skin for perhaps
the two-hundredth time since his birth; and Mowgli, who never
forgot that he owed his life to Kaa for a night's work at Cold
Lairs, which you may perhaps remember, went to congratulate
him. Skin-changing always makes a snake moody and de-
pressed till the new skin begins to shine and look beautiful.
Kaa never made fun of Mowgli any more, but accepted him,
as the other Jungle-People did, for the Master of the Jungle,
and brought him all the news that a python of his size would
naturally hear. What Kaa did not know about the Middle
Jungle, as they call it, — the life that runs close to the earth or
under it, the boulder, burrow, and the tree-bole life, — might
have been written upon the smallest of his scales.

That afternoon Mowgli was sitting in the circle of Kaa's great
coils, fingering the flaked and broken old skin that lay all
looped and twisted among the rocks just as Kaa had left it.
Kaa had very courteously packed himself under Mowgli's
broad, bare shoulders, so that the boy was really resting in a
living arm-chair.

'Even to the scales of the eyes it is perfect,' said Mowgli,
under his breath, playing with the old skin. 'Strange to see the
covering of one's own head at one's own feet!'

'Ay, but I lack feet,' said Kaa; 'and since this is the custom
of all my people, I do not find it strange. Does thy skin never
feel old and harsh?'

'Then go I and wash, Flathead; but, it is true, in the great heats I have wished I could slough my skin without pain, and run skinless.'

'I wash, and *also* I take off my skin. How looks the new coat?'

Mowgli ran his hand down the diagonal checkerings of the immense back. 'The Turtle is harder-backed, but not so gay,' he said judgmatically. 'The Frog, my name-bearer, is more gay, but not so hard. It is very beautiful to see — like the mottling in the mouth of a lily.'

'It needs water. A new skin never comes to full colour before the first bath. Let us go bathe.'

'I will carry thee,' said Mowgli; and he stooped down, laughing, to lift the middle section of Kaa's great body, just where the barrel was thickest. A man might just as well have tried to heave up a two-foot water-main; and Kaa lay still, puffing with quiet amusement. Then the regular evening game began — the Boy in the flush of his great strength, and the Python in his sumptuous new skin, standing up one against the other for a wrestling match — a trial of eye and strength. Of course, Kaa could have crushed a dozen Mowglis if he had let himself go; but he played carefully, and never loosed one-tenth of his power. Ever since Mowgli was strong enough to endure a little rough handling, Kaa had taught him this game, and it suppled his limbs as nothing else would. Sometimes Mowgli would stand lapped almost to his throat in Kaa's shifting coils, striving to get one arm free and catch him by the throat. Then Kaa would give way limply, and Mowgli, with quick-moving feet, would try to cramp the purchase of that huge tail as it flung backward feeling for a rock or a stump. They would rock to and fro, head to head, each waiting for his chance, till the beautiful statue-like group melted in a whirl of black-and-yellow coils and struggling legs and arms, to rise up again and again. 'Now! now! now!' said Kaa, making feints with his head that even Mowgli's quick hand could not turn aside. 'Look! I touch thee here, Little Brother! Here, and here! Are thy hands numb? Here again!'

The game always ended in one way — with a straight, driving blow of the head that knocked the boy over and over. Mowgli could never learn the guard for that lightning lunge, and, as Kaa said, there was not the least use in trying.

'Good hunting!' Kaa grunted at last; and Mowgli, as usual, was shot away half a dozen yards, gasping and laughing. He rose with his fingers full of grass, and followed Kaa to the wise snake's pet bathing-place — a deep, pitchy-black pool surrounded with rocks, and made interesting by sunken tree-stumps. The boy slipped in, Jungle-fashion, without a sound, and dived across; rose, too, without a sound, and turned on his back, his arms behind his head, watching the moon rising above the rocks, and breaking up her reflection in the water with his toes. Kaa's diamond-shaped head cut the pool like a razor, and came out to rest on Mowgli's shoulder. They lay still, soaking luxuriously in the cool water.

'It is *very* good,' said Mowgli at last, sleepily. 'Now, in the Man-Pack, at this hour, as I remember, they laid them down upon hard pieces of wood in the inside of a mud-trap, and, having carefully shut out all the clean winds, drew foul cloth over their heavy heads and made evil songs through their noses. It is better in the Jungle.'

A hurrying cobra slipped down over a rock and drank, gave them 'Good hunting!' and went away.

'Ssh!' said Kaa, as though he had suddenly remembered something. 'So the Jungle gives thee all that thou hast ever desired, Little Brother?'

'Not all,' said Mowgli, laughing; 'else there would be a new and strong Shere Khan to kill once a moon. Now, I could kill with my own hands, asking no help of buffaloes. And also I have wished the sun to shine in the middle of the Rains, and the Rains to cover the sun in the deep of summer; and also I have never gone empty but I wished that I had killed a goat; and also I have never killed a goat but I wished it had been buck; nor buck but I wished it had been nilghai. But thus do we feel, all of us.'

'Thou hast no other desire?' the big snake demanded.

'What more can I wish? I have the Jungle, and the favour of the Jungle! Is there more anywhere between sunrise and sunset?'

'Now, the Cobra said ——' Kaa began.

'What cobra? He that went away just now said nothing. He was hunting.'

'It was another.'

'Hast thou many dealings with the Poison People? I give them their own path. They carry death in the fore-tooth, and that is not good — for they are so small. But what hood is this thou hast spoken with?'

Kaa rolled slowly in the water like a steamer in a beam sea. 'Three or four moons since,' said he, 'I hunted in Cold Lairs, which place thou hast not forgotten. And the thing I hunted fled shrieking past the tanks and to that house whose side I once broke for thy sake, and ran into the ground.'

'But the people of Cold Lairs do not live in burrows.' Mowgli knew that Kaa was talking of the Monkey-People.

'This thing was not living, but seeking to live,' Kaa replied, with a quiver of his tongue. 'He ran into a burrow that led very far. I followed, and having killed, I slept. When I waked I went forward.'

'Under the earth?'

'Even so, coming at last upon a White Hood [a white cobra], who spoke of things beyond my knowledge, and showed me many things I had never before seen.'

'New game? Was it good hunting?' Mowgli turned quickly on his side.

'It was no game, and would have broken all my teeth; but the White Hood said that a man — he spoke as one that knew the breed — that a man would give the breath under his ribs for only the sight of those things.'

'We will look,' said Mowgli. 'I now remember that I was once a man.'

'Slowly — slowly. It was haste killed the Yellow Snake that are the sun. We two spoke together under the earth, and I spoke of thee, naming thee as a man. Said the White Hood (and he is indeed as old as the Jungle): "It is long since I have seen a man. Let him come, and he shall see all these things, for the least of which very many men would die."'

'That *must* be new game. And yet the Poison People do not tell us when game is afoot. They are an unfriendly folk.'

'It is *not* game. It is — it is — I cannot say what it is.'

'We will go there. I have never seen a White Hood, and I wish to see the other things. Did he kill them?'

'They are all dead things. He says he is the keeper of them all.'

'Ah! As a wolf stands above meat he has taken to his own lair. Let us go.'

Mowgli swam to bank, rolled on the grass to dry himself, and the two set off for Cold Lairs, the deserted city of which you may have heard. Mowgli was not the least afraid of the Monkey-People in those days, but the Monkey-People had the liveliest horror of Mowgli. Their tribes, however, were raiding in the Jungle, and so Cold Lairs stood empty and silent in the moonlight. Kaa led up to the ruins of the queens' pavilion that stood on the terrace, slipped over the rubbish, and dived down the half-choked staircase that went underground from the centre of the pavilion. Mowgli gave the Snake Call, — 'We be of one blood, ye and I', — and followed on his hands and knees. They crawled a long distance down a sloping passage that turned and twisted several times, and at last came to where the root of some great tree, growing thirty feet overhead, had forced out a solid stone in the wall. They crept through the gap, and found themselves in a large vault, whose domed roof had been also broken away by tree-roots so that a few streaks of light dropped down into the darkness.

'A safe lair,' said Mowgli, rising to his firm feet, 'but over-far to visit daily. And now what do we see?'

'Am I nothing?' said a voice in the middle of the vault; and Mowgli saw something white move till, little by little, there stood up the hugest cobra he had ever set eyes on — a creature nearly eight feet long, and bleached by being in darkness to an old ivory-white. Even the spectacle-marks of his spread hood had faded to faint yellow. His eyes were as red as rubies, and altogether he was most wonderful.

'Good hunting!' said Mowgli, who carried his manners with his knife, and that never left him.

'What of the city?' said the White Cobra, without answering the greeting. 'What of the great, the walled city — the city of a hundred elephants and twenty thousand horses, and cattle past counting — the city of the King of Twenty Kings? I grow deaf here, and it is long since I heard their war-gongs.'

'The Jungle is above our heads,' said Mowgli. 'I know only Hathi and his sons among elephants. Bagheera has slain all the horses in one village, and — what is a King?'

'I told thee,' said Kaa softly to the Cobra, — 'I told thee, four moons ago, that thy city was not.'

'The city — the great city of the forest whose gates are guarded by the King's towers — can never pass. They builded it before my father's father came from the egg, and it shall endure when my son's sons are as white as I! Salomdhi, son of Chandrabija, son of Viyeja, son of Yegasuri, made it in the days of Bappa Rawal. Whose cattle are *ye*?'

'It is a lost trail,' said Mowgli, turning to Kaa. 'I know not his talk.'

'Nor I. He is very old. Father of Cobras, there is only the Jungle here, as it has been since the beginning.'

'Then who is *he*,' said the White Cobra, 'sitting down before me, unafraid, knowing not the name of the King, talking our talk through a man's lips? Who is he with the knife and the snake's tongue?'

'Mowgli they call me,' was the answer. 'I am of the Jungle. The wolves are my people, and Kaa here is my brother. Father of Cobras, who art thou?'

'I am the Warden of the King's Treasure. Kurrun Raja builded the stone above me, in the days when my skin was dark, that I might teach death to those who came to steal. Then they let down the treasure through the stone, and I heard the song of the Brahmins my masters.'

'Umm!' said Mowgli to himself. 'I have dealt with one Brahmin already, in the Man-Pack, and — I know what I know. Evil comes here in a little.'

'Five times since I came here has the stone been lifted, but always to let down more, and never to take away. There are no riches like these riches — the treasures of a hundred kings. But it is long and long since the stone was last moved, and I think that my city has forgotten.'

'There is no city. Look up. Yonder are roots of the great trees tearing the stones apart. Trees and men do not grow together,' Kaa insisted.

'Twice and thrice have men found their way here,' the White Cobra answered savagely; 'but they never spoke till I came upon them groping in the dark, and then they cried only a little time. But *ye* come with lies, Man and Snake both, and would have me believe the city is not, and that my wardship ends. Little do men change in the years. But *I* change never! Till the stone is lifted, and the Brahmins come down singing the songs that I know, and feed me with warm milk, and take me to the light again, I — I — *I*, and no other, am the Warden of the King's Treasure! The city is dead, ye say, and here are the roots of the trees? Stoop down, then, and take what ye will. Earth has no treasure like to these. Man with the snake's tongue, if thou canst go alive by the way that thou hast entered at, the lesser Kings will be thy servants!'

'Again the trail is lost,' said Mowgli coolly. 'Can any jackal have burrowed so deep and bitten this great White Hood? He is surely mad. Father of Cobras, I see nothing here to take away.'

'By the Gods of the Sun and Moon, it is the madness of death upon the boy!' hissed the Cobra. 'Before thine eyes close I will allow thee this favour. Look thou, and see what man has never seen before!'

'They do not well in the Jungle who speak to Mowgli of favours,' said the boy, between his teeth; 'but the dark changes all, as I know. I will look, if that please thee."

He stared with puckered-up eyes round the vault, and then lifted up from the floor a handful of something that glittered.

'Oho!' said he, 'this is like the stuff they play with in the Man-Pack: only this is yellow and the other was brown.'

He let the gold pieces fall, and moved forward. The floor of the vault was buried some five or six feet deep in coined gold and silver that had burst from the sacks it had been originally stored in, and, in the long years, the metal had packed and settled as sand packs at low tide. On it and in it, and rising through it, as wrecks lift through the sand, were jewelled elephant-howdahs of embossed silver, studded with plates of hammered gold, and adorned with carbuncles and turquoises. There were palanquins and litters for carrying queens, framed and braced with silver and enamel, with jade-handled poles and amber curtain-rings; there were golden candlesticks hung with pierced emeralds that quivered on the branches; there were studded images, five feet high, of forgotten gods, silver with jewelled eyes; there were coats of mail, gold inlaid on steel, and fringed with rotted and blackened seed-pearls; there were helmelts, crested and beaded with pigeon's-blood rubies; there were shields of lacquer, of tortoise-shell and rhinoceros-hide, strapped and bossed with red gold and set with emeralds at the edge; there were sheaves of diamond-hilted swords, daggers, and hunting-knives; there were golden sacrificial bowls and ladles, and portable altars of a shape that never sees the light of day; there were jade cups and bracelets; there were incense-burners, combs, and pots for perfume, henna, and eye-powder, all in embossed gold; there were nose-rings, armlets, head-bands, finger-rings, and girdles past any counting; there were belts, seven fingers broad, of square-cut diamonds and rubies, and wooden boxes, trebly clamped with iron, from which the wood had fallen away in powder, showing the pile of uncut star-sapphires, opals, cat's-eyes, sapphires, rubies, diamonds, emeralds, and garnets within.

The White Cobra was right. No mere money would begin to pay the value of this treasure, the sifted pickings of centuries of war, plunder, trade, and taxation. The coins alone were price-less, leaving out of count all the precious stones; and the dead weight of the gold and silver alone might be two or three hundred tons. Every native ruler in India to-day, however poor, has a hoard to which he is always adding; and though, once in a long while, some enlightened prince may send off forty or fifty bullock-cart loads of silver to be exchanged for Government securities, the bulk of them keep their treasure and the know-ledge of it very closely to themselves.

But Mowgli naturally did not understand what these things meant. The knives interested him a little, but they did not balance so well as his own, and so he dropped them. At last he found something really fascinating laid on the front of a how-dah half buried in the coins. It was a three-foot ankus, or ele-phant-goad — something like a small boat-hook. The top was one round, shining ruby, and eight inches of the handle below it were studded with rough turquoises close together, giving a most satisfactory grip. Below them was a rim of jade with a flower-pattern running round it — only the leaves were emer-alds, and the blossoms were rubies sunk in the cool, green stone. The rest of the handle was a shaft of pure ivory, while the point — the spike and hook — was gold-inlaid steel with pic-tures of elephant-catching; and the pictures attracted Mowgli, who saw that they had something to do with his friend Hathi the Silent.

The White Cobra had been following him closely.

'Is not this worth dying to behold?' he said. 'Have I not done thee a great favour?'

'I do not understand,' said Mowgli. 'The things are hard and cold, and by no means good to eat. But this' — he lifted the ankus — 'I desire to take away, that I may see it in the sun. Thou sayest they are all thine? Wilt thou give it to me, and I will bring thee frogs to eat?'

The White Cobra fairly shook with evil delight. 'Assuredly I will give it,' he said. 'All that is here I will give thee — till thou goest away.'

'But I go now. This place is dark and cold, and I wish to take the thorn-pointed thing to the Jungle.'

'Look by thy foot! What is that there?'

Mowgli picked up something white and smooth. 'It is the bone of a man's head,' he said quietly. 'And here are two more.'

'They came to take the treasure away many years ago. I spoke to them in the dark, and they lay still.'

'But what do I need of this that is called treasure? If thou wilt give me the ankus to take away, it is good hunting. If not, it is good hunting none the less. I do not fight with the Poison People, and I was also taught the Master Word of thy tribe.'

'There is but one Master Word here. It is mine!'

Kaa flung himself forward with blazing eyes. 'Who bade me bring the Man?' he hissed.

'I surely,' the old Cobra lisped. 'It is long since I have seen Man, and this Man speaks our tongue.'

'But there was no talk of killing. How can I go to the Jungle and say that I have led him to his death?' said Kaa.

'I talk not of killing till the time. And as to thy going or not going, there is the hole in the wall. Peace, now, thou fat monkey-killer! I have but to touch thy neck, and the Jungle will know thee no longer. Never Man came here that went away with the breath under his ribs. I am the Warden of the Treasure of the King's City!'

'But, thou white worm of the dark, I tell thee there is neither king nor city! The Jungle is all about us!' cried Kaa.

'There is still the Treasure. But this can be done. Wait awhile, Kaa of the Rocks, and see the boy run. There is room for great sport here. Life is good. Run to and fro awhile, and make sport, boy!'

Mowgli put his hand on Kaa's head quietly.

'The white thing has dealt with men of the Man-Pack until now. He does not know me,' he whispered. 'He has asked for this hunting. Let him have it.' Mowgli had been standing with the ankus held point down. He flung it from him quickly, and it dropped crossways just behind the great snake's hood, pinning him to the floor. In a flash, Kaa's weight was upon the writhing body, paralysing it from hood to tail. The red eyes burned, and the six spare inches of the head struck furiously right and left.

'Kill!' said Kaa, as Mowgli's hand went to his knife.

'No,' he said, as he drew the blade; 'I will never kill again save for food. But look you, Kaa!' He caught the snake behind the hood, forced the mouth open with the blade of the knife, and showed the terrible poison-fangs of the upper jaw lying black and withered in the gum. The White Cobra had outlived his poison, as a snake will.

'*Thuu*' ('It is dried up'),[1] said Mowgli; and motioning Kaa away, he picked up the ankus, setting the White Cobra free.

'The King's Treasure needs a new Warden,' he said gravely. 'Thuu, thou hast not done well. Run to and fro and make sport, Thuu!'

'I am ashamed. Kill me!' hissed the White Cobra.

'There has been too much talk of killing. We will go now. I take the thorn-pointed thing. Thuu, because I have fought and worsted thee.'

'See, then, that the thing does not kill thee at last. It is Death! Remember, it is Death! There is enough in that thing to kill the

---

[1] Literally a rotted-out tree-stump.

men of all my city. Not long wilt thou hold it, Jungle Man, nor he who takes it from thee. They will kill, and kill, and kill for its sake! My strength is dried up, but the ankus will do my work. It is Death! It is Death! It is Death!'

Mowgli crawled out through the hole into the passage again, and the last that he saw was the White Cobra striking furiously with his harmless fangs at the stolid golden faces of the gods that lay on the floor, and hissing, 'It is Death!'

They were glad to get to the light of day once more; and when they were back in their own Jungle and Mowgli made the ankus glitter in the morning light, he was almost as pleased as though he had found a bunch of new flowers to stick in his hair.

'This is brighter than Bagheera's eyes,' he said delightedly, as he twirled the ruby. 'I will show it to him; but what did the Thuu mean when he talked of death?'

'I cannot say. I am sorrowful to my tail's tail that he felt not thy knife. There is always evil at Cold Lairs — above ground or below. But now I am hungry. Dost thou hunt with me this dawn?' said Kaa.

'No; Bagheera must see this thing. Good hunting!' Mowgli danced off, flourishing the great ankus, and stopping from time to time to admire it, till he came to that part of the Jungle Bagheera chiefly used, and found him drinking after a heavy kill. Mowgli told him all his adventures from beginning to end, and Bagheera sniffed at the ankus between whiles. When Mowgli came to the White Cobra's last words, the panther purred approvingly.

'Then the White Hood spoke the thing which is?' Mowgli asked quickly.

'I was born in the King's cages at Oodeypore, and it is in my stomach that I know some little of Man. Very many men would kill thrice in a night for the sake of that one big red stone alone.'

'But the stone makes it heavy to the hand. My little bright

knife is better; and — see! the red stone is not good to eat. Then *why* would they kill?'

'Mowgli, go thou and sleep. Thou hast lived among men, and ——'

'I remember. Men kill because they are not hunting; — for idleness and pleasure. Wake again, Bagheera. For what use was this thorn-pointed thing made?'

Bagheera half opened his eyes — he was very sleepy — with a malicious twinkle.

'It was made by men to thrust into the head of the sons of Hathi, so that the blood should pour out. I have seen the like in the street of Oodeypore, before our cages. That thing has tasted the blood of many such as Hathi.'

'But why do they thrust into the heads of elephants?'

'To teach them Man's Law. Having neither claws nor teeth, men make these things — and worse.'

'Always more blood when I come near, even to the things the Man-Pack have made,' said Mowgli disgustedly. He was getting a little tired of the weight of the ankus. 'If I had known this, I would not have taken it. First it was Messua's blood on the thongs, and now it is Hathi's. I will use it no more. Look!'

The ankus flew sparkling, and buried itself point down thirty yards away, between the trees. 'So my hands are clean of Death,' said Mowgli, rubbing his palms on the fresh, moist earth. 'The Thuu said Death would follow me. He is old and white and mad.'

'White or black, or death or life, *I* am going to sleep, Little Brother. I cannot hunt all night and howl all day, as do some folk.'

Bagheera went off to a hunting-lair that he knew, about two miles off. Mowgli made an easy way for himself up a convenient tree, knotted three or four creepers together, and in less time than it takes to tell was swinging in a hammock fifty feet above ground. Though he had no positive objection to strong daylight, Mowgli followed the custom of his friends, and used it as little as he could. When he waked among the very loud-voiced peoples that live in the trees, it was twilight once more, and he had been dreaming of the beautiful pebbles he had thrown away.

'At least I will look at the thing again,' he said, and slid down a creeper to the earth; but Bagheera was before him. Mowgli could hear him snuffing in the half-light.

'Where is the thorn-pointed thing?' cried Mowgli.

'A man has taken it. Here is the trail.'

'Now we shall see whether the Thuu spoke truth. If the pointed thing is Death, that man will die. Let us follow.'

'Kill first,' said Bagheera. 'An empty stomach makes a careless eye. Men go very slowly, and the Jungle is wet enough to hold the lightest mark.'

They killed as soon as they could, but it was nearly three hours before they finished their meat and drink and buckled down to the trail. The Jungle-People know that nothing makes up for being hurried over your meals.

'Think you the pointed thing will turn in the man's hand and kill him?' Mowgli asked. 'The Thuu said it was Death.'

'We shall see when we find,' said Bagheera, trotting with his head low. 'It is single-foot' (he meant that there was only one man), 'and the weight of the thing has pressed his heel far into the ground.'

'Hai! This is as clear as summer lightning,' Mowgli answered; and they fell into the quick, choppy trail-trot in and out through the checkers of the moonlight, following the marks of those two bare feet.

'Now he runs swiftly,' said Mowgli. 'The toes are spread apart.' They went on over some wet ground. 'Now why does he turn aside here?'

'Wait!' said Bagheera, and flung himself forward with one superb bound as far as ever he could. The first thing to do when a trail ceases to explain itself is to cast forward without leaving your own confusing foot-marks on the ground. Bagheera turned as he landed, and faced Mowgli, crying, 'Here comes another trail to meet him. It is a smaller foot, this second trail, and the toes turn inward.'

Then Mowgli ran up and looked. 'It is the foot of a Gond hunter,' he said. 'Look! Here he dragged his bow on the grass. That is why the first trail turned aside so quickly. Big Foot hid from Little Foot.'

'That is true,' said Bagheera. 'Now, lest by crossing each other's tracks we foul the signs, let each take one trail. I am Big Foot, Little Brother, and thou art Little Foot, the Gond.'

Bagheera leaped back to the original trail, leaving Mowgli stooping above the curious narrow track of the wild little man of the woods.

'Now,' said Bagheera, moving step by step along the chain of footprints, 'I, Big Foot, turn aside here. Now I hide me behind a rock and stand still, not daring to shift my feet. Cry thy trail, Little Brother.'

'Now, I, Little Foot, come to the rock,' said Mowgli, running up his trail. 'Now, I sit down under the rock, leaning upon my right hand, and resting my bow between my toes. I wait long, for the mark of my feet is deep here.'

'I also,' said Bagheera, hidden behind the rock. 'I wait, resting the end of the thorn-pointed thing upon a stone. It slips, for here is a scratch upon the stone. Cry thy trail, Little Brother.'

'One, two twigs and a big branch are broken here,' said Mowgli, in an undertone. 'Now, how shall I cry *that*? Ah! It is plain now. I, Little Foot, go away making noises and tramplings so that Big Foot may hear me.' He moved away from the rock pace by pace among the trees, his voice rising in the distance as he approached a little cascade. 'I — go — far — away — to — where —the — noise — of — falling — water — covers — my — noise; and — here — I — wait. Cry thy trail, Bagheera, Big Foot!'

The panther had been casting in every direction to see how

Big Foot's trail led away from behind the rock. Then he gave tongue:

'I come from behind the rock upon my knees, dragging the thorn-pointed thing. Seeing no one, I run. I, Big Foot, run swiftly. The trail is clear. Let each follow his own. I run!'

Bagheera swept on along the clearly-marked trail, and Mowgli followed the steps of the Gond. For some time there was silence in the Jungle.

'Where art thou, Little Foot?' cried Bagheera. Mowgli's voice answered him not fifty yards to the right.

'Um!' said the panther, with a deep cough. 'The two run side by side, drawing nearer!'

They raced on another half-mile, always keeping about the same distance, till Mowgli, whose head was not so close to the ground as Bagheera's, cried: 'They have met. Good hunting — look! Here stood Little Foot, with his knee on a rock — and yonder is Big Foot indeed!'

Not ten yards in front of them, stretched across a pile of broken rocks, lay the body of a villager of the district, a long, small-feathered Gond arrow through his back and breast.

'Was the Thuu so old and so mad, Little Brother?' said Bagheera gently. 'Here is one death, at least.'

'Follow on. But where is the drinker of elephant's blood — the red-eyed thorn?'

'Little Foot has it — perhaps. It is single-foot again now.'

The single trail of a light man who had been running quickly and bearing a burden on his left shoulder held on round a long, low spur of dried grass, where each footfall seemed, to the sharp eyes of the trackers, marked in hot iron.

Neither spoke till the trail ran up to the ashes of a camp-fire hidden in a ravine.

'Again!' said Bagheera, checking as though he had been turned into stone.

The body of a little wizened Gond lay with its feet in the ashes, and Bagheera looked inquiringly at Mowgli.

'That was done with a bamboo,' said the boy, after one glance. 'I have used such a thing among the buffaloes when I served in the Man-Pack. The Father of Cobras — I am sorrowful that I made a jest of him —knew the breed well, as I might have known. Said I not that men kill for idleness?'

'Indeed, they killed for the sake of the red and blue stones,' Bagheera answered. 'Remember, I was in the King's cages at Oodeypore.'

'One, two, three, four tracks,' said Mowgli, stooping over the ashes. 'Four tracks of men with shod feet. They do not go so quickly as Gonds. Now, what evil had the little woodman done to them? See, they talked together, all five, standing up, before they killed him. Bagheera, let us go back. My stomach is heavy in me, and yet it heaves up and down like an oriole's nest at the end of a branch.'

'It is not good hunting to leave game afoot. Follow!' said the panther. 'Those eight shod feet have not gone far.'

No more was said for fully an hour, as they worked up the broad trail of the four men with shod feet.

It was clear, hot daylight now, and Bagheera said, 'I smell smoke.'

'Men are always more ready to eat than to run,' Mowgli answered, trotting in and out between the low scrub bushes of the new Jungle they were exploring. Bagheera, a little to his left, made an indescribable noise in his throat.

'Here is one that has done with feeding,' said he. A tumbled bundle of gay-coloured clothes lay under a bush, and round it was some spilt flour.

'That was done by the bamboo again,' said Mowgli. 'See! that white dust is what men eat. They have taken the kill from this one, — he carried their food, — and given him for a kill to Chil, the Kite.'

'It is the third,' said Bagheera.

'I will go with new, big frogs to the Father of Cobras, and feed him fat,' said Mowgli to himself. 'The drinker of elephant's blood is Death himself — but still I do not understand!'

'Follow!' said Bagheera.

They had not gone half a mile farther when they heard Ko, the Crow, singing the death-song in the top of a tamarisk under whose shade three men were lying. A half-dead fire smoked in the centre of the circle, under an iron plate which held a blackened and burned cake of unleavened bread. Close to the fire, and blazing in the sunshine, lay the ruby-and-turquoise ankus.

'The thing works quickly; all ends here,' said Bagheera. 'How did *these* die, Mowgli? There is no mark on any.'

A Jungle-dweller gets to learn by experience as much as many doctors know of poisonous plants and berries. Mowgli sniffed the smoke that came up from the fire, broke off a morsel of the blackened bread, tasted it, and spat it out again.

'Apple of Death,' he coughed. 'The first must have made it ready in the food for *these*, who killed him, having first killed the Gond.'

'Good hunting, indeed! The kills follow close,' said Bagheera.

'Apple of Death' is what the Jungle call thorn-apple or dhatura, the readiest poison in all India.

'What now?' said the panther. 'Must thou and I kill each other for yonder red-eyed slayer?'

'Can it speak?' said Mowgli in a whisper. 'Did I do it a wrong when I threw it away? Between us two it can do no wrong, for we do not desire what men desire. If it be left here, it will assuredly continue to kill men one after another as fast as nuts fall in a high wind. I have no love to men, but even I would not have them die six in a night.'

'What matter? They are only men. They killed one another, and were well pleased,' said Bagheera. 'That first little woodman hunted well.'

'They are cubs none the less; and a cub will drown himself to bite the moon's light on the water. The fault was mine,' said

Mowgli, who spoke as though he knew all about everything. 'I will never again bring into the Jungle strange things — not though they be as beautiful as flowers. This' — he handled the ankus gingerly — 'goes back to the Father of Cobras. But first we must sleep, and we cannot sleep near these sleepers. Also we must bury *him*, lest he run away and kill another six. Dig me a hole under that tree.'

'But, Little Brother,' said Bagheera, moving off to the spot, 'I tell thee it is no fault of the blood-drinker. The trouble is with the men.'

'All one,' said Mowgli. 'Dig the hole deep. When we wake I will take him up and carry him back.'

.   .   .   .   .

Two nights later, as the White Cobra sat mourning in the darkness of the vault, ashamed, and robbed, and alone, the turquoise ankus whirled through the hole in the wall, and clashed on the floor of golden coins.

'Father of Cobras,' said Mowgli (he was careful to keep the other side of the wall), 'get thee a young and ripe one of thine own people to help thee guard the King's Treasure, so that no man may come away alive any more.'

'Ah-ha! It returns, then. I said the thing was Death. How comes it that thou art still alive?' the old Cobra mumbled, twining lovingly round the ankus-haft.

'By the Bull that bought me, I do not know! That thing has killed six times in a night. Let him go out no more.'

THE SONG OF THE LITTLE HUNTER

Ere Mor the Peacock flutters, ere the Monkey-People cry,
   Ere Chil the Kite swoops down a furlong sheer,
Through the Jungle very softly flits a shadow and a sigh —
   He is Fear, O Little Hunter, he is Fear!
Very softly down the glade runs a waiting, watching shade,
   And the whisper spreads and widens far and near;
And the sweat is on thy brow, for he passes even now —
   He is Fear, O Little Hunter, he is Fear!

Ere the moon has climbed the mountain, ere the rocks are ribbed with
   light,
   When the downward-dipping trails are dank and drear,
Comes a breathing hard behind thee — *snuffle-snuffle* through the night —
   It is Fear, O Little Hunter, it is Fear!
On thy knees and draw the bow; bid the shrilling arrow go;
   In the empty, mocking thicket plunge the spear;
But thy hands are loosed and weak, and the blood has left thy cheek —
   It is Fear, O Little Hunter, it is Fear!

When the heat-cloud sucks the tempest, when the slivered pine-trees fall,
   When the blinding, blaring rain-squalls lash and veer;
Through the war-gongs of the thunder rings a voice more loud than all —
   It is Fear, O Little Hunter, it is Fear!
Now the spates are banked and deep; now the footless boulders leap —
   Now the lightning shows each littlest leaf-rib clear —
But thy throat is shut and dried, and thy heart against thy side
   Hammers: Fear, O Little Hunter — this is Fear!

RED DOG

For our white and our excellent nights — for the nights of swift running,
    Fair ranging, far seeing, good hunting, sure cunning!
For the smells of the dawning, untainted, ere dew has departed!
For the rush through the mist, and the quarry blind-started!
For the cry of our mates when the sambhur has wheeled and is standing at
  bay,

        For the risk and the riot of night!
        For the sleep at the lair-mouth by day,
          It is met, and we go to the fight.
            Bay! O Bay!

IT was after the letting in of the Jungle that the pleasantest part of Mowgli's life began. He had the good conscience that comes from paying debts; all the Jungle was his friend, and just a little afraid of him. The things that he did and saw and heard when he was wandering from one people to another, with or without his four companions, would make many many stories, each as long as this one. So you will never be told how he met the Mad Elephant of Mandla, who killed two-and-twenty bullocks drawing eleven carts of coined silver to the Government Treasury, and scattered the shiny rupees in the dust; how he fought Jacala, the Crocodile, all one long night in the Marshes of the North, and broke his skinning-knife on the brute's back-plates; how he found a new and longer knife round the neck of a man who had been killed by a wild boar, and how he tracked that boar and killed him as a fair price for the knife; how he was caught up once in the Great Famine, by the moving of the deer, and nearly crushed to death in the swaying hot herds; how he saved Hathi the Silent from being once more trapped in a pit with a stake at the bottom, and how, next day, he himself fell into a very cunning leopard-trap, and how Hathi broke the thick wooden bars to pieces above him; how he milked the wild buffaloes in the swamp, and how ——

But we must tell one tale at a time. Father and Mother Wolf died, and Mowgli rolled a big boulder against the mouth of their cave, and cried the Death Song over them; Baloo grew very old and stiff, and even Bagheera, whose nerves were steel and whose muscles were iron, was a shade slower on the kill than he had been. Akela turned from gray to milky white with pure age; his ribs stuck out, and he walked as though he had been made of wood, and Mowgli killed for him. But the young wolves, the children of the disbanded Seeonee Pack, throve and increased, and when there were about forty of them, master-less, full-voiced, clean-footed five-year-olds, Akela told them that they ought to gather themselves together and follow the Law, and run under one head, as befitted the Free People.

This was not a question in which Mowgli concerned himself, for, as he said, he had eaten sour fruit, and he knew the tree it hung from: but when Phao, son of Phaona (his father was the Gray Tracker in the days of Akela's headship), fought his way to the leadership of the Pack, according to the Jungle Law, and the old calls and songs began to ring under the stars once more, Mowgli came to the Council Rock for memory's sake. When he chose to speak the Pack waited till he had finished, and he sat at Akela's side on the Rock above Phao. Those were days of good hunting and good sleeping. No stranger cared to break into the Jungles that belonged to Mowgli's people, as they called the Pack, and the young wolves grew fat and strong, and there were many cubs to bring to the Looking-over. Mowgli always attended a Looking-over, remembering the night when a black panther bought a naked brown baby into the Pack, and the long call, 'Look — look well, O Wolves', made his heart flutter. Otherwise, he would be far away in the Jungle with his four brothers, tasting, touching, seeing, and feeling new things.

One twilight when he was trotting leisurely across the ranges to give Akela the half of a buck that he had killed, while the Four jogged behind him, sparring a little, and tumbling one another over for joy of being alive, he heard a cry that had never been heard since the bad days of Shere Khan. It was what they call in the Jungle the *pheeal*, a hideous kind of shriek that the jackal gives when he is hunting behind a tiger, or when there is a big killing afoot. If you can imagine a mixture of hate, triumph, fear, and despair, with a kind of leer running through it, you will get some notion of the *pheeal* that rose and sank and wavered and quavered far away across the Waingunga. The Four stopped at once, bristling and growling. Mowgli's hand went to his knife, and he checked, the blood in his face, his eyebrows knotted.

'There is no Striped One dare kill here,' he said.

'That is not the cry of the Forerunner,' answered Gray Brother. 'It is some great killing. Listen!'

It broke out again, half sobbing and half chuckling, just as though the jackal had soft human lips. Then Mowgli drew deep breath, and ran to the Council Rock, overtaking on his way hurrying wolves of the Pack. Phao and Akela were on the Rock together, and below them, every nerve strained, sat the others. The mothers and the cubs were cantering off to their lairs, for when the *pheeal* cries it is no time for weak things to be abroad.

They could hear nothing except the Waingunga rushing and gurgling in the dark, and the light evening winds among the tree-tops, till suddenly across the river a wolf called. It was no wolf of the Pack, for they were all at the Rock. The note changed to a long, despairing bay; and 'Dhole!' it said, 'Dhole! dhole! dhole!' They heard tired feet on the rocks, and a gaunt wolf, streaked with red on his flanks, his right fore-paw useless, and his jaws white with foam, flung himself into the circle and lay gasping at Mowgli's feet.

'Good hunting! Under whose Headship?' said Phao gravely.

'Good hunting! Won-tolla am I,' was the answer. He meant that he was a solitary wolf, fending for himself, his mate, and his cubs in some lonely lair, as do many wolves in the south. Won-tolla means an Outlier — one who lies out from any

Pack. Then he panted, and they could see his heart-beats shake him backward and forward.

'What moves?' said Phao, for that is the question all the Jungle asks after the *pheeal* cries.

'The dhole, the dhole of the Dekkan — Red Dog, the Killer! They came north from the south saying the Dekkan was empty and killing out by the way. When this moon was new there were four to me — my mate and three cubs. She would teach them to kill on the grass plains, hiding to drive the buck, as we do who are of the open. At midnight I heard them together, full tongue on the trail. At the dawn-wind I found them stiff in the grass — four, Free People, four when this moon was new. Then sought I my Blood-Right and found the dhole.'

'How many?' said Mowgli quickly; the Pack growled deep in their throats.

'I do not know. Three of them will kill no more, but at the last they drove me like the buck; on my three legs they drove me. Look, Free People!'

He thrust out his mangled fore-foot, all dark with dried blood. There were cruel bites low down on his side, and his throat was torn and worried.

'Eat,' said Akela, rising up from the meat Mowgli had brought him, and the Outlier flung himself on it.

'This shall be no loss,' he said humbly, when he had taken off the first edge of his hunger. 'Give me a little strength, Free People, and I also will kill. My lair is empty that was full when the moon was new, and the Blood Debt is not all paid.'

Phao heard his teeth crack on a haunch-bone and grunted approvingly.

'We shall need those jaws,' said he. 'Were there cubs with the dhole?'

'Nay, nay. Red Hunters all: grown dogs of their Pack, heavy and strong for all that they eat lizards in the Dekkan.'

What Won-tolla had said meant that the dhole, the red hunting-dog of the Dekkan, was moving to kill, and the Pack knew well that even the tiger will surrender a new kill to the dhole. They drive straight through the Jungle, and what they meet they pull down and tear to pieces. Though they are not as big nor half as cunning as the wolf, they are very strong and very numerous. The dhole, for instance, do not begin to call themselves a pack till they are a hundred strong; whereas forty wolves make a very fair pack indeed. Mowgli's wanderings had taken him to the edge of the high grassy downs of the Dekkan, and he had seen the fearless dholes sleeping and playing and scratching themselves in the little hollows and tussocks that they use for lairs. He despised and hated them because they did not smell like the Free People, because they did not live in caves, and, above all, because they had hair between their toes while he and his friends were clean-footed. But he knew, for Hathi had told him, what a terrible thing a dhole hunting-pack was. Even Hathi moves aside from their line, and until they are killed, or till game is scarce, they will go forward.

Akela knew something of the dholes, too, for he said to Mowgli quietly, 'It is better to die in a Full Pack than leaderless and alone. This is good hunting, and — my last. But, as men live, thou hast very many more nights and days, Little Brother. Go north and lie down, and if any live after the dhole has gone by he shall bring thee word of the fight.'

'Ah,' said Mowgli, quite gravely, 'must I go to the marshes and catch little fish and sleep in a tree, or must I ask help of the *Bandar-log* and crack nuts, while the Pack fight below?'

'It is to the death,' said Akela. 'Thou hast never met the dhole — the Red Killer. Even the Striped One ——'

'*Aowa! Aowa!*' said Mowgli pettingly. 'I have killed one striped ape, and sure am I in my stomach that Shere Khan would have left his own mate for meat to the dhole if he had winded a pack across three ranges. Listen now: There was a wolf, my father, and there was a wolf, my mother, and there was an old gray wolf (not too wise: he is white now) was my father and my mother. Therefore I —' he raised his voice, 'I say that when the dhole come, and if the dhole come, Mowgli and the Free People are of one skin for that hunting; and I say, by the Bull that bought me — by the Bull Bagheera paid for me in the old days which ye of the Pack do not remember — *I* say, that the Trees and the River may hear and hold fast if I forget; *I* say that this my knife shall be as a tooth to the Pack — and I do not think it is so blunt. This is my Word which has gone from me.'

'Thou dost not know the dhole, man with a wolf's tongue,' said Won-tolla. 'I look only to clear the Blood Debt against them ere they have me in many pieces. They move slowly, killing out as they go, but in two days a little strength will come back to me and I turn again for the Blood Debt. But for *ye*, Free People, my word is that ye go north and eat but little for a while till the dhole are gone. There is no meat in this hunting.'

'Hear the Outlier!' said Mowgli with a laugh. 'Free People, we must go north and dig lizards and rats from the bank, lest by any chance we meet the dhole. He must kill out our hunting-grounds, while we lie hid in the north till it please him to give us our own again. He is a dog — and the pup of a dog — red, yellow-bellied, lairless, and haired between every toe! He counts his cubs six and eight at the litter, as though he were Chilkai, the little leaping rat. Surely we must run away, Free People, and beg leave of the peoples of the north for the offal of dead cattle! Ye know the saying: "North are the vermin; south are the lice. *We* are the Jungle." Choose ye, O choose. It is good hunting! For the Pack — for the Full Pack — for the lair and the litter: for the in-kill and the out-kill; for the mate that drives the doe and the little, little cub within the cave; it is met! — it is met! — it is met!'

The Pack answered with one deep, crashing bark that sounded in the night like a big tree falling. 'It is met!' they cried.

'Stay with these,' said Mowgli to the Four. 'We shall need every tooth. Phao and Akela must make ready the battle. I go to count the dogs.'

'It is death!' Won-tolla cried, half rising. 'What can such a
hairless one do against the Red Dog? Even the Striped One,
remember ——'

'Thou art indeed an Outlier,' Mowgli called back; 'but we
will speak when the dholes are dead. Good hunting all!'

He hurried off into the darkness, wild with excitement,
hardly looking where he set foot, and the natural consequence
was that he tripped full length over Kaa's great coils where the
python lay watching a deer-path near the river.

'*Kssha!*' said Kaa angrily. 'Is this jungle-work, to stamp and
tramp and undo a night's hunting — when the game are moving
so well, too?'

'The fault was mine,' said Mowgli, picking himself up. 'Indeed I was seeking thee, Flathead, but each time we meet thou
art longer and broader by the length of my arm. There is none
like thee in the Jungle, wise, old, strong, and most beautiful
Kaa.'

'Now whither does *this* trail lead?' Kaa's voice was gentler.
'Not a moon since there was a Manling with a knife threw
stones at my head and called me bad little tree-cat names, because I lay asleep in the open.'

'Ay, and turned every driven deer to all the winds, and
Mowgli was hunting, and this same Flathead was too deaf
to hear his whistle. and leave the deer-roads free,' Mowgli
answered composedly, sitting down among the painted
coils.

'Now this same Manling comes with soft, tickling words to
this same Flathead, telling him that he is wise and strong and
beautiful, and this same old Flathead believes and makes a
place, thus, for this same stone-throwing Manling, and ——
Art thou at ease now? Could Bagheera give thee so good a
resting-place?'

Kaa had, as usual, made a sort of soft half-hammock of himself under Mowgli's weight. The boy reached out in the darkness, and gathered in the supple cable-like neck till Kaa's head

rested on his shoulder, and then he told him all that had happened in the Jungle that night.

'Wise I may be,' said Kaa at the end; 'but deaf I surely am. Else I should have heard the *pheeal*. Small wonder the Eaters of Grass are uneasy. How many be the dhole?'

'I have not yet seen. I came hot-foot to thee. Thou art older than Hathi. But oh, Kaa,' — here Mowgli wriggled with sheer joy, — 'it will be good hunting. Few of us will see another moon.'

'Dost *thou* strike in this? Remember thou art a Man; and remember what Pack cast thee out. Let the Wolf look to the Dog. *Thou* art a Man.'

'Last year's nuts are this year's black earth,' said Mowgli. 'It is true that I am a Man, but it is in my stomach that this night I have said that I am a Wolf. I called the River and the Trees to remember. I am of the Free People, Kaa, till the dhole has gone by.'

'Free People,' Kaa grunted. 'Free thieves! And thou hast tied thyself into the death-knot for the sake of the memory of the dead wolves? This is no good hunting.'

'It is my Word which I have spoken. The Trees know, the River knows. Till the dhole have gone by, my Word comes not back to me.'

'*Ngssh!* This changes all trails. I had thought to take thee away with me to the northern marshes, but the Word — even the Word of a little, naked, hairless Manling — is the Word. Now I, Kaa, say ——'

'Think well, Flathead, lest thou tie thyself into the death-knot also. I need no Word from thee, for well I know ——'

'Be it so, then,' said Kaa. 'I will give no Word; but what is in thy stomach to do when the dhole come?'

'They must swim the Waingunga. I thought to meet them with my knife in the shallows, the Pack behind me; and so stabbing and thrusting, we a little might turn them downstream, or cool their throats.'

'The dhole do not turn and their throats are hot,' said Kaa. 'There will be neither Manling nor Wolf-cub when that hunting is done, but only dry bones.'

'*Alala!* If we die, we die. It will be most good hunting. But my stomach is young, and I have not seen many Rains. I am not wise nor strong. Hast thou a better plan, Kaa?'

'I have seen a hundred and a hundred Rains. Ere Hathi cast his milk-tushes my trail was big in the dust. By the First Egg, I am older than many trees, and I have seen all that the Jungle has done.'

'But *this* is new hunting,' said Mowgli. 'Never before have the dhole crossed our trail.'

'What is has been. What will be is no more than a forgotten year striking backward. Be still while I count those my years.'

For a long hour Mowgli lay back among the coils, while Kaa, his head motionless on the ground, thought of all that he had seen and known since the day he came from the egg. The light seemed to go out of his eyes and leave them like stale opals, and now and again he made little stiff passes with his head, right and left, as though he were hunting in his sleep. Mowgli dozed quietly, for he knew that there is nothing like sleep before hunting, and he was trained to take it at any hour of the day or night.

Then he felt Kaa's back grow bigger and broader below him as the huge python puffed himself out, hissing with the noise of a sword drawn from a steel scabbard.

'I have seen all the dead seasons,' Kaa said at last, 'and the great trees and the old elephants, and the rocks that were bare and sharp-pointed ere the moss grew. Art *thou* still alive, Manling?'

'It is only a little after moonset,' said Mowgli. 'I do not understand ——'

'*Hssh!* I am again Kaa. I knew it was but a little time. Now we will go to the river, and I will show thee what is to be done against the dhole.'

He turned, straight as an arrow, for the main stream of the Waingunga, plunging in a little above the pool that hid the Peace Rock, Mowgli at his side.

'Nay, do not swim. I go swiftly. My back, Little Brother.'

Mowgli tucked his left arm round Kaa's neck, dropped his right close to his body, and straightened his feet. Then Kaa breasted the current as he alone could, and the ripple of the checked water stood up in a frill round Mowgli's neck, and his feet were waved to and fro in the eddy under the python's lashing sides. A mile or two above the Peace Rock the Waingunga narrows between a gorge of marble rocks from eighty to a hundred feet high, and the current runs like a mill-race between and over all manner of ugly stones. But Mowgli did not trouble his head about the water; little water in the world could have given him a moment's fear. He was looking at the gorge on either side and sniffing uneasily, for there was a sweetish-sourish smell in the air, very like the smell of a big ant-hill on a hot day. Instinctively he lowered himself in the water, only raising his head to breathe from time to time, and Kaa came to anchor with a double twist of his tail round a sunken rock, holding Mowgli in the hollow of a coil, while the water raced on.

'This is the Place of Death,' said the boy. 'Why do we come here?'

'They sleep,' said Kaa. 'Hathi will not turn aside for the Striped One. Yet Hathi and the Striped One together turn aside for the dhole, and the dhole, they say, turn aside for nothing. And yet for whom do the Little People of the Rocks turn aside? Tell me, Master of the Jungle, who is the Master of the Jungle?'

'These,' Mowgli whispered. 'It is the Place of Death. Let us go.'

'Nay, look well, for they are asleep. It is as it was when I was not the length of thy arm.'

The split and weatherworn rocks of the gorge of the Waingunga had been used since the beginning of the Jungle by the

Little People of the Rocks — the busy, furious, black wild bees of India; and, as Mowgli knew well, all trails turned off half a mile before they reached the gorge. For centuries the Little People had hived and swarmed from cleft to cleft, and swarmed again, stâining the white marble with stale honey, and made their combs tall and deep in the dark of the inner caves, where neither man nor beast nor fire nor water had ever touched them. The length of the gorge on both sides was hung as it were with black shimmery velvet curtains, and Mowgli sank as he looked, for those were the clotted millions of the sleeping bees. There were other lumps and festoons and things like decayed tree-trunks studded on the face of the rock, the old combs of past years, or new cities built in the shadow of the windless gorge, and huge masses of spongy, rotten trash had rolled down and stuck among the trees and creepers that clung to the rock-face. As he listened he heard more than once the rustle and slide of a honey-loaded comb turning over or falling away somewhere in the dark galleries; then a booming of angry wings, and the sullen drip, drip, drip, of the wasted honey, guttering along till it lipped over some ledge in the open air and sluggishly trickled down on the twigs. There was a tiny little beach, not five feet broad, on one side of the river, and that was piled high with the rubbish of uncounted years. There were dead bees, drones, sweepings, and stale combs, and wings of marauding moths that had strayed in after honey, all tumbled in smooth piles of the finest black dust. The mere sharp smell of it was enough to frighten anything that had no wings, and knew what the Little People were.

Kaa moved up-stream again till he came to a sandy bar at the head of the gorge.

'Here is this season's kill,' said he. 'Look!'

On the bank lay the skeletons of a couple of young deer and a buffalo. Mowgli could see that neither wolf nor jackal had touched the bones, which were laid out naturally.

'They came beyond the line; they did not know the Law,'

murmured Mowgli, 'and the Little People killed them. Let us go ere they wake.'

'They do not wake till the dawn,' said Kaa. 'Now I will tell thee. A hunted buck from the south, many, many Rains ago, came hither from the south, not knowing the Jungle, a Pack on his trail. Being made blind by fear, he leaped from above, the Pack running by sight, for they were hot and blind on the trail. The sun was high, and the Little People were many and very angry. Many, too, were those of the Pack who leaped into the Waingunga, but they were dead ere they took water. Those who did not leap died also in the rocks above. But the buck lived.'

'How?'

'Because he came first, running for his life, leaping ere the Little People were aware, and was in the river when they gathered to kill. The Pack, following, was altogether lost under the weight of the Little People.'

'The buck lived?' Mowgli repeated slowly.

'At least he did not die *then*, though none waited his coming down with a strong body to hold him safe against the water, as a certain old fat, deaf, yellow Flathead would wait for a Manling — yea, though there were all the dholes of the Dekkan on his trail. What is in thy stomach?' Kaa's head was close to Mowgli's ear; and it was a little time before the boy answered.

'It is to pull the very whiskers of Death, but — Kaa, thou art, indeed, the wisest of all the Jungle.'

'So many have said. Look now, if the dhole follow thee ——'

'As surely they will follow. Ho! ho! I have many little thorns under my tongue to prick into their hides.'

'If they follow thee hot and blind, looking only at thy shoulders, those who do not die up above will take water either here or lower down, for the Little People will rise up and cover them. Now the Waingunga is hungry water, and they will have no Kaa to hold them, but will go down, such as live, to the shallows by the Seeonee Lairs, and there thy Pack may meet them by the throat.'

'*Ahai! Eowawa!* Better could not be till the Rains fall in the dry season. There is now only the little matter of the run and the leap. I will make me known to the dholes, so that they shall follow me very closely.'

'Hast thou seen the rocks above thee? From the landward side?'

'Indeed, no. That I had forgotten.'

'Go look. It is all rotten ground, cut and full of holes. One of thy clumsy feet set down without seeing would end the hunt. See, I leave thee here, and for thy sake only I will carry word to the Pack that they may know where to look for the dhole. For myself, I am not of one skin with *any* wolf.'

When Kaa disliked an acquaintance he could be more unpleasant than any of the Jungle-People, except perhaps Bagheera. He swam down-stream, and opposite the Rock he came on Phao and Akela listening to the night noises.

'*Hssh!* Dogs,' he said cheerfully. 'The dholes will come down-stream. If ye be not afraid ye can kill them in the shallows.'

'When come they?' said Phao. 'And where is my Mancub?' said Akela.

'They come when they come,' said Kaa. 'Wait and see. As for *thy* Man-cub, from whom thou hast taken a Word and so laid him open to Death, *thy* Man-cub is with *me*, and if he be not already dead the fault is none of thine, bleached dog! Wait here for the dhole, and be glad that the Man-cub and I strike on thy side.'

Kaa flashed up-stream again, and moored himself in the middle of the gorge, looking upward at the line of the cliff. Presently he saw Mowgli's head move against the stars, and then there was a whizz in the air, the keen, clean *schloop* of a body falling feet first, and next minute the boy was at rest again in the loop of Kaa's body.

'It is no leap by night,' said Mowgli quietly. 'I have jumped twice as far for sport; but that is an evil place above — low bushes and gullies that go down very deep, all full of the Little People. I have put big stones one above the other by the side of three gullies. These I shall throw down with my feet in running, and the Little People will rise up behind me, very angry.'

'That is Man's talk and Man's cunning,' said Kaa. 'Thou art wise, but the Little People are always angry.'

'Nay, at twilight all wings near and far rest for a while. I will play with the dhole at twlight, for the dhole hunts best by day. He follows now Won-tolla's blood-trail.'

'Chil does not leave a dead ox, nor the dhole the blood-trail,' said Kaa.

'Then I will make him a new blood-trail, of his own blood if I can, and give him dirt to eat. Thou wilt stay here, Kaa, till I come again with my dholes?'

'Ay, but what if they kill thee in the Jungle, or the Little People kill thee before thou canst leap down to the river?'

'When to-morrow comes we will kill for to-morrow,' said Mowgli, quoting a Jungle saying; and again, 'When I am dead it is time to sing the Death Song. Good hunting, Kaa!'

He loosed his arm from the python's neck and went down the gorge like a log in a freshet, paddling toward the far bank, where he found slack-water, and laughing aloud from sheer happiness. There was nothing Mowgli liked better than, as he himself said, 'to pull the whiskers of Death,' and make the Jungle know that he was their overlord. He had often, with Baloo's help, robbed bees' nests in single trees, and he knew that the Little People hated the smell of wild garlic. So he gathered a small bundle of it, tied it up with a bark string, and then followed Won-tolla's blood-trail, as it ran southerly from the Lairs, for some five miles, looking at the trees with his head on one side, and chuckling as he looked.

'Mowgli the Frog have I been,' said he to himself; 'Mowgli the Wolf have I said that I am. Now Mowgli the Ape must I be before I am Mowgli the Buck. At the end I shall be Mowgli the

Man. Ho!' and he slid his thumb along the eighteen-inch blade of his knife.

Won-tolla's trail, all rank with dark blood-spots, ran under a forest of thick trees that grew close together and stretched away north-eastward, gradually growing thinner and thinner to within two miles of the Bee Rocks. From the last tree to the low scrub of the Bee Rocks was open country, where there was hardly cover enough to hide a wolf. Mowgli trotted along under the trees, judging distances between branch and branch, occasionally climbing up a trunk and taking a trial leap from one tree to another till he came to the open ground, which he studied very carefully for an hour. Then he turned, picked up Wontolla's trail where he had left it, settled himself in a tree with an outrunning branch some eight feet from the ground, and sat still, sharpening his knife on the sole of his foot and singing to himself.

A little before mid-day, when the sun was very warm, he heard the patter of feet and smelt the abominable smell of the dhole-pack as they trotted pitilessly along Won-tolla's trail. Seen from above, the red dhole does not look half the size of a wolf, but Mowgli knew how strong his feet and jaws were. He watched the sharp bay head of the leader snuffing along the trail, and gave him 'Good hunting!'

The brute looked up, and his companions halted behind him, scores and scores of red dogs with low-hung tails, heavy shoulders, weak quarters, and bloody mouths. The dholes are a very silent people as a rule, and they have no manners even in their own Jungle. Fully two hundred must have gathered below him, but he could see that the leaders sniffed hungrily on Won-tolla's trail, and tried to drag the pack forward. That would never do, or they would be at the Lairs in broad daylight, and Mowgli meant to hold them under his tree till dusk.

'By whose leave do ye come here?' said Mowgli.

'All Jungles are our Jungle,' was the reply and the dhole that gave it bared his white teeth. Mowgli looked down with a smile, and imitated perfectly the sharp chitter-chatter of Chikai, the leaping rat of the Dekkan, meaning the dholes to understand that he considered them no better than Chikai. The pack closed up round the tree-trunk and the leader bayed savagely, calling Mowgli a tree-ape. For an answer Mowgli stretched down one naked leg and wriggled his bare toes just above the leader's head. That was enough, and more than enough, to wake the pack to stupid rage. Those who have hair between their toes do not care to be reminded of it. Mowgli caught his foot away as the leader leaped up, and said sweetly; 'Dog, red dog! Go back to the Dekkan and eat lizards. Go to Chikai thy brother — dog, dog — red, red dog! There is hair between every toe!' He twiddled his toes a second time.

'Come down ere we starve thee out, hairless ape!' yelled the pack, and this was exactly what Mowgli wanted. He laid himself down along the branch, his cheek to the bark, his right arm free, and there he told the pack what he thought and knew about them, their manners, their customs, their mates, and their puppies. There is no speech in the world so rancorous and so stinging as the language the Jungle-People use to show scorn and contempt. When you come to think of it you will see how this must be so. As Mowgli told Kaa, he had many little thorns under his tongue, and slowly and deliberately he drove the dholes from silence to growls, from growls to yells, and from yells to hoarse slavery ravings. They tried to answer his taunts, but a cub might as well have tried to answer Kaa in a rage; and all the while Mowgli's right hand lay crooked at his side, ready for action, his feet locked round the branch. The big bay leader had leaped many times in the air, but Mowgli dared not risk a false blow. At last, made furious beyond his natural strength, he bounded up seven or eight feet clear of the ground. Then Mowgli's hand shot out like the head of a tree-snake, and gripped him by the scruff of his neck, and the branch shook with the jar as his weight fell back, almost wrenching Mowgli to the ground. But he never loosed his grip, and inch by inch he hauled the beast, hanging like a drowned jackal, up on the branch. With his left hand he reached for his knife and cut off the red, bushy tail, flinging the dhole back to earth again. That was all he needed. The pack would not go forward on Wontolla's trail now till they had killed Mowgli or Mowgli had killed them. He saw them settle down in circles with a quiver of the haunches that meant they were going to stay, and so he climbed to a higher crotch, settled his back comfortably, and went to sleep.

After three or four hours he waked and counted the pack. They were all there, silent, husky, and dry, with eyes of steel. The sun was beginning to sink. In half an hour the Little People of the Rocks would be ending their labours, and, as you know, the dhole does not fight best in the twilight.

'I did not need such faithful watchers,' he said politely, standing up on a branch, 'but I will remember this. Ye be true dholes, but to my thinking over much of one kind. For that reason I do not give the big lizard-eater his tail again. Art thou not pleased, Red Dog?'

'I myself will tear out thy stomach!' yelled the leader, scratching at the foot of the tree.

'Nay, but consider, wise rat of the Dekkan. There will now be many litters of little tailless red dogs, yea, with raw red stumps that sting when the sand is hot. Go home, Red Dog, and cry that an ape has done this. Ye will not go? Come, then, with me, and I will make you very wise!'

He moved, *Bandar-log* fashion, into the next tree, and so on into the next and the next, the pack following with lifted hungry heads. Now and then he would pretend to fall, and the pack would tumble one over the other in their haste to be at the death. It was a curious sight — the boy with the knife that shone in the low sunlight as it sifted through the upper branches and the silent pack with their red coats all aflame, huddling and following below. When he came to the last tree he took the garlic and rubbed himself all over carefully, and the dholes yelled with scorn. 'Ape with a wolf's tongue, dost thou think to cover thy scent?' they said. 'We follow to the death.'

'Take thy tail,' said Mowgli, flinging it back along the course he had taken. The pack instinctively rushed after it. 'And follow now — to the death.'

He had slipped down the tree-trunk, and headed like the wind in bare feet for the Bee Rocks, before the dholes saw what he would do.

They gave one deep howl, and settled down to the long, lobbing canter that can at the last run down anything that runs. Mowgli knew their pack-pace to be much slower than that of the wolves, or he would never have risked a two-mile run in full sight. They were sure that the boy was theirs at last, and he was sure that he held them to play with as he pleased. All his trouble was to keep them sufficiently hot behind him to prevent their turning off too soon. He ran cleanly, evenly, and springily; the tailless leader not five yards behind him; and the pack tailing out over perhaps a quarter of a mile of ground, crazy and blind with the rage of slaughter, So he kept his distance by ear, reserving his last effort for the rush across the Bee Rocks.

The Little People had gone to sleep in the early twilight, for it was not the season of late blossoming flowers; but as Mowgli's first foot-falls rang hollow on the hollow ground he heard a sound as though all the earth were humming. Then he ran as he had never run in his life before, spurned aside one — two — three of the piles of stones into the dark, sweet-smelling gullies; heard a roar like the roar of the sea in a cave; saw with the tail of his eye the air grow dark behind him; saw the current of the Waingunga far below, and a flat, diamond-shaped head in the water; leaped outward with all his strength, the tailless dhole snapping at his shoulder in mid-air, and dropped feet first to the safety of the river, breathless and triumphant. There was not a sting upon him, for the smell of the garlic had checked the Little People for just the few seconds that he was among them. When he rose Kaa's coils were steadying him and things were bounding over the edge of the cliff — great lumps, it seemed, of clustered bees falling like plummets; but before any lump touched water the bees flew upward and the body of a dhole whirled down-stream. Overhead they could hear furious short yells that were drowned in a roar like breakers — the roar of the wings of the Little People of the Rocks. Some of the dholes, too, had fallen into the gullies that communicated with the underground caves, and there choked and fought and snapped among the tumbled honeycombs, and at last, borne up, even when they were dead, on the heaving waves of bees beneath them, shot out of some hole in the river-face, to roll over on the black rubbish-heaps. There were dholes who had leaped short into the trees on the cliffs, and the bees blotted out their shapes; but the greater number of them, maddened by the stings, had flung themselves into the river; and, as Kaa said, the Waingunga was hungry water.

Kaa held Mowgli fast till the boy had recovered his breath, 'We may not stay here,' he said. 'The Little People are roused indeed. Come!'

Swimming low and diving as often as he could, Mowgli went down the river, knife in hand.

'Slowly, slowly,' said Kaa. 'One tooth does not kill a hundred unless it be a cobra's, and many of the dholes took water swiftly when they saw the Little People rise.'

'The more work for my knife, then. *Phai!* How the Little People follow!' Mowgli sank again. The face of the water was blanketed with wild bees, buzzing sullenly and stinging all they found.

'Nothing was ever yet lost by silence,' said Kaa — no sting could penetrate his scales — 'and thou hast all the long night for the hunting. Hear them howl!'

Nearly half the pack had seen the trap their fellows rushed into, and turning sharp aside had flung themselves into the water where the gorge broke down in steep banks. Their cries of rage and their threats against the 'tree-ape' who had brought them to their shame mixed with the yells and growls of those who had been punished by the Little People. To remain ashore was death, and every dhole knew it. Their pack was swept along the current, down to the deep eddies of the Peace Pool, but even there the angry Little People followed and forced them to the water again. Mowgli could hear the voice of the tailless leader bidding his people hold on and kill out every wolf in Seeonee. But he did not waste his time in listening.

'One kills in the dark behind us!' snapped a dhole. 'Here is tainted water!'

Mowgli had dived forward like an otter, twitched a struggling dhole under water before he could open his mouth, and dark rings rose as the body plopped up, turning on its side. The dholes tried to turn, but the current prevented them, and the Little People darted at their heads and ears, and they could hear the challenge of the Seeonee Pack growing louder and deeper in the gathering darkness. Again Mowgli dived, and again a dhole went under, and rose dead, and again the clamour broke out at the rear of the pack; some howling that it was best to go ashore, others calling on their leader to lead them back to the Dekkan, and others bidding Mowgli show himself and be killed.

'They come to the fight with two stomachs and several voices,' said Kaa. 'The rest is with thy brethren below yonder. The Little People go back to sleep. They have chased us far. Now I, too, turn back, for I am not of one skin with any wolf. Good hunting, Little Brother, and remember the dhole bites low.'

A wolf came running along the bank on three legs, leaping up and down, laying his head sideways close to the ground, hunching his back, and breaking high into the air, as though he were playing with his cubs. It was Won-tolla, the Outlier, and he said never a word, but continued his horrible sport beside the dholes. They had been long in the water now, and were swimming wearily, their coats drenched and heavy, their bushy tails dragging like sponges, so tired and shaken that they, too, were silent, watching the pair of blazing eyes that moved abreast.

'This is no good hunting,' said one, panting.

'Good hunting!' said Mowgli, as he rose boldly at the brute's side, and sent the long knife home behind the shoulder, pushing hard to avoid his dying snap.

'Art thou there, Man-cub?' said Won-tolla across the water.

'Ask of the dead, Outlier,' Mowgli replied. 'Have none come down-stream? I have filled these dogs' mouths with dirt; I have tricked them in the broad daylight, and their leader lacks his tail, but here be some few for thee still. Whither shall I drive them?'

'I will wait,' said Won-tolla. 'The night is before me.'

Nearer and nearer came the bay of the Seeonee wolves. 'For the Pack, for the Full Pack it is met!' and a bend in the river drove the dholes forward among the sands and shoals opposite the Lairs.

Then they saw their mistake. They should have landed half a mile higher up, and rushed the wolves on dry ground. Now it was too late. The bank was lined with burning eyes, and except for the horrible *pheeal* that had never stopped since sundown, there was no sound in the Jungle. It seemed as though Won-tolla were fawning on them to come ashore; and 'Turn and take hold!' said the leader of the dholes. The entire pack flung themselves at the shore, threshing and squattering through the shoal water, till the face of the Waingunga was all white and torn, and the great ripples went from side to side, like bow-waves from a boat. Mowgli followed the rush, stabbing and slicing as the dholes, huddled together, rushed up the river-beach in one wave.

Then the long fight began, heaving and straining and splitting and scattering and narrowing and broadening along the red, wet sands, and over and between the tangled tree-roots, and through and among the bushes, and in and out of the grass clumps; for even now the dholes were two to one. But they met wolves fighting for all that made the Pack, and not only the short, high, deep-chested, white-tusked hunters of the Pack, but the anxious-eyed lahinis — the she-wolves of the lair, as the saying is — fighting for their litters, with here and there a yearling wolf, his first coat still half woolly, tugging and grappling by their sides. A wolf, you must know, flies at the throat or snaps at the flank, while a dhole, by preference, bites at the belly; so when the dholes were struggling out of the water and had to raise their heads, the odds were with the wolves. On dry land the wolves suffered; but in the water or ashore, Mowgli's knife came and went without ceasing. The Four had worried their way to his side. Gray Brother, crouched between the boy's knees, was protecting his stomach, while the others guarded his back and either side, or stood over him when the shock of a leaping, yelling dhole who had thrown himself full on the steady blade bore him down. For the rest, it was one tangled confusion — a locked and swaying mob that moved from right to left and from left to right along the bank; and also ground round and round slowly on its own centre. Here would be a heaving mound, like a water-blister in a whirlpool, which would break like a water-blister, and throw up four or five mangled dogs, each striving to get back to the centre; here would be a single wolf borne down by two or three dholes laboriously dragging them forward, and sinking the while; here a yearling cub would be held up by the pressure round him, though he had been killed early, while his mother, crazed with dumb rage, rolled over and over, snapping, and passing on; and in the middle of the thickest press, perhaps, one wolf and one dhole, forgetting everything else, would be manœuvring for first hold till they were whirled away by a rush of furious fighters. Once Mowgli passed Akela, a dhole on either flank, and his all but toothless jaws closed over the loins of a third; and once he saw Phao, his teeth set in the throat of a dhole, tugging the unwilling beast forward till the yearlings could finish him. But the bulk of the fight was blind flurry and smother in the dark; hit, trip, and tumble, yelp, groan, and worry-worry-worry, round him and behind him and above him. As the night wore on, the quick, giddy-go-round motion increased. The dholes were cowed and afraid to attack the stronger wolves, but did not yet dare to run away. Mowgli felt that the end was coming soon, and contented himself with striking merely to cripple. The yearlings were growing bolder; there was time now and again to breathe, and pass a word to a friend, and the mere flicker of the knife would sometimes turn a dog aside.

'The meat is very near the bone,' Gray Brother yelled. He was bleeding from a score of flesh-wounds.

'But the bone is yet to be cracked,' said Mowgli. '*Eowawa! Thus* do we do in the Jungle!' The red blade ran like a flame along the side of a dhole whose hind-quarters were hidden by the weight of a clinging wolf.

'My kill!' snorted the wolf through his wrinkled nostrils. 'Leave him to me.'

'Is thy stomach still empty, Outlier?' said Mowgli. Won-tolla was fearfully punished, but his grip had paralysed the dhole, who could not turn round and reach him.

'By the Bull that bought me,' said Mowgli, with a bitter laugh, 'it is the tailless one!' And indeed it was the big bay-coloured leader.

'It is not wise to kill cubs and lahinis,' Mowgli went on philosophically, wiping the blood out of his eyes, 'unless one has also killed the Outlier; and it is in my stomach that this Won-tolla kills thee.'

A dhole leaped to his leader's aid; but before his teeth had found Won-tolla's flank, Mowgli's knife was in his throat, and Gray Brother took what was left.

'And thus do we do in the Jungle,' said Mowgli.

Won-tolla said not a word, only his jaws were closing and closing on the backbone as his life ebbed. The dhole shuddered, his head dropped, and he lay still, and Won-tolla dropped above him.

'*Huh!* The Blood Debt is paid,' said Mowgli. 'Sing the song, Won-tolla.'

'He hunts no more,' said Gray Brother; 'and Akela, too, is silent this long time.'

'The bone is cracked!' thundered Phao, son of Phaona. 'They go! Kill, kill out, O hunters of the Free People!'

Dhole after dhole was slinking away from those dark and bloody sands to the river, to the thick Jungle, up-stream or down-stream as he saw the road clear.

'The debt! The debt!' shouted Mowgli. 'Pay the debt! They have slain the Lone Wolf! Let not a dog go!'

He was flying to the river, knife in hand, to check any dhole who dared to take water, when, from under a mound of nine dead, rose Akela's head and fore-quarters, and Mowgli dropped on his knees beside the Lone Wolf.

'Said I not it would be my last fight?' Akela gasped. 'It is good hunting. And thou, Little Brother?'

'I live, having killed many.'

'Even so. I die, and I would — I would die by thee, Little Brother.'

Mowgli took the terrible scarred head on his knees, and put his arms round the torn neck.

'It is long since the old days of Shere Khan, and a Man-cub that rolled naked in the dust.'

'Nay, nay, I am a wolf. I am of one skin with the Free People,' Mowgli cried. 'It is no will of mine that I am a man.'

'Thou art a man, Little Brother, wolfling of my watching. Thou art a man, or else the Pack had fled before the dhole. My life I owe to thee, and to-day thou hast saved the Pack even as once I saved thee. Hast thou forgotten? All debts are paid now. Go to thine own people. I tell thee again, eye of my eye, this hunting is ended. Go to thine own people.'

'I will never go. I will hunt alone in the Jungle. I have said it.'

'After the summer come the Rains, and after the Rains comes the spring. Go back before thou art driven.'

'Who will drive me?'

'Mowgli will drive Mowgli. Go back to thy people. Go to Man.'

'When Mowgli drives Mowgli I will go,' Mowgli answered.

'There is no more to say,' said Akela. 'Little Brother, canst thou raise me to my feet? I also was a leader of the Free People.'

Very carefully and gently Mowgli lifted the bodies aside, and raised Akela to his feet, both arms round him, and the Lone Wolf drew a long breath, and began the Death Song that a leader of the Pack should sing when he dies. It gathered strength as he went on, lifting and lifting, and ringing far across the river, till it came to the last 'Good hunting!' and Akela shook himself clear of Mowgli for an instant, and, leaping into the air, fell backward dead upon his last and most terrible kill.

Mowgli sat with his head on his knees, careless of anything else, while the remnant of the flying dholes were being overtaken and run down by the merciless lahinis. Little by little the cries died away, and the wolves returned limping, as their wounds stiffened, to take stock of the losses. Fifteen of the Pack, as well as half a dozen lahinis, lay dead by the river, and of the others not one was unmarked. And Mowgli sat through it all till the cold daybreak, when Phao's wet, red muzzle was dropped in his hand, and Mowgli drew back to show the gaunt body of Akela.

'Good hunting!' said Phao, as though Akela were still alive, and then over his bitten shoulder to the others: 'Howl, dogs! A Wolf has died to-night!'

But of all the pack of two hundred fighting dholes, whose boast was that all Jungles were their Jungle, and that no living thing could stand before them, not one returned to the Dekkan to carry that word.

CHIL'S SONG

[This is the song that Chil sang as the kites dropped down one after another to the river-bed, when the great fight was finished. Chil is good friends with everybody, but he is a cold-blooded kind of creature at heart, because he knows that almost everybody in the Jungle comes to him in the long-run.]

These were my companions going forth by night —
    (*For Chil! Look you, for Chil!*)
Now come I to whistle them the ending of the fight.
    (*Chil! Vanguards of Chil!*)
Word they gave me overhead of quarry newly slain,
Word I gave them underfoot of buck upon the plain.
Here's an end of every trail — they shall not speak again!

They that called the hunting-cry — they that followed fast —
    (*For Chil! Look you, for Chil!*)
They that bade the sambhur wheel, or pinned him as he passed —
    (*Chil! Vanguards of Chil!*)
They that lagged behind the scent — they that ran before,
They that shunned the level horn — they that overbore.
Here's an end of every trail — they shall not follow more.

These were my companions. Pity 'twas they died!
    (*For Chil! Look you, for Chil!*)
Now come I to comfort them that knew them in their pride.
    (*Chil! Vanguards of Chil!*)
Tattered flank and sunken eye, open mouth and red,
Locked and lank and lone they lie, the dead upon their dead.
Here's an end of every trail — and here my hosts are fed.

THE SPRING RUNNING

Man goes to Man! Cry the challenge through the Jungle!
  He that was our Brother goes away.
Hear, now, and judge, O ye People of the Jungle, —
  Answer, who shall turn him — who shall stay?

Man goes to Man! He is weeping in the Jungle:
  He that was our Brother sorrows sore!
Man goes to Man! (Oh, we loved him in the Jungle!)
  To the Man-Trail where we may not follow more.

THE second year after the great fight with Red Dog and the death of Akela, Mowgli must have been nearly seventeen years old. He looked older, for hard exercise, the best of good eating, and baths whenever he felt in the least hot or dusty, had given him strength and growth far beyond his age. He could swing by one hand from a top branch for half an hour at a time, when he had occasion to look along the tree-roads. He could stop a young buck in mid-gallop and throw him sideways by the head. He could even jerk over the big, blue wild boars that lived in the Marshes of the North. The Jungle-People who used to fear him for his wits feared him now for his strength, and when he moved quietly on his own affairs the mere whisper of his coming cleared the wood-paths. And yet the look in his eyes was always gentle. Even when he fought, his eyes never blazed as Bagheera's did. They only grew more and more interested and excited; and that was one of the things that Bagheera himself did not understand.

He asked Mowgli about it, and the boy laughed and said: 'When I miss the kill I am angry. When I must go empty for two days I am very angry. Do not my eyes talk then?'

'The mouth is hungry,' said Bagheera, 'but the eyes say nothing. Hunting, eating, or swimming, it is all one — like a stone in wet or dry weather.' Mowgli looked at him lazily from under his long eyelashes, and, as usual, the panther's head dropped. Bagheera knew his master.

They were lying out far up the side of a hill overlooking the Waingunga, and the morning mists hung below them in bands of white and green. As the sun rose it changed into bubbling seas of red gold, churned off, and let the low rays stripe the dried grass on which Mowgli and Bagheera were resting. It was the end of the cold weather, the leaves and the trees looked worn and faded, and there was a dry, ticking rustle everywhere when the wind blew. A little leaf tap-tap-tapped furiously against a twig, as a single leaf caught in a current will. It roused Bagheera, for he snuffed the morning air with a deep, hollow cough, threw himself on his back, and struck with his fore-paws at the nodding leaf above.

'The year turns,' he said. 'The Jungle goes forward. The Time of New Talk is near. That leaf knows. It is very good.'

'The grass is dry,' Mowgli answered, pulling up a tuft. 'Even Eye-of-the-Spring [that is a little trumpet-shaped, waxy red flower that runs in and out among the grasses] — even Eye-of-the-Spring is shut, and . . . Bagheera, *is* it well for the Black Panther so to lie on his back and beat with his paws in the air, as though he were the tree-cat?'

'Aowh?' said Bagheera. He seemed to be thinking of other things.

'I say, *is* it well for the Black Panther so to mouth and cough, and howl and roll? Remember, we be the Masters of the Jungle, thou and I.'

'Indeed, yes; I hear, Man-cub.' Bagheera rolled over hurriedly and sat up, the dust on his ragged black flanks. (He was just casting his winter coat.) 'We be surely the Masters of the Jungle! Who is so strong as Mowgli? Who so wise?' There was a curious drawl in the voice that made Mowgli turn to see whether by any chance the Black Panther were making fun of him, for the Jungle is full of words that sound like one thing, but mean another. 'I said we be beyond question the Masters of the Jungle,' Bagheera repeated. 'Have I done wrong? I did not know that the Man-cub no longer lay upon the ground. Does he fly, then?'

Mowgli sat with his elbows on his knees, looking out across the valley at the daylight. Somewhere down in the woods below a bird was trying over in a husky, reedy voice the first few notes of his spring song. It was no more than a shadow of the liquid, tumbling call he would be pouring later, but Bagheera heard it.

'I said the Time of New Talk is near,' growled the panther, switching his tail.

'I hear,' Mowgli answered. 'Bagheera, why dost thou shake all over? The sun is warm.'

'That is Ferao, the scarlet woodpecker,' said Bagheera. '*He* has not forgotten. Now I, too, must remember my song,' and he began purring and crooning to himself, harking back dissatis-fied again and again.

'There is no game afoot,' said Mowgli.

'Little Brother, are *both* thine ears stopped? That is no kill-ing-word, but my song that I make ready against the need.'

'I had forgotten. I shall know when the Time of New Talk is here, because then thou and the others all run away and leave me alone.' Mowgli spoke rather savagely.

'But indeed, Little Brother,' Bagheera began, 'we do not always ——'

'I say ye do,' said Mowgli, shooting out his forefinger an-grily. 'Ye *do* run away, and I, who am the Master of the Jungle, must needs walk alone. How was it last season, when I would gather sugar-cane from the fields of a Man-Pack? I sent a run-ner — I sent thee! — to Hathi, bidding him to come upon such a night and pluck the sweet grass for me with his trunk.'

'He came only two nights later,' said Bagheera, cowering a little; 'and of that long, sweet grass that pleased thee so he gathered more than any Man-cub could eat in all the nights of the Rains. That was no fault of mine.'

'He did not come upon the night when I sent him the word.

No, he was trumpeting and running and roaring through the valleys in the moonlight. His trail was like the trail of three elephants, for he would not hide among the trees. He danced in the moonlight before the houses of the Man-Pack. I saw him, and yet he would not come to me; and *I* am the Master of the Jungle!'

'It was the Time of New Talk,' said the panther, always very humble. 'Perhaps, Little Brother, thou didst not that time call him by a Master Word? Listen to Ferao, and be glad!'

Mowgli's bad temper seemed to have boiled itself away. He lay back with his head on his arms, his eyes shut. 'I do not know — nor do I care,' he said sleepily. 'Let us sleep, Bagheera. My stomach is heavy in me. Make me a rest for my head.'

The panther lay down again with a sigh, because he could hear Ferao practising and repractising his song against the Springtime of New Talk, as they say.

In an Indian Jungle the seasons slide one into the other almost without division. There seem to be only two — the wet and the dry; but if you look closely below the torrents of rain and the clouds of char and dust you will find all four going round in their regular ring. Spring is the most wonderful, because she has not to cover a clean, bare field with new leaves and flowers, but to drive before her and to put away the hanging-on, over-surviving raffle of half-green things which the gentle winter has suffered to live, and to make the partly-dressed stale earth feel new and young once more. And this she does so well that there is no spring in the world like the Jungle spring.

There is one day when all things are tired, and the very smells, as they drift on the heavy air, are old and used. One cannot explain this, but it feels so. Then there is another day — to the eye nothing whatever has changed — when all the smells are new and delightful, and the whiskers of the Jungle-People quiver to their roots, and the winter hair comes away from their sides in long, draggled locks. Then, perhaps, a little rain falls, and all the trees and the bushes and the bamboos and the mosses and the juicy-leaved plants wake with a noise of growing that you can almost hear, and under this noise runs, day and night, a deep hum. *That* is the noise of the spring — a vibrating boom which is neither bees, nor falling water, nor the wind in tree-tops, but the purring of the warm, happy world.

Up to this year Mowgli had always delighted in the turn of the seasons. It was he who generally saw the first Eye-of-the-Spring deep down among the grasses, and the first bank of spring clouds, which are like nothing else in the Jungle. His voice could be heard in all sorts of wet, star-lighted, blossoming places, helping the big frogs through their choruses, or mocking the little upside-down owls that hoot through the white nights. Like all his people, spring was the season he chose for his flit-tings — moving, for the mere joy of rushing through the warm air, thirty, forty, or fifty miles between twilight and the morning star, and coming back panting and laughing and wreathed with strange flowers. The Four did not follow him on these wild ringings of the Jungle, but went off to sing songs with other wolves. The Jungle-People are very busy in the spring, and Mowgli could hear them grunting and screaming and whistling according to their kind. Their voices then are different from their voices at other times of the year, and that is one of the reasons why spring in the Jungle is called the Time of New Talk.

But that spring, as he told Bagheera, his stomach was changed in him. Ever since the bamboo shoots turned spotty-brown he had been looking forward to the morning when the smells should change. But when the morning came, and Mor the Peacock, blazing in bronze and blue and gold, cried it aloud all along the misty woods, and Mowgli opened his mouth to send on the cry, the words choked between his teeth, and a feel-ing came over him that began at his toes and ended in his hair — a feeling of pure unhappiness, so that he looked himself over to be sure that he had not trod on a thorn. Mor cried the new smells, the other birds took it over, and from the rocks by the Waingunga he heard Bagheera's hoarse scream — something between the scream of an eagle and the neighing of a horse. There was a yelling and scattering of *Bandar-log* in the new-budding branches above, and there stood Mowgli, his chest, filled to answer Mor, sinking in little gasps as the breath was driven out of it by this unhappiness.

He stared all round him, but he could see no more than the mocking *Bandar-log* scudding through the trees, and Mor, his tail spread in full splendour, dancing on the slopes below.

'The smells have changed,' screamed Mor. 'Good hunting, Little Brother! Where is thy answer?'

'Little Brother, good hunting!' whistled Chil the Kite and his mate, swooping down together. The two baffed under Mowgli's nose so close that a pinch of downy white feathers brushed away.

A light spring rain — elephant-rain they call it — drove across the Jungle in a belt half a mile wide, left the new leaves wet and nodding behind, and died out in a double rainbow and a light roll of thunder. The spring hum broke out for a minute, and was silent, but all the Jungle-Folk seemed to be giving tongue at once. All except Mowgli.

'I have eaten good food,' he said to himself. 'I have drunk good water. Nor does my throat burn and grow small, as it did when I bit the blue-spotted root that Oo the Turtle said was clean food. But my stomach is heavy, and I have given very bad talk to Bagheera and others, people of the Jungle and my people. Now, too, I am hot and now I am cold, and now I am neither hot nor cold, but angry with that which I cannot see. Huhu! It is time to make a running! To-night I will cross the ranges; yes, I will make a spring running to the Marshes of the North, and back again. I have hunted too easily too long. The Four shall come with me, for they grow as fat as white grubs.'

He called, but never one of the Four answered. They were far beyond earshot, singing over the spring songs — the Moon and Sambhur Songs — with the wolves of the Pack; for in the springtime the Jungle-People make very little difference between the day and the night. He gave the sharp, barking note, but his only answer was the mocking *maiou* of the little spotted tree-cat winding in and out among the branches for early birds' nests. At this he shook all over with rage, and half drew his knife. Then he became very haughty, though there was no one to see him, and stalked severely down the hillside, chin up and eyebrows down. But never a single one of his people asked him a question, for they were all too busy with their own affairs.

'Yes,' said Mowgli to himself, though in his heart he knew that he had no reason. 'Let the Red Dhole come from the Dekkan, or the Red Flower dance among the bamboos, and all the Jungle runs whining to Mowgli, calling him great elephant-names. But now, because Eye-of-the-Spring is red, and Mor, forsooth, must show his naked legs in some spring dance, the Jungle goes mad as Tabaqui. . . . By the Bull that bought me! am I the Master of the Jungle, or am I not? Be silent! What do ye here?'

A couple of young wolves of the Pack were cantering down a path, looking for open ground in which to fight. (You will remember that the Law of the Jungle forbids fighting where the Pack can see.) Their neck-bristles were as stiff as wire, and they bayed furiously, crouching for the first grapple. Mowgli leaped forward, caught one outstretched throat in either hand, expecting to fling the creatures backward as he had often done in games or Pack hunts. But he had never before interfered with a spring fight. The two leaped forward and dashed him aside, and without word to waste rolled over and over close locked.

Mowgli was on his feet almost before he fell, his knife and his white teeth were bared, and at that minute he would have killed them both for no reason but that they were fighting when he wished them to be quiet, although every wolf has full right under the Law to fight. He danced round them with lowered shoulders and quivering hand, ready to send in a double blow when the first flurry of the scuffle should be over; but while he waited the strength seemed to ebb from his body, the knife-point lowered, and he sheathed the knife and watched.

'I have surely eaten poison,' he sighed at last. 'Since I broke up the Council with the Red Flower — since I killed Shere Khan — none of the Pack could fling me aside. And these be only tail-wolves in the Pack, little hunters! My strength is gone from me, and presently I shall die. Oh, Mowgli, why dost thou not kill them both?'

The fight went on till one wolf ran away, and Mowgli was left alone on the torn and bloody ground, looking now at his knife, and now at his legs and arms, while the feeling of unhappiness he had never known before covered him as water covers a log.

He killed early that evening and ate but little, so as to be in good fettle for his spring running, and he ate alone because all the Jungle-People were away singing or fighting. It was a perfect white night, as they call it. All green things seemed to have made a month's growth since the morning. The branch that was yellow-leaved the day before dripped sap when Mowgli broke it. The mosses curled deep and warm over his feet, the young grass had no cutting edges, and all the voices of the Jungle boomed like one deep harp-string touched by the moon — the Moon of New Talk, who splashed her light full on rock and pool, slipped it between trunk and creeper, and sifted it through a million leaves. Forgetting his unhappiness, Mowgli sang aloud with pure delight as he settled into his stride. It was more like flying than anything else, for he had chosen the long downward slope that leads to the Northern Marshes through the heart of the main Jungle, where the springy ground deadened the fall of his feet. A man-taught man would have picked his way with many stumbles through the cheating moonlight, but Mowgli's muscles, trained by years of experience, bore him up as though he were a feather. When a rotten log or a hidden stone turned under his foot he saved himself, never checking his pace, without effort and without thought. When he tired of ground-going he threw up his hands monkey-fashion to the nearest creeper, and seemed to float rather than to climb up into the thin branches, whence he would follow a tree-road till his mood changed, and he shot downward in a long, leafy curve to the levels again. There were still, hot hollows surrounded by wet rocks where he could hardly breathe for the heavy scents of the night flowers and the bloom along the creeper buds; dark avenues where the moonlight lay in belts as regular as checkered marbles in a church aisle; thickets where the wet young growth stood breast-high about him and threw its arms round his waist; and hilltops crowned with broken rock, where he leaped from stone to stone above the lairs of the frightened little foxes. He would hear, very faint and far off, the *chug-drug* of a boar sharpening his tusks on a bole; and would come across the great gray brute all alone, scribing and rending the bark of a tall tree, his mouth dripping with foam, and his eyes blazing like fire. Or he would turn aside to the sound of clashing horns and hissing grunts, and dash past a couple of furious sambhur, staggering to and fro with lowered heads, striped with blood that showed black in the moonlight. Or at some rushing ford he would hear Jacala the Crocodile bellowing like a bull, or disturb a twined knot of the Poison People, but before they could strike he would be away and across the glistening shingle, and deep in the Jungle again.

So he ran, sometimes shouting, sometimes singing to himself, the happiest thing in all the Jungle that night, till the smell of the flowers warned him that he was near the marshes, and those lay far beyond his farthest hunting-grounds.

Here, again, a man-trained man would have sunk overhead in three strides, but Mowgli's feet had eyes in them, and they passed him from tussock to tussock and clump to quaking clump without asking help from the eyes in his head. He ran out to the middle of the swamp, disturbing the duck as he ran, and sat down on a moss-coated tree-trunk lapped in the black water. The marsh was awake all round him, for in the spring the Bird-People sleep very lightly, and companies of them were coming or going the night through. But no one took any notice of Mowgli sitting among the tall reeds humming songs without words, and looking at the soles of his hard brown feet in case of neglected thorns. All his unhappiness seemed to have been left behind in his own Jungle, and he was just beginning a full-throat song when it came back again — ten times worse than before.

This time Mowgli was frightened. 'It is here also!' he said half aloud. 'It has followed me,' and he looked over his shoulder to see whether the It were not standing behind him. 'There is no one here.' The night noises of the marsh went on, but never a bird or beast spoke to him, and the new feeling of misery grew.

'I have surely eaten poison,' he said in an awe-stricken voice. 'It must be that carelessly I have eaten poison, and my strength is going from me. I was afraid — and yet it was not *I* that was afraid — Mowgli was afraid when the two wolves fought. Akela, or even Phao, would have silenced them; yet Mowgli was afraid. That is true sign I have eaten poison. . . . But what do they care in the Jungle? They sing and howl and fight, and run in companies under the moon, and I — *Hai-mai!* — I am dying in the marshes, of that poison which I have eaten.' He was so sorry for himself that he nearly wept. 'And after,' he went on, 'they will find me lying in the black water. Nay, I will go back to my own Jungle, and I will die upon the Council Rock, and Bagheera, whom I love, if he is not screaming in the valley — Bagheera, perhaps, may watch by what is left for a little, lest Chil use me as he used Akela.'

A large, warm tear splashed down on his knee, and, miserable as he was, Mowgli felt happy that he was so miserable, if you can understand that upside-down sort of happiness. 'As Chil the Kite used Akela,' he repeated, 'on the night I saved the Pack from Red Dog.' He was quiet for a little, thinking of the last words of the Lone Wolf, which you, of course, remember. 'Now Akela said to me many foolish things before he died, for when we die our stomachs change. He said . . . None the less, I *am* of the Jungle!'

In his excitement, as he remembered the fight on Waingunga bank, he shouted the last words aloud, and a wild buffalo-cow among the reeds sprang to her knees, snorting, 'Man!'

'Uhh!' said Mysa, the Wild Buffalo (Mowgli could hear him turn in his wallow), '*that* is no man. It is only the hairless wolf of the Seeonee Pack. On such nights runs he to and fro.'

'Uhh!' said the cow, dropping her head again to graze, 'I thought it was Man.'

'I say no. Oh, Mowgli, is it danger?' lowed Mysa.

'Oh, Mowgli, is it danger?' the boy called back mockingly. 'That is all Mysa thinks for: Is it danger? But for Mowgli, who goes to and fro in the Jungle by night, watching, what do ye care?'

'How loud he cries!' said the cow.

'Thus do they cry,' Mysa answered contemptuously, 'who, having torn up the grass, know not how to eat it.'

'For less than this,' Mowgli groaned to himself, — 'for less than this even last Rains I had pricked Mysa out of his wallow, and ridden him through the swamp on a rush halter.' He stretched a hand to break one of the feathery reeds, but drew it back with a sigh. Mysa went on steadily chewing the cud, and the long grass ripped where the cow grazed. 'I will not die *here*,' he said angrily. 'Mysa, who is of one blood with Jacala and the pig, would see me. Let us go beyond the swamp and see what comes. Never have I run such a spring running — hot and cold together. Up, Mowgli!'

He could not resist the temptation of stealing across the reeds to Mysa and pricking him with the point of his knife. The great dripping bull broke out of his wallow like a shell exploding, while Mowgli laughed till he sat down.

'Say now that the hairless wolf of the Seeonee Pack once herded thee, Mysa,' he called.

'Wolf! *Thou?*' the bull snorted, stamping in the mud. 'All the Jungle knows thou wast a herder of tame cattle — such a man's brat as shouts in the dust by the crops yonder. *Thou* of the Jungle! What hunter would have crawled like a snake among the leeches, and for a muddy jest — a jackal's jest — have shamed me before my cow? Come to firm ground, and I will — I will . . .' Mysa frothed at the mouth, for Mysa has nearly the worst temper of any one in the Jungle.

Mowgli watched him puff and blow with eyes that never changed. When he could make himself heard through the spattering mud, he said: 'What Man-Pack lair here by the marshes, Mysa? This is new Jungle to me.'

'Go north, then,' roared the angry bull, for Mowgli had pricked him rather sharply. 'It was a naked cow-herd's jest. Go and tell them at the village at the foot of the marsh.'

'The Man-Pack do not love Jungle-tales, nor do I think, Mysa, that a scratch more or less on thy hide is any matter for a council. But I will go and look at this village. Yes, I will go. Softly now. It is not every night that the Master of the Jungle comes to herd thee.'

He stepped out to the shivering ground on the edge of the marsh, well knowing that Mysa would never charge over it, and laughed, as he ran, to think of the bull's anger.

'My strength is not altogether gone,' he said. 'It may be that the poison is not to the bone. There is a star sitting low yonder.' He looked at it between his half-shut hands. 'By the Bull that bought me, it is the Red Flower — the Red Flower that I lay beside before — before I came even to the first Seeonee Pack! Now that I have seen, I will finish the running.'

The marsh ended in a broad plain where a light twinkled. It was a long time since Mowgli had concerned himself with the doings of men, but this night the glimmer of the Red Flower drew him forward.

'I will look,' said he, 'as I did in the old days, and I will see how far the Man-Pack has changed.'

Forgetting that he was no longer in his own Jungle, where he could do what he pleased, he trod carelessly through the dew-loaded grasses till he came to the hut where the light stood. Three or four yelping dogs gave tongue, for he was on the outskirts of a village.

'Ho!' said Mowgli, sitting down noiselessly, after sending back a deep wolf-growl that silenced the curs. 'What comes will come. Mowgli, what hast thou to do any more with the lairs of the Man-Pack?' He rubbed his mouth, remembering where a stone had struck it years ago when the other Man-Pack had cast him out.

The door of the hut opened, and a woman stood peering out into the darkness. A child cried, and the woman said over her shoulder, 'Sleep. It was but a jackal that waked the dogs. In a little time morning comes.'

Mowgli in the grass began to shake as though he had fever. He knew that voice well, but to make sure he cried softly, surprised to find how man's talk came back, 'Messua! O Messua!'

'Who calls?' said the woman, a quiver in her voice.

'Hast thou forgotten?' said Mowgli. His throat was dry as he spoke.

'If it be *thou*, what name did I give thee? Say!' She had half shut the door, and her hand was clutching at her breast.

'Nathoo! Ohé Nathoo!' said Mowgli, for, as you remember, that was the name Messua gave him when he first came to the Man-Pack.

'Come, my son,' she called, and Mowgli stepped into the light, and looked full at Messua, the woman who had been good to him, and whose life he had saved from the Man-Pack so long before. She was older, and her hair was gray, but her eyes and her voice had not changed. Woman-like, she expected to find Mowgli where she had left him, and her eyes travelled upward in a puzzled way from his chest to his head, that touched the top of the door.

'My son,' she stammered; and then, sinking to his feet: 'But it is no longer my son. It is a Godling of the Woods! Ahai!'

As he stood in the red light of the oil-lamp, strong, tall, and beautiful, his long black hair sweeping over his shoulders, the knife swinging at his neck, and his head crowned with a wreath of white jasmine, he might easily have been mistaken for some wild god of a Jungle legend. The child half asleep on a cot sprang up and shrieked aloud with terror. Messua turned to soothe him, while Mowgli stood still, looking in at the water-jars and the cooking-pots, the grain-bin, and all the other human belongings that he found himself remembering so well.

'What wilt thou eat or drink?' Messua murmured. 'This is all thine. We owe our lives to thee. But art thou him I called Nathoo, or a Godling, indeed?'

'I am Nathoo,' said Mowgli. 'I am very far from my own place. I saw this light, and came hither. I did not know thou wast here.'

'After we came to Khanhiwara,' Messua said timidly, 'the English would have helped us against those villagers that sought to burn us. Rememberest thou?'

'Indeed, I have not forgotten.'

'But when the English Law was made ready, we went to the village of those evil people, and it was no more to be found.'

'That also I remember,' said Mowgli, with a quiver of his nostril.

'My man, therefore, took service in the fields, and at last — for, indeed, he was a strong man, — we held a little land here. It is not so rich as the old village, but we do not need much — we two.'

'Where is he — the man that dug in the dirt when he was afraid on that night?'

'He is dead — a year.'

'And he?' Mowgli pointed to the child.

'My son that was born two Rains ago. If thou art a Godling, give him the Favour of the Jungle, that he may be safe among thy — thy people, as we were safe on that night.'

She lifted up the child, who, forgetting his fright, reached out to play with the knife that hung on Mowgli's chest, and Mowgli put the little fingers aside very carefully.

'And if thou art Nathoo whom the tiger carried away,' Messua went on, choking, 'he is then thy younger brother. Give him an elder brother's blessing.'

'*Hai-mai!* What do I know of the thing called a blessing? I am neither a Godling nor his brother, and — O mother, mother, my heart is heavy in me.' He shivered as he set down the child.

'Like enough,' said Messua, bustling among the cooking-pots. 'This comes of running about the marshes by night. Beyond question, the fever had soaked thee to the marrow.' Mowgli smiled a little at the idea of anything in the Jungle hurting him. 'I will make a fire, and thou shalt drink warm milk. Put away the jasmine wreath: the smell is heavy in so small a place.'

Mowgli sat down, muttering, with his face in his hands. All manner of strange feelings that he had never felt before were running over him, exactly as though he had been poisoned, and he felt dizzy and a little sick. He drank the warm milk in long gulps, Messua patting him on the shoulder from time to time, not quite sure whether he were her son Nathoo of the long-ago days, or some wonderful Jungle being, but glad to feel that he was at least flesh and blood.

'Son,' she said at last — her eyes were full of pride, — 'have any told thee that thou art beautiful beyond all men?'

'Hah?' said Mowgli, for naturally he had never heard anything of the kind. Messua laughed softly and happily. The look in his face was enough for her.

'I am the first, then? It is right, though it comes seldom, that a mother should tell her son these good things. Thou art very beautiful. Never have I looked upon such a man.'

Mowgli twisted his head and tried to see over his own hard shoulder, and Messua laughed again so long that Mowgli, not knowing why, was forced to laugh with her, and the child ran from one to the other, laughing too.

'Nay, thou must not mock thy brother,' said Messua, catching him to her breast. 'When thou art one-half as fair we will marry thee to the youngest daughter of a king, and thou shalt ride great elephants.'

Mowgli could not understand one word in three of the talk here; the warm milk was taking effect on him after his long run, so he curled up and in a minute was deep asleep, and Messua put the hair back from his eyes, threw a cloth over him, and was happy. Jungle-fashion, he slept out the rest of that night and all the next day; for his instincts, which never wholly slept, warned him there was nothing to fear. He waked at last with a bound that shook the hut, for the cloth over his face made him dream of traps; and there he stood, his hand on his knife, the sleep all heavy in his rolling eyes, ready for any fight.

Messua laughed, and set the evening meal before him. There were only a few coarse cakes baked over the smoky fire, some rice, and a lump of sour preserved tamarinds — just enough to go on with till he could get to his evening kill. The smell of the dew in the marshes made him hungry and restless. He wanted to finish his spring running, but the child insisted on sitting in his arms, and Messua would have it that his long, blue-black hair must be combed out. So she sang, as she combed, foolish little baby-songs, now calling Mowgli her son, and now begging him to give some of his Jungle power to the child. The hut door was closed, but Mowgli heard a sound he knew well, and saw Messua's jaw drop with horror as a great gray paw came under the bottom of the door, and Gray Brother outside whined a muffled and penitent whine of anxiety and fear.

'Out and wait! Ye would not come when I called,' said Mowgli in Jungle-talk, without turning his head, and the great gray paw disappeared.

'Do not — do not bring thy — thy servants with thee,' said Messua. 'I — we have always lived at peace with the Jungle.'

'It is peace,' said Mowgli, rising. 'Think of that night on the road to Khanhiwara. There were scores of such folk before thee and behind thee. But I see that even in springtime the Jungle-People do not always forget. Mother, I go.'

Messua drew aside humbly — he was indeed a wood-god, she thought; but as his hand was on the door the mother in her made her throw her arms round Mowgli's neck again and again.

'Come back!' she whispered. 'Son or no son, come back, for I love thee — Look, he too grieves.'

The child was crying because the man with the shiny knife was going away.

'Come back again,' Messua repeated. 'By night or by day this door is never shut to thee.'

Mowgli's throat worked as though the cords in it were being pulled, and his voice seemed to be dragged from it as he answered, 'I will surely come back.'

'And now,' he said, as he put by the head of the fawning wolf on the threshold, 'I have a little cry against thee, Gray Brother. Why came ye not all four when I called so long ago?'

'So long ago? It was but last night. I — we — were singing in the Jungle the new songs, for this is the Time of New Talk. Rememberest thou?'

'Truly, truly.'

'And as soon as the songs were sung,' Gray Brother went on earnestly, 'I followed thy trail. I ran from all the others and followed hot-foot. But, O Little Brother, what hast *thou* done, eating and sleeping with the Man-Pack?'

'If ye had come when I called, this had never been,' said Mowgli, running much faster.

'And now what is to be?' said Gray Brother.

Mowgli was going to answer when a girl in a white cloth came down some path that led from the outskirts of the village. Gray Brother dropped out of sight at once, and Mowgli backed noiselessly into a field of high-springing crops. He could almost have touched her with his hand when the warm, green stalks closed before his face and he disappeared like a ghost. The girl screamed, for she thought she had seen a spirit, and then she gave a deep sigh. Mowgli parted the stalks with his hands and watched her till she was out of sight.

'And now I do not know,' he said, sighing in his turn. '*Why* did ye not come when I called?'

'We follow thee — we follow thee,' Gray Brother mumbled, licking at Mowgli's heel. 'We follow thee always, except in the Time of New Talk.'

'And would ye follow me to the Man-Pack?' Mowgli whispered.

'Did I not follow thee on the night our old Pack cast thee out? Who waked thee lying among the crops?'

'Ay, but again?'

'Have I not followed thee to-night?'

'Ay, but again and again, and it may be again, Gray Brother?'

Gray Brother was silent. When he spoke he growled to himself, 'The Black One spoke truth.'

'And he said?'

'Man goes to Man at the last. Raksha, our mother, said ——'

'So also said Akela on the night of Red Dog,' Mowgli muttered.

'So also says Kaa, who is wiser than us all.'

'What dost thou say, Gray Brother?'

'They cast thee out once, with bad talk. They cut thy mouth with stones. They sent Buldeo to slay thee. They would have thrown thee into the Red Flower. Thou, and not I, hast said that they are evil and senseless. Thou, and not I — I follow my own people — didst let in the Jungle upon them. Thou, and not I, didst make song against them more bitter even than our song against Red Dog.'

'I ask thee what *thou* sayest?'

They were talking as they ran. Gray Brother cantered on a while without replying, and then he said, — between bound and bound as it were, — 'Man-cub — Master of the Jungle — Son of Raksha, Lair-brother to me — though I forget for a little while in the spring, thy trail is my trail, thy lair is my lair, thy kill is my kill, and thy death-fight is my death-fight. I speak for the Three. But what wilt thou say to the Jungle?'

'That is well thought. Between the sight and the kill it is not good to wait. Go before and cry them all to the Council Rock, and I will tell them what is in my stomach. But they may not come — in the Time of New Talk they may forget me.'

'Hast thou, then, forgotten nothing?' snapped Gray Brother over his shoulder, as he laid himself down to gallop, and Mowgli followed, thinking.

At any other season the news would have called all the Jungle together with bristling necks, but now they were busy hunting and fighting and killing and singing. From one to another Gray Brother ran, crying, 'The Master of the Jungle goes back to Man! Come to the Council Rock.' And the happy, eager People only answered, 'He will return in the summer heats. The Rains will drive him to lair. Run and sing with us, Gray Brother.'

'But the Master of the Jungle goes back to Man,' Gray Brother would repeat.

'*Eee — Yoawa?* Is the Time of New Talk any less sweet for that?' they would reply. So when Mowgli, heavy-hearted, came up through the well-remembered rocks to the place where he had been brought into the Council, he found only the Four, Baloo, who was nearly blind with age, and the heavy, cold-blooded Kaa coiled around Akela's empty seat.

'Thy trail ends here, then, Manling?' said Kaa, as Mowgli threw himself down, his face in his hands. 'Cry thy cry. We be of one blood, thou and I — man and snake together.'

'Why did I not die under Red Dog?' the boy moaned. 'My strength is gone from me, and it is not any poison. By night and by day I hear a double step upon my trail. When I turn my head it is as though one had hidden himself from me that instant. I go to look behind the trees and he is not there. I call and none cry again; but it is as though one listened and kept back the answer. I lie down, but I do not rest. I run the spring running, but I am not made still. I bathe, but I am not made cool. The kill sickens me, but I have no heart to fight except I kill. The Red Flower is in my body, my bones are water — and — I know not what I know.'

'What need of talk?' said Baloo slowly, turning his head to where Mowgli lay. 'Akela by the river said it, that Mowgli should drive Mowgli back to the Man-Pack. I said it. But who listens now to Baloo? Bagheera — where is Bagheera this night? — he knows also. It is the Law.'

'When we met at Cold Lairs, Manling, I knew it,' said Kaa, turning a little in his mighty coils. 'Man goes to Man at the last, though the Jungle does not cast him out.'

The Four looked at one another and at Mowgli, puzzled but obedient.

'The Jungle does not cast me out, then?' Mowgli stammered.

Gray Brother and the Three growled furiously, beginning, 'So long as we live none shall dare ——' But Baloo checked them.

'I taught thee the Law. It is for me to speak,' he said; 'and, though I cannot now see the rocks before me, I see far. Little Frog, take thine own trail; make thy lair with thine own blood and pack and people; but when there is need of foot or tooth or eye, or a word carried swiftly by night, remember, Master of the Jungle, the Jungle is thine at call.'

'The Middle Jungle is thine also,' said Kaa. 'I speak for no small people.'

'*Hai-mai*, my brothers,' cried Mowgli, throwing up his arms with a sob. 'I know not what I know! I would not go; but I am drawn by both feet. How shall I leave these nights?'

'Nay, look up, Little Brother,' Baloo repeated. 'There is no shame in this hunting. When the honey is eaten we leave the empty hive.'

'Having cast the skin,' said Kaa, 'we may not creep into it afresh. It is the Law.'

'Listen, dearest of all to me,' said Baloo. 'There is neither word nor will here to hold thee back. Look up! Who may question the Master of the Jungle? I saw thee playing among the white pebbles yonder when thou wast a little frog; and Bagheera, that bought thee for the price of a young bull newly killed, saw thee also. Of that Looking-over we two only remain; for Raksha, thy lair-mother, is dead with thy lair-father; the old Wolf-Pack is long since dead; thou knowest whither Shere Khan went, and Akela died among the dholes, where, but for thy wisdom and strength, the second Seeonee Pack would also have died. There remains nothing but old bones. It is no longer the Man-cub that asks leave of his Pack, but the Master of the Jungle that changes his trail. Who shall question Man in his ways?'

'But Bagheera and the Bull that bought me,' said Mowgli. 'I would not ——'

His words were cut short by a roar and a crash in the thicket below, and Bagheera, light, strong, and terrible as always, stood before him.

'*Therefore*,' he said, stretching out a dripping right paw, 'I did not come. It was a long hunt, but he lies dead in the bushes now — a bull in his second year — the Bull that frees thee, Little Brother. All debts are paid now. For the rest, my word is Baloo's word.' He licked Mowgli's foot. 'Remember, Bagheera loved thee,' he cried, and bounded away. At the foot of the hill he cried again long and loud, 'Good hunting on a new trail, Master of the Jungle! Remember, Bagheera loved thee.'

'Thou hast heard,' said Baloo. 'There is no more. Go now; but first come to me. O wise Little Frog, come to me!'

'It is hard to cast the skin,' said Kaa as Mowgli sobbed and sobbed, with his head on the blind bear's side and his arms round his neck, while Baloo tried feebly to lick his feet.

'The stars are thin,' said Gray Brother, snuffing at the dawn wind. 'Where shall we lair to-day? for, from now, we follow new trails.'

THE OUTSONG

(This is the song that Mowgli heard behind him in the Jungle till he came
to Messua's door again.)

BALOO

For the sake of him who showed
One wise Frog the Jungle-Road,
Keep the Law the Man-Pack make —
For thy blind old Baloo's sake!
Clean or tainted, hot or stale,
Hold it as it were the Trail,
Through the day and through the night,
Questing neither left nor right.
For the sake of him who loves
Thee beyond all else that moves,
When thy Pack would make thee pain,
Say: 'Tabaqui sings again.'
When thy Pack would work thee ill,
Say: 'Shere Khan is yet to kill.'
When the knife is drawn to slay,
Keep the Law and go thy way.
(Root and honey, palm and spathe,
Guard a cub from harm and scathe!)
Wood and Water, Wind and Tree,
Jungle-Favour go with thee!

KAA

Anger is the egg of Fear —
Only lidless eyes are clear.
Cobra-poison none may leech.
Even so with Cobra-speech.
Open talk shall call to thee
Strength, whose mate is Courtesy.
Send no lunge beyond thy length;
Lend no rotten bough thy strength.
Gauge thy gape with buck or goat,
Lest thine eye should choke thy throat.
After gorging, wouldst thou sleep?
Look thy den is hid and deep,

Lest a wrong, by thee forgot,
Draw thy killer to the spot.
East and West and North and South,
Wash thy hide and close thy mouth.
 (Pit and rift and blue pool-brim,
Middle-Jungle follow him!)
Wood and Water, Wind and Tree,
Jungle-Favour go with thee!

BAGHEERA

In the cage my life began;
Well I know the worth of Man.
By the Broken Lock that freed —
Man-cub, 'ware the Man-cub's breed!
Scenting-dew or starlight pale,
Choose no tangled tree-cat trail.
Pack or council, hunt or den,
Cry no truce with Jackal-Men.
Feed them silence when they say:
'Come with us an easy way.'
Feed them silence when they seek
Help of thine to hurt the weak.
Make no *bandar*'s boast of skill;
Hold thy peace above the kill.
Let nor call nor song nor sign
Turn thee from thy hunting-line.
(Morning mist or twilight clear,
Serve him, Wardens of the Deer!)
Wood and Water, Wind and Tree,
Jungle-Favour go with thee!

THE THREE

On the trail that thou must tread
To the thresholds of our dread,
Where the Flower blossoms red;
Through the night when thou shalt lie
Prisoned from our Mother-sky,
Hearing us, thy loves, go by;
In the dawns when thou shalt wake
To the toil thou canst not break,
Heartsick for the Jungle's sake;
Wood and Water, Wind and Tree,
Wisdom, Strength, and Courtesy,
Jungle-Favour go with thee!

IN THE RUKH

OF the wheels of public service that turn under the Indian Government, there is none more important than the Department of Woods and Forests. The reboisement of all India is in its hands; or will be when Government has the money to spend. Its servants wrestle with wandering sand-torrents and shifting dunes; wattling them at the sides, damming them in front, and pegging them down atop with coarse grass and spindling pine after the rules of Nancy. They are responsible for all the timber in the State forests of the Himalayas, as well as for the denuded hillsides that the monsoons wash into dry gullies and aching ravines; each cut a mouth crying aloud what carelessness can do. They experiment with battalions of foreign trees, and coax the blue gum to take root and, perhaps, dry up the Canal fever. In the plains the chief part of their duty is to see that the belt fire-lines in the forest reserves are kept clean, so that when drought comes and the cattle starve, they may throw the reserve open to the villager's herds and allow the man himself to gather sticks. They poll and lop for the stacked railway-fuel along the lines that burn no coal; they calculate the profit of their plantations to five points of decimals; they are the doctors and mid-wives of the huge teak forests of Upper Burma, the rubber of the Eastern Jungles, and the gall-nuts of the South; and they are always hampered by lack of funds. But since a Forest Officer's business takes him far from the beaten roads and the regular stations, he learns to grow wise in more than wood-lore alone; to know the people and the polity of the jungle; meeting tiger, bear, leopard, wild-dog, and all the deer, not once or twice after days of beating, but again and again in the execution of his duty. He spends much time in saddle or under canvas — the friend of newly planted trees, the associate of uncouth rangers and hairy trackers — till the woods, that show his care, in turn set their mark upon him, and he ceases to sing the naughty French songs he learned at Nancy, and grows silent with the silent things of the underbrush.

Gisborne of the Woods and Forests had spent four years in the service. At first he loved it without comprehension, because it led him into the open on horseback and gave him authority. Then he hated it furiously, and would have given a year's pay for one month of such society as India affords. That crisis over, the forests took him back again, and he was content to serve them, to deepen and widen his fire-lines, to watch the green mist of his new plantation against the older foliage, to dredge out the choked stream, and to follow and strengthen the last struggle of the forest where it broke down and died among the long pig-grass. On some still day that grass would be burned off, and a hundred beasts that had their homes there would rush out before the pale flames at high noon. Later, the forest would creep forward over the blackened ground in orderly lines of saplings, and Gisborne, watching, would be well pleased. His bungalow, a thatched white-walled cottage of two rooms, was set at one end of the great *rukh* and overlooking it. He made no pretence at keeping a garden, for the *rukh* swept up to his door, curled over in a thicket of bamboo, and he rode from his verandah into its heart without the need of any carriage-drive.

Abdul Gafur, his fat Mohammedan butler, fed him when he was at home, and spent the rest of the time gossiping with the little band of native servants whose huts lay behind the bungalow. There were two grooms, a cook, a water-carrier, and a sweeper, and that was all. Gisborne cleaned his own guns and kept no dog. Dogs scared the game, and it pleased the man to be able to say where the subjects of his kingdom would drink at moonrise, eat before dawn, and lie up in the day's heat. The rangers and forest-guards lived in little huts far away in the *rukh*, only appearing when one of them had been injured by a falling tree or a wild beast. There Gisborne was alone.

In spring the *rukh* put out few new leaves, but lay dry and still untouched by the finger of the year, waiting for rain. Only there was then more calling and roaring in the dark on a quiet night; the tumult of a battle-royal among the tigers, the bellowing of arrogant buck, or the steady wood-chopping of an old boar sharpening his tushes against a bole. Then Gisborne laid aside his little-used gun altogether, for it was to him a sin to kill. In summer, through the furious May heats, the *rukh* reeled in the haze, and Gisborne watched for the first sign of curling smoke that should betray a forest fire. Then came the Rains with a roar, and the *rukh* was blotted out in fetch after fetch of warm mist, and the broad leaves drummed the night through under the big drops; and there was a noise of running water, and of juicy green stuff crackling where the wind struck it, and the lightning wove patterns behind the dense matting of the foliage, till the sun broke loose again and the *rukh* stood with hot flanks smoking to the newly washed sky. Then the heat and the dry cold subdued everything to tiger-colour again. So Gisborne learned to know his *rukh* and was very happy. His pay came month by month, but he had very little need for money. The currency notes accumulated in the drawer where he kept his home-letters and the recapping-machine. If he drew anything, it was to make a purchase from the Calcutta Botanical Gardens, or to pay a ranger's widow a sum that the Government of India would never have sanctioned for her man's death.

Payment was good, but vengeance was also necessary, and he took that when he could. One night of many nights a runner, breathless and gasping, came to him with the news that a forest-guard lay dead by the Kanye stream, the side of his head smashed in as though it had been an egg-shell. Gisborne went out at dawn to look for the murderer. It is only travellers and now and then young soldiers who are known to the world as great hunters. The Forest Officers take their *shikar* as part of the day's work, and no one hears of it. Gisborne went on foot to the place of the kill: the widow was wailing over the corpse as it lay on a bedstead, while two or three men were looking at footprints on the moist ground. 'That is the Red One,' said a man. 'I knew he would turn to man in time, but surely there is game enough even for him. This must have been done for devilry.'

'The Red One lies up in the rocks at the back of the *sal* trees,' said Gisborne. He knew the tiger under suspicion.

'Not now, Sahib, not now. He will be raging and ranging to and fro. Remember that the first kill is a triple kill always. Our blood makes them mad. He may be behind us even as we speak.'

'He may have gone to the next hut,' said another. 'It is only four *koss*. Wallah, who is this?'

Gisborne turned with the others. A man was walking down the dried bed of the stream, naked except for the loin-cloth, but crowned with a wreath of the tasselled blossoms of the white convolvulus creeper. So noiselessly did he move over the little pebbles, that even Gisborne, used to the soft-footedness of trackers, started.

'The tiger that killed,' he began, without any salute, 'has gone to drink, and now he is asleep under a rock beyond that hill.' His voice was clear and bell-like, utterly different from the usual whine of the native, and his face as he lifted it in the sunshine might have been that of an angel strayed among the woods. The widow ceased wailing above the corpse and looked round-eyed at the stranger, returning to her duty with double strength.

'Shall I show the Sahib?' he said simply.

'If thou art sure ——' Gisborne began.

'Sure indeed. I saw him only an hour ago — the dog. It is before his time to eat man's flesh. He has yet a dozen sound teeth in his evil head.'

The men kneeling above the footprints slunk off quietly, for fear that Gisborne should ask them to go with him, and the young man laughed a little to himself.

'Come, Sahib,' he cried, and turned on his heel, walking before his companion.

'Not so fast. I cannot keep that pace,' said the white man. 'Halt there. Thy face is new to me.'

'That may be. I am but newly come into this forest.'

'From what village?'

'I am without a village. I came from over there.' He flung out his arm toward the north.

'A gipsy then?'

'No, Sahib. I am a man without caste, and for matter of that without a father.'

'What do men call thee?'

'Mowgli, Sahib. And what is the Sahib's name?'

'I am the warden of this *rukh* — Gisborne is my name.'

'How? Do they number the trees and the blades of grass here?'

'Even so; lest such gipsy fellows as thou set them afire.'

'I! I would not hurt the jungle for any gift. That is my home.'

He turned to Gisborne with a smile that was irresistible, and held up a warning hand.

'Now, Sahib, we must go a little quietly. There is no need to wake the dog, though he sleeps heavily enough. Perhaps it were better if I went forward alone and drove him down wind to the Sahib!'

'Allah! Since when have tigers been driven to and fro like cattle by naked men?' said Gisborne, aghast at the man's audacity.

He laughed again softly. 'Nay, then, come along with me and shoot him in thy own way with the big English rifle.'

Gisborne stepped in his guide's track, twisted, crawled, and clomb and stooped and suffered through all the many agonies of a jungle-stalk. He was purple and dripping with sweat when Mowgli at the last bade him raise his head and peer over a blue-baked rock near a tiny hill pool. By the waterside lay the tiger extended and at ease, lazily licking clean again an enormous elbow and fore-paw. He was old, yellow-toothed, and not a little mangy, but in that setting and sunshine, imposing enough.

Gisborne had no false ideas of sport where the man-eater was concerned. This thing was vermin, to be killed as speedily as possible. He waited to recover his breath, rested the rifle on the rock and whistled. The brute's head turned slowly not twenty feet from the rifle-mouth, and Gisborne planted his shots, businesslike, one behind the shoulder and the other a little below the eye. At that range the heavy bones were no guard against the rending bullets.

'Well, the skin was not worth keeping at any rate,' said he, as the smoke cleared away and the beast lay kicking and gasping in the last agony.

'A dog's death for a dog,' said Mowgli quietly. 'Indeed there is nothing in that carrion worth taking away.'

'The whiskers. Dost thou not take the whiskers?' said Gisborne, who knew how the rangers valued such things.

'I? Am I a lousy *shikarri* of the jungle to paddle with a tiger's muzzle? Let him lie. Here come his friends already.'

A dropping kite whistled shrilly overhead, as Gisborne snapped out the empty shells, and wiped his face.

'And if thou art not a *shikarri*, where didst thou learn thy knowledge of the tiger-folk?' said he. 'No tracker could have done better.'

'I hate all tigers,' said Mowgli curtly. 'Let the Sahib give me his gun to carry. *Arré*, it is a very fine one. And where does the Sahib go now?'

'To my house.'

'May I come? I have never yet looked within a white man's house.'

Gisborne returned to his bungalow, Mowgli striding noiselessly before him, his brown skin glistening in the sunlight.

He stared curiously at the verandah and the two chairs there, fingered the split bamboo shade curtains with suspicion, and entered, looking always behind him. Gisborne loosed a curtain to keep out the sun. It dropped with a clatter, but almost before it touched the flagging of the verandah Mowgli had leaped clear, and was standing with heaving chest in the open.

'It is a trap,' he said quickly.

Gisborne laughed. 'White men do not trap men. Indeed thou art altogether of the jungle.'

'I see,' said Mowgli, 'it has neither catch nor fall. I — I never beheld these things till to-day.'

He came in on tiptoe and stared with large eyes at the furniture of the two rooms. Abdul Gafur, who was laying lunch, looked at him with deep disgust.

'So much trouble to eat, and so much trouble to lie down after you have eaten!' said Mowgli with a grin. 'We do better in the jungle. It is very wonderful. There are very many rich things here. Is the Sahib not afraid that he may be robbed? I have never seen such wonderful things.' He was staring at a dusty Benares brass plate on a rickety bracket.

'Only a thief from the jungle would rob here,' said Abdul Gafur, setting down a plate with a clatter. Mowgli opened his eyes wide and stared at the white-bearded Mohammedan.

'In my country when goats bleat very loud we cut their throats,' he returned cheerfully. 'But have no fear, thou. I am going.'

He turned and disappeared into the *rukh*. Gisborne looked after him with a laugh that ended in a little sigh. There was not much outside his regular work to interest the Forest Officer, and this son of the forest, who seemed to know tigers as other people know dogs, would have been a diversion.

'He's a most wonderful chap,' thought Gisborne; 'he's like the illustrations in the Classical Dictionary. I wish I could have made him a gun-boy. There's no fun in shikarring alone, and this fellow would have been a perfect *shikarri*. I wonder what in the world he is.'

That evening he sat on the verandah under the stars smoking as he wondered. A puff of smoke curled from the pipe-bowl. As it cleared he was aware of Mowgli sitting with arms crossed on the verandah edge. A ghost could not have drifted up more noiselessly. Gisborne started and let the pipe drop.

'There is no man to talk to out there in the *rukh*,' said Mowgli; 'I came here, therefore.' He picked up the pipe and returned it to Gisborne.

'Oh,' said Gisborne, and after a long pause, 'What news is there in the *rukh*? Hast thou found another tiger?'

'The nilghai are changing their feeding-ground against the new moon, as is their custom. The pig are feeding near the Kanye river now, because they will not feed with the nilghai, and one of their sows has been killed by a leopard in the long grass at the water-head. I do not know any more.'

'And how didst thou know all these things?' said Gisborne, leaning forward and looking at the eyes that glittered in the starlight.

'How should I not know? The nilghai has his custom and his use, and a child knows that pig will not feed with him.'

'I do not know this,' said Gisborne.

'Tck! Tck! And thou art in charge — so the men of the huts tell me — in charge of all this *rukh*.' He laughed to himself.

'It is well enough to talk and to tell child's tales,' Gisborne retorted, nettled at the chuckle. 'To say that this and that goes on in the *rukh*. No man can deny thee.'

'As for the sow's carcase, I will show thee her bones to-morrow,' Mowgli returned, absolutely unmoved. 'Touching the matter of the nilghai, if the Sahib will sit here very still I will drive one nilghai up to this place, and by listening to the sounds carefully, the Sahib can tell whence that nilghai has been driven.'

'Mowgli, the jungle has made thee mad,' said Gisborne. 'Who can drive nilghai?'

'Still — sit still, then. I go.'

'Gad, the man's a ghost!' said Gisborne; for Mowgli had faded out into the darkness and there was no sound of feet. The *rukh* lay out in great velvety folds in the uncertain shimmer of the star-dust — so still that the least little wandering wind among the tree-tops came up as the sigh of a child sleeping equably. Abdul Gafur in the cook-house was clicking plates together.

'Be still there!' shouted Gisborne, and composed himself to listen as a man can who is used to the stillness of the *rukh*. It had been his custom, to preserve his self-respect in his isolation, to dress for dinner each night, and the stiff white shirt-front creaked with his regular breathing till he shifted a little sideways. Then the tobacco of a somewhat foul pipe began to purr, and he threw the pipe from him. Now, except for the night-breath in the *rukh*, everything was dumb.

From an inconceivable distance, and drawled through immeasurable darkness, came the faint, faint echo of a wolf's howl. Then silence again for, it seemed, long hours. At last, when his legs below the knees had lost all feeling, Gisborne heard something that might have been a crash far off through the undergrowth. He doubted till it was repeated again and yet again.

'That's from the west,' he muttered; 'there's something on foot there.' The noise increased — crash on crash, plunge on plunge — with the thick grunting of a hotly pressed nilghai, flying in panic terror and taking no heed to his course.

A shadow blundered out from between the tree-trunks, wheeled back, turned again grunting, and with a clatter on the bare ground dashed up almost within reach of his hand. It was a bull nilghai, dripping with dew — his withers hung with a torn trail of creeper, his eyes shining in the light from the house. The creature checked at sight of the man, and fled along the edge of the *rukh* till he melted in the darkness. The first idea in Gisborne's bewildered mind was the indecency of thus dragging out for inspection the big blue bull of the *rukh* — the putting him through his paces in the night which should have been his own.

Then said a smooth voice at his ear as he stood staring:

'He came from the water-head where he was leading the herd. From the west he came. Does the Sahib believe now, or shall I bring up the herd to be counted? The Sahib is in charge of this *rukh*.'

Mowgli had reseated himself on the verandah, breathing a little quickly. Gisborne looked at him with open mouth. 'How was that accomplished?' he said.

'The Sahib saw. The bull was driven — driven as a buffalo is. Ho! ho! He will have a fine tale to tell when he returns to the herd.'

'That is a new trick to me. Canst thou run as swiftly as the nilghai, then?'

'The Sahib has seen. If the Sahib needs more knowledge at any time of the movings of the game, I, Mowgli, am here. This is a good *rukh*, and I shall stay.'

'Stay, then, and if thou hast need of a meal at any time my servants shall give thee one.'

'Yes, indeed, I am fond of cooked food,' Mowgli answered quickly. 'No man may say that I do not eat boiled and roast as much as any other man. I will come for that meal. Now, on my part, I promise that the Sahib shall sleep safely in his house by night, and no thief shall break in to carry away his so rich treasures.'

The conversation ended itself on Mowgli's abrupt departure. Gisborne sat long smoking, and the upshot of his thoughts was that in Mowgli he had found at last that ideal ranger and forest-guard for whom he and the Department were always looking.

'I must get him into the Government service somehow. A man who can drive nilghai would know more about the *rukh* than fifty men. He's a miracle — a *lusus naturæ* — but a forest-guard he must be if he'll only settle down in one place,' said Gisborne.

Abdul Gafur's opinion was less favourable. He confided to Gisborne at bedtime that strangers from God-knew-where were more than likely to be professional thieves, and that he personally did not approve of naked outcastes who had not the proper manner of addressing white people. Gisborne laughed and bade him go to his quarters, and Abdul Gafur retreated growling. Later in the night he found occasion to rise up and beat his thirteen-year-old daughter. Nobody knew the cause of dispute, but Gisborne heard the cry.

Through the days that followed Mowgli came and went like a shadow. He had established himself and his wild house-keeping close to the bungalow, but on the edge of the *rukh*, where Gisborne, going out on to the verandah for a breath of cool air, would see him sometimes sitting in the moonlight, his forehead on his knees, or lying out along the fling of a branch, closely pressed to it as some beast of the night. Thence Mowgli would throw him a salutation and bid him sleep at ease, or descending would weave prodigious stories of the manners of the beasts in the *rukh*. Once he wandered into the stables and was found looking at the horses with deep interest.

'That,' said Abdul Gafur pointedly, 'is sure sign that some day he will steal one. Why, if he lives about this house, does he not take an honest employment? But no, he must wander up and down like a loose camel, turning the heads of fools and opening the jaws of the unwise to folly.' So Abdul Gafur would give harsh orders to Mowgli when they met, would bid him fetch water and pluck fowls, and Mowgli, laughing unconcernedly, would obey.

'He has no caste,' said Abdul Gafur. 'He will do anything. Look to it, Sahib, that he does not do too much. A snake is a snake, and a jungle-gipsy is a thief till the death.'

'Be silent, then,' said Gisborne. 'I allow thee to correct thy own household if there is not too much noise, because I know thy customs and use. My custom thou dost not know. The man is without doubt a little mad.'

'Very little mad indeed,' said Abdul Gafur. 'But we shall see what comes thereof.'

A few days later on, his business took Gisborne into the *rukh* for three days. Abdul Gafur being old and fat was left at home. He did not approve of lying up in rangers' huts, and was inclined to levy contributions in his master's name of grain and oil and milk from those who could ill afford such benevolences. Gisborne rode off early one dawn a little vexed that his man of the woods was not at the verandah to accompany him. He liked him — liked his strength, fleetness, and silence of foot, and his ever-ready open smile; his ignorance of all forms of ceremony and salutations, and the child-like tales that he would tell (and Gisborne would credit now) of what the game was doing in the *rukh*. After an hour's riding through the greenery, he heard a rustle behind him, and Mowgli trotted at his stirrup.

'We have a three days' work toward,' said Gisborne, 'among the new trees.'

'Good,' said Mowgli. 'It is always good to cherish young trees. They make cover if the beasts leave them alone. We must shift the pig again.'

'Again? How?' Gisborne smiled.

'Oh, they were rooting and tusking among the young *sal* last night, and I drove them off. Therefore I did not come to the verandah this morning. The pig should not be on this side of the *rukh* at all. We must keep them below the head of the Kanye river.'

'If a man could herd clouds he might do that thing; but, Mowgli, if, as thou sayest, thou art herder in the *rukh* for no gain and for no pay ——'

'It is the Sahib's *rukh*,' said Mowgli, quickly looking up.

Gisborne nodded thanks and went on: 'Would it not be better to work for pay from the Government? There is a pension at the end of long service.'

'Of that I have thought,' said Mowgli, 'but the rangers live in huts with shut doors, and all that is all too much a trap to me. Yet I think ——'

'Think well then and tell me later. Here we will stay for breakfast.'

Gisborne dismounted, took his morning meal from his home-made saddle-bags, and saw the day open hot above the *rukh*. Mowgli lay in the grass at his side staring up to the sky.

Presently he said in a lazy whisper: 'Sahib, is there any order at the bungalow to take out the white mare to-day?'

'No, she is fat and old and a little lame beside. Why?'

'She is being ridden now and *not* slowly on the road that runs to the railway line.'

'Bah, that is two *koss* away. It is a woodpecker.'

Mowgli put up his forearm to keep the sun out of his eyes.

'The road curves in with a big curve from the bungalow. It is not more than a *koss*, at the farthest, as the kite goes; and sound flies with the birds. Shall we see?'

'What folly! To run a *koss* in this sun to see a noise in the forest.'

'Nay, the pony is the Sahib's pony. I meant only to bring her here. If she is not the Sahib's pony, no matter. If she is, the Sahib can do what he wills. She is certainly being ridden hard.'

'And how wilt thou bring her here, madman?'

'Has the Sahib forgotten? By the road of the nilghai and no other.'

'Up then and run if thou art so full of zeal.'

'Oh, I do not run!' He put out his hand to sign for silence, and still lying on his back called aloud thrice — with a deep gurgling cry that was new to Gisborne.

'She will come,' he said at the end. 'Let us wait in the shade.' The long eyelashes drooped over the wild eyes as Mowgli began to doze in the morning hush. Gisborne waited patiently: Mowgli was surely mad, but as entertaining a companion as a lonely Forest Officer could desire.

'Ho! ho!' said Mowgli lazily, with shut eyes. 'He has dropped off. Well, first the mare will come and then the man.' Then he yawned as Gisborne's pony stallion neighed. Three minutes later Gisborne's white mare, saddled, bridled, but riderless, tore into the glade where they were sitting, and hurried to her companion.

'She is not very warm,' said Mowgli, 'but in this heat the sweat comes easily. Presently we shall see her rider, for a man goes more slowly than a horse — especially if he chance to be a fat man and old.'

'Allah! This is the devil's work,' cried Gisborne, leaping to his feet, for he heard a yell in the jungle.

'Have no care, Sahib. He will not be hurt. He also will say that it is devil's work. Ah! Listen! Who is that?'

It was the voice of Abdul Gafur in an agony of terror, crying out upon unknown things to spare him and his gray hairs.

'Nay, I cannot move another step,' he howled. 'I am old and my turban is lost. *Arré! Arré!* But I will move. Indeed I will hasten. I will run! Oh, Devils of the Pit, I am a Mussulman!'

The undergrowth parted and gave up Abdul Gafur, turbanless, shoeless, with his waist-cloth unbound, mud and grass in his clutched hands, and his face purple. He saw Gisborne, yelled anew, and pitched forward, exhausted and quivering, at his feet. Mowgli watched him with a sweet smile.

'This is no joke,' said Gisborne sternly. 'The man is like to die, Mowgli.'

'He will not die. He is only afraid. There was no need that he should have come out of a walk.'

Abdul Gafur groaned and rose up, shaking in every limb.

'It was witchcraft — witchcraft and devildom!' he sobbed, fumbling with his hand in his breast. 'Because of my sin I have been whipped through the woods by devils. It is all finished. I repent. Take them, Sahib!' He held out a roll of dirty paper.

'What is the meaning of this, Abdul Gafur?' said Gisborne, already knowing what would come.

'Put me in the jail-khana — the notes are all here — but lock me up safely that no devils may follow. I have sinned against the Sahib and his salt which I have eaten; and but for those accursed wood-demons, I might have bought land afar off and lived in peace all my days.' He beat his head upon the ground in an agony of despair and mortification. Gisborne turned the roll of notes over and over. It was his accumulated back-pay for the last nine months — the roll that lay in the drawer with the home-letters and the recapping machine. Mowgli watched Abdul Gafur, laughing noiselessly to himself. 'There is no need to put me on the horse again. I will walk home slowly with the Sahib and then he can send me under guard to the jail-khana. The Government gives many years for this offence,' said the butler sullenly.

Loneliness in the *rukh* affects very many ideas about very many things. Gisborne stared at Abdul Gafur, remembering that he was a very good servant, and that a new butler must be broken into the ways of the house from the beginning, and at the best would be a new face and a new tongue.

'Listen, Abdul Gafur,' he said. 'Thou hast done great wrong, and altogether lost thy *izzat* and thy reputation. But I think that this came upon thee suddenly.'

'Allah! I had never desired the notes before. The Evil took me by the throat while I looked.'

'That also I can believe. Go then back to my house, and when I return I will send the notes by a runner to the Bank, and there shall be no more said. Thou art too old for the jail-khana. Also thy household is guiltless.'

For answer Abdul Gafur sobbed between Gisborne's cowhide riding-boots.

'Is there no dismissal then?' he gulped.

'That we shall see. It hangs upon thy conduct when we return. Get upon the mare and ride slowly back.'

'But the devils! The *rukh* is full of devils.'

'No matter, my father. They will do thee no more harm unless, indeed, the Sahib's orders be not obeyed,' said Mowgli. 'Then, perchance, they may drive thee home — by the road of the nilghai.'

Abdul Gafur's lower jaw dropped as he twisted up his waist-cloth, staring at Mowgli.

'Are they *his* devils? His devils! And I had thought to return and lay the blame upon this warlock!'

'That was well thought of, Huzrut; but before we make a trap we see first how big the game is that may fall into it. Now I thought no more than that a man had taken one of the Sahib's horses. I did not know that the design was to make me a thief before the Sahib, or my devils had haled thee here by the leg. It is not too late now.'

Mowgli looked inquiringly at Gisborne; but Abdul Gafur waddled hastily to the white mare, scrambled on her back and fled, the woodways crashing and echoing behind him.

'That was well done,' said Mowgli. 'But he will fall again unless he holds by the mane.'

'Now it is time to tell me what these things mean,' said Gisborne a little sternly. 'What is this talk of thy devils? How can men be driven up and down the *rukh* like cattle? Give answer.'

'Is the Sahib angry because I have saved him his money?'

'No, but there is trick-work in this that does not please me.'

'Very good. Now if I rose and stepped three paces into the *rukh* there is no one, not even the Sahib, could find me till I choose. As I would not willingly do this, so I would not willingly tell. Have patience a little, Sahib, and some day I will show thee everything, for, if thou wilt, some day we will drive the buck together. There is no devil-work in the matter at all. Only . . . I know the *rukh* as a man knows the cooking-place in his house.'

Mowgli was speaking as he would speak to an impatient child. Gisborne, puzzled, baffled, and a great deal annoyed, said nothing, but stared on the ground and thought. When he looked up the man of the woods had gone.

'It is not good,' said a level voice from the thicket, 'for friends to be angry. Wait till the evening, Sahib, when the air cools.'

Left to himself thus, dropped as it were in the heart of the *rukh*, Gisborne swore, then laughed, remounted his pony, and rode on. He visited a ranger's hut, overlooked a couple of new plantations, left some orders as to the burning of a patch of dry grass, and set out for a camping-ground of his own choice, a pile of splintered rocks roughly roofed over with branches and leaves, not far from the banks of the Kanye stream. It was twilight when he came in sight of his resting-place, and the *rukh* was waking to the hushed ravenous life of the night.

A camp-fire flickered on the knoll, and there was the smell of a very good dinner in the wind.

'Um,' said Gisborne, 'that's better than cold meat at any rate. Now the only man who'd be likely to be here'd be Muller, and, officially, he ought to be looking over the Changamanga *rukh*. I suppose that's why he's on my ground.'

The gigantic German who was the head of the Woods and Forests of all India, Head Ranger from Burma to Bombay, had a habit of flitting bat-like without warning from one place to another, and turning up exactly where he was least looked for. His theory was that sudden visitations, the discovery of short-comings and a word-of-mouth upbraiding of a subordinate were infinitely better than the slow processes of correspondence, which might end in a written and official reprimand — a thing in after years to be counted against a Forest Officer's record. As he explained it: 'If I only talk to my boys like a Dutch uncle, dey say, "It was only dot damned old Muller," and dey do better next dime. But if my fat-head clerk he write and say dot Muller der Inspecdor-General fail to onderstand and is much annoyed, first dot does no goot because I am not dere, and, second, der fool dot comes after me he may say to my best boys: "Look here, you haf been wigged by my bredecessor." I tell you der big brass-hat pizness does not make der trees grow.'

Muller's deep voice was coming out of the darkness behind the firelight as he bent over the shoulders of his pet cook. 'Not so much sauce, you son of Belial! Worcester sauce he is a gondi-ment and not a fluid. Ah, Gisborne, you haf come to a very bad dinner. Where is your camp?' and he walked up to shake hands.

'I'm the camp, sir,' said Gisborne. 'I didn't know you were about here.'

Muller looked at the young man's trim figure. 'Goot! That is very goot! One horse and some cold things to eat. When I was young I did my camp so. Now you shall dine with me. I went into Headquarters to make up my rebort last month. I haf written half — ho! ho! — and der rest I haf leaved to my glerks and come out for a walk. Der Government is mad about dose reborts. I dold der Viceroy so at Simla.'

Gisborne chuckled, remembering the many tales that were told of Muller's conflicts with the Supreme Government. He was the chartered libertine of all the offices, for as a Forest Officer he had no equal.

'If I find you, Gisborne, sitting in your bungalow und hatch-ing reborts to me about der blantations instead of riding der blantations, I will dransfer you to der middle of der Bikaneer Desert to reforest *him*. I am sick of reborts und chewing paper when we should do our work.'

'There's not much danger of my wasting time over my an-nuals. I hate them as much as you do, sir.'

The talk went over at this point to professional matters. Muller had some questions to ask, and Gisborne orders and hints to receive, till dinner was ready. It was the most civilised meal Gisborne had eaten for months. No distance from the base of supplies was allowed to interfere with the work of Muller's cook; and that table spread in the wilderness began with devilled small fresh-water fish, and ended with coffee and cognac.

'Ah!' said Muller at the end, with a sigh of satisfaction as he lighted a cheroot and dropped into his much-worn camp-chair. 'When I am making reborts I am Freethinker und Atheist, but here in der *rukh* I am more than Christian. I am Bagan also.'

He rolled the cheroot-butt luxuriously under his tongue, dropped his hands on his knees, and stared before him into the dim shifting heart of the *rukh*, full of stealthy noises; the snapping of twigs like the snapping of the fire behind him; the sigh and rustle of a heat-bended branch recovering her straightness in the cool night; the incessant mutter of the Kanye stream, and the undernote of the many-peopled grass uplands out of sight beyond a swell of hill. He blew out a thick puff of smoke, and began to quote Heine to himself.

'Yes, it is very goot. Very goot. "Yes, I work miracles, and, by Gott, dey come off too." I remember when dere was no *rukh* more big than your knee, from here to der plough-lands, und in drought-time der cattle ate bones of dead cattle up and down. Now der trees haf come back. Dey were planted by a Freethinker, because he know just de cause dot made der effect. But der trees dey had der cult of der old gods — "und der Christian Gods howl loudly". Dey could not live in der *rukh*, Gisborne.'

A shadow moved in one of the bridle-paths — moved and stepped out into the starlight.

'I haf said true. Hush! Here is Faunus himself come to see der Insbector-General. Himmel, he is der god! Look!'

It was Mowgli, crowned with his wreath of white flowers and walked with a half-peeled branch — Mowgli, very mistrustful of the fire-light and ready to fly back to the thicket on the least alarm.

'That's a friend of mine,' said Gisborne. 'He's looking for me. Ohé, Mowgli!'

Muller had barely time to gasp before the man was at Gisborne's side, crying: 'I was wrong to go. I was wrong, but I did not know then that the mate of him that was killed by this river was awake looking for thee. Else I should not have gone away. She tracked thee from the back-range, Sahib.'

'He is a little mad,' said Gisborne, 'and he speaks of all the beasts about here as if he was a friend of theirs.'

'Of course — of course. If Faunus does not know, who should know?' said Muller gravely. 'What does he say about tigers — dis god who knows you so well?'

Gisborne relighted his cheroot, and before he had finished the story of Mowgli and his exploits it was burned down to moustache-edge. Muller listened without interruption. 'Dot is not madness,' he said at last when Gisborne had described the driving of Abdul Gafur. 'Dot is not madness at all.'

'What is it, then? He left me in a temper this morning because I asked him to tell how he did it. I fancy the chap's possessed in some way.'

'No, dere is no bossession, but it is most wonderful. Normally dey die young — dese beople. Und you say now dot your thief-servant did not say what drove der pony, and of course der nilghai he could not speak.'

'No, but, confound it, there wasn't anything. I listened, and I can hear most things. The bull and the man simply came headlong — mad with fright.'

For answer Muller looked Mowgli up and down from head to foot, then beckoned him nearer. He came as a buck treads a tainted trail.

'There is no harm,' said Muller in the vernacular. 'Hold out an arm.'

He ran his hand down to the elbow, felt that, and nodded. 'So I thought. Now the knee.' Gisborne saw him feel the kneecap and smile. Two or three white scars just above the ankle caught his eye.

'Those came when thou wast very young?' he said.

'Ay,' Mowgli answered with a smile. 'They were love-tokens from the little ones.' Then to Gisborne over his shoulder: 'This Sahib knows everything. Who is he?'

'That comes after, my friend. Now where are *they*?' said Muller.

Mowgli swept his hand round his head in a circle.

'So! And thou canst drive nilghai? See! There is my mare in

her pickets. Canst thou bring her to me without frightening her?'

'Can I bring the mare to the Sahib without frightening her?' Mowgli repeated, raising his voice a little above its normal pitch. 'What is more easy if the heel-ropes are loose?'

'Loosen the head and heel-pegs,' shouted Muller to the groom. They were hardly out of the ground before the mare, a huge black Australian, flung up her head and cocked her ears.

'Careful! I do not wish her driven into the *rukh*,' said Muller.

Mowgli stood still fronting the blaze of the fire — in the very form and likeness of that Greek god who is so lavishly described in the novels. The mare whickered, drew up one hind leg, found that the heel-ropes were free, and moved swiftly to her master, on whose bosom she dropped her head, sweating lightly.

'She came of her own accord. My horses will do that,' cried Gisborne.

'Feel if she sweats,' said Mowgli.

Gisborne laid a hand on the damp flank.

'It is enough,' said Muller.

'It is enough,' Mowgli repeated, and a rock behind him threw back the word.

'That's uncanny, isn't it?' said Gisborne.

'No, only wonderful — most wonderful. Still you do not know, Gisborne?'

'I confess I don't.'

'Well, then, I shall not tell. He says dot some day he will show you what it is. It would be gruel if I told. But why he is not dead I do not understand. Now listen thou.' Muller faced Mowgli, and returned to the vernacular. 'I am the head of all the *rukhs* in the country of India and others across the Black Water. I do not know how many men be under me — perhaps five thousand, perhaps ten. Thy business is this, — to wander no more up and down the *rukh* and drive beasts for sport or for show, but to take service under me, who am the Government in

the matter of Woods and Forests, and to live in the *rukh* as a
forest-guard; to drive the villagers' goats away when there is no
order to feed them in the *rukh*; to admit them when there is an
order; to keep down, as thou canst keep down, the boar and
the nilghai when they become too many; to tell Gisborne Sahib
how and where tigers move, and what game there is in the
forests; and to give sure warning of all fires in the *rukh*, for
thou canst give warning more quickly than any other. For that
work there is a payment each month in silver, and at the end,
when thou hast gathered a wife and cattle and, maybe, children,
a pension. What answer?'

'That's just what I ——' Gisborne began.

'My Sahib spoke this morning of such a service. I walked all
day alone considering the matter, and my answer is ready here.
I serve, *if* I serve in this *rukh* and no other: *with* Gisborne Sahib
and with no other.'

'It shall be so. In a week comes the written order that pledges
the honour of the Government for the pension. After that thou
wilt take up thy hut where Gisborne Sahib shall appoint.'

'I was going to speak to you about it,' said Gisborne.

'I did not want to be told when I saw that man. Dere will
never be a forest-guard like him. He is a miracle. I tell you, Gisborne, some day you will find it so. Listen, he is blood-brother
to every beast in der *rukh*!'

'I should be easier in my mind if I could understand him.'

'Dot will come. Now I tell you dot only once in my service,
and dot is thirty years, haf I met a boy dot began as this man
began. Und he died. Sometimes you hear of dem in der census
reports, but dey all die. Dis man haf lived, and he is an an-
achronism, for he is before der Iron Age, and der Stone Age.
Look here, he is at der beginnings of der history of man —
Adam in der Garden, und now we want only an Eva! No! He
is older than dot child-tale, shust as der *rukh* is older dan der
gods. Gisborne, I am a Bagan now, once for all.'

Through the rest of the long evening Muller sat smoking

and smoking, and staring and staring into the darkness, his lips moving in multiplied quotations, and great wonder upon his face. He went to his tent, but presently came out again in his majestic pink sleeping-suit, and the last words that Gisborne heard him address to the *rukh* through the deep hush of midnight were these, delivered with immense emphasis:—

> 'Dough we shivt und bedeck und bedrape us,
>   Dou art noble und nude und andeek;
> Libidina dy moder, Briapus
>   Dy fader, a God und a Greek.

Now I know dot, Bagan *or* Christian, I shall nefer know der inwardness of der *rukh*!'

. . . . .

It was midnight in the bungalow a week later when Abdul Gafur, ashy gray with rage, stood at the foot of Gisborne's bed and whispering bade him awake.

'Up, Sahib,' he stammered. 'Up and bring thy gun. Mine honour is gone. Up and kill before any see.'

The old man's face had changed, so that Gisborne stared stupidly.

'It was for this, then, that that jungle outcaste helped me to polish the Sahib's table, and drew water and plucked fowls. They have gone off together for all my beatings, and now he sits among his devils dragging her soul to the Pit. Up, Sahib, and come with me!'

He thrust a rifle into Gisborne's half-wakened hand and almost dragged him from the room on to the verandah.

'They are there in the *rukh*; even within gunshot of the house. Come softly with me.'

'But what is it? What is the trouble, Abdul?'

'Mowgli, and his devils. Also my own daughter,' said Abdul Gafur. Gisborne whistled and followed his guide. Not for nothing, he knew, had Abdul Gafur beaten his daughter of nights, and not for nothing had Mowgli helped in the housework a man whom his own powers, whatever those were, had convicted of theft. Also, a forest wooing goes quickly.

There was the breathing of a flute in the *rukh*, as it might have been the song of some wandering wood-god, and, as they came nearer, a murmur of voices. The path ended in a little semi-circular glade walled partly by high grass and partly by trees. In the centre, upon a fallen trunk, his back to the watchers and his arm round the neck of Abdul Gafur's daughter, sat Mowgli, newly crowned with flowers, playing upon a rude bamboo flute, to whose music four huge wolves danced solemnly on their hind legs.

'Those are his devils,' Abdul Gafur whispered. He held a bunch of cartridges in his hand. The beasts dropped to a long-drawn quavering note and lay still with steady green eyes, glaring at the girl.

'Behold,' said Mowgli, laying aside the flute. 'Is there anything of fear in that? I told thee, little Stout-heart, that there was not, and thou didst believe. Thy father said — and oh, if thou couldst have seen thy father being driven by the road of the nilghai! — thy father said that they were devils; and by Allah, who is thy God, I do not wonder that he so believed.'

The girl laughed a little rippling laugh, and Gisborne heard Abdul grind his few remaining teeth. This was not at all the girl that Gisborne had seen with a half-eye slinking about the compound veiled and silent, but another — a woman full blown in a night as the orchid puts out in an hour's moist heat.

'But they are my playmates and my brothers, children of that mother that gave me suck, as I told thee behind the cook-house,' Mowgli went on. 'Children of the father that lay between me and the cold at the mouth of the cave when I was a little naked child. Look' — a wolf raised his gray jowl, slavering at Mowgli's knee — 'my brother knows that I speak of them. Yes, when I was a little child he was a cub rolling with me on the clay.'

'But thou hast said that thou art human-born,' cooed the girl, nestling closer to the shoulder. 'Thou art human-born?'

'Said! Nay, I know that I am human-born, because my heart is in thy hold, little one.' Her head dropped under Mowgli's chin. Gisborne put up a warning hand to restrain Abdul Gafur, who was not in the least impressed by the wonder of the sight.

'But I was a wolf among wolves none the less till a time came when Those of the Jungle bade me go because I was a man.'

'Who bade thee go? That is not like a true man's talk.'

'The very beasts themselves. Little one, thou wouldst never believe that telling, but so it was. The beasts of the Jungle bade me go, but these four followed me because I was their brother. Then was I a herder of cattle among men, having learned their language. Ho! ho! The herds paid toll to my brothers, till a woman, an old woman, beloved, saw me playing by night with my brethren in the crops. They said that I was possessed of devils, and drove me from that village with sticks and stones, and the four came with me by stealth and not openly. That was when I had learned to eat cooked meat and to talk boldly. From village to village I went, heart of my heart, a herder of cattle, a tender of buffaloes, a tracker of game, but there was no man that dared lift a finger against me twice.' He stooped down and patted one of the heads. 'Do thou also like this. There is neither hurt nor magic in them. See, they know thee.'

'The woods are full of all manner of devils,' said the girl with a shudder.

'A lie. A child's lie,' Mowgli returned confidently. 'I have lain out in the dew under the stars and in the dark night, and I know. The jungle is my house. Shall a man fear his own roof-beams or a woman her man's hearth? Stoop down and pat them.'

'They are dogs and unclean,' she murmured, bending forward with averted head.

'Having eaten the fruit, now we remember the Law!' said

Abdul Gafur bitterly. 'What is the need of this waiting, Sahib? Kill!'

'H'sh, thou. Let us learn what has happened,' said Gisborne.

'That is well done,' said Mowgli, slipping his arm round the girl again. 'Dogs or no dogs, they were with me through a thousand villages.'

'Ahi, and where was thy heart then? Through a thousand villages. Thou hast seen a thousand maids. I — have I thy heart?'

'What shall I swear by? By Allah, of whom thou speakest?'

'Nay, by the life that is in thee, and I am well content. Where was thy heart in those days?'

Mowgli laughed a little. 'In my belly, because I was young and always hungry. So I learned to track and to hunt, sending and calling my brothers back and forth as a king calls his armies. Therefore I drove the nilghai for the foolish young Sahib, and the big fat mare for the big fat Sahib, when they questioned my power. It were as easy to have driven the men themselves. Even now,' his voice lifted a little — 'even now I know that behind me stand thy father and Gisborne Sahib. Nay, do not run, for no ten men dare move a pace forward. Remembering that thy father beat thee more than once, shall I give the word and drive him again in rings through the *rukh*?' A wolf stood up with bared teeth.

Gisborne felt Abdul Gafur tremble at his side. Next, his place was empty, and the fat man was skimming down the glade.

'Remains only Gisborne Sahib,' said Mowgli, still without turning; 'but I have eaten Gisborne Sahib's bread, and presently I shall be in his service, and my brothers will be his servants to drive game and carry the news. Hide thou in the grass.'

The girl fled, the tall grass closed behind her and the guardian wolf that followed, and Mowgli turning with his three retainers faced Gisborne as the Forest Officer came forward.

'That is all the magic,' he said, pointing to the three. 'The fat

Sahib knew that we who are bred among wolves run on our elbows and our knees for a season. Feeling my arms and legs, he felt the truth which thou didst not know. Is it so wonderful, Sahib?'

'Indeed it is all more wonderful than magic. These, then, drove the nilghai?'

'Ay, as they would drive Eblis if I gave the order. They are my eyes and feet to me.'

'Look to it, then, that Eblis does not carry a double rifle. They have yet something to learn, thy devils, for they stand one behind the other, so that two shots would kill the three.'

'Ah, but they know they will be thy servants as soon as I am a forest-guard.'

'Guard or no guard, Mowgli, thou hast done a great shame to Abdul Gafur. Thou hast dishonoured his house and blackened his face.'

'For that, it was blackened when he took thy money, and made blacker still when he whispered in thy ear a little while since to kill a naked man. I myself will talk to Abdul Gafur, for I am a man of the Government service, with a pension. He shall make the marriage by whatsoever rite he will, or he shall run once more. I will speak to him in the dawn. For the rest, the Sahib has his house and this is mine. It is time to sleep again, Sahib.'

Mowgli turned on his heel and disappeared into the grass, leaving Gisborne alone. The hint of the wood-god was not to be mistaken; and Gisborne went back to the bungalow, where Abdul Gafur, torn by rage and fear, was raving in the verandah.

'Peace, peace,' said Gisborne, shaking him, for he looked as though he were going to have a fit. 'Muller Sahib has made the man a forest-guard, and as thou knowest there is a pension at the end of that business, and it is Government service.'

'He is an outcaste — a *mlech* — a dog among dogs; an eater of carrion! What pension can pay for that?'

'Allah knows; and thou hast heard that the mischief is done.

Wouldst thou blaze it to all the other servants? Make the *shadi* swiftly, and the girl will make him a Mussulman. He is very comely. Canst thou wonder that after thy beatings she went to him?'

'Did he say that he would chase me with his beasts?'

'So it seemed to me. If he be a wizard, he is at least a very strong one.'

Abdul Gafur thought awhile, and then broke down and howled, forgetting that he was a Mussulman: —

'Thou art a Brahmin. I am thy cow. Make thou the matter plain, and save my honour if it can be saved!'

A second time then Gisborne plunged into the *rukh* and called Mowgli. The answer came from high overhead, and in no submissive tones.

'Speak softly,' said Gisborne, looking up. 'There is yet time to strip thee of thy place and hunt thee with thy wolves. The girl must go back to her father's house to-night. To-morrow there will be the *shadi*, by the Mussulman law, and then thou canst take her away. Bring her to Abdul Gafur.'

'I hear.' There was a murmur of two voices conferring among the leaves. 'Also, we will obey — for the last time.'

.   .   .   .   .   .

A year later Muller and Gisborne were riding through the *rukh* together, talking of their business. They came out among the rocks near the Kanye stream; Muller riding a little in advance. Under the shade of a thorn thicket sprawled a naked brown baby, and from the brake immediately behind him peered the head of a gray wolf. Gisborne had just time to strike up Muller's rifle, and the bullet tore spattering through the branches above.

'Are you mad?' thundered Muller. 'Look!'

'I see,' said Gisborne quietly. 'The mother's somewhere near. You'll wake the whole pack, by Jove!'

The bushes parted once more, and a woman unveiled snatched up the child.

'Who fired, Sahib?' she cried to Gisborne.

'This Sahib. He had not remembered thy man's people.'

'Not remembered? But indeed it may be so, for we who live with them forget that they are strangers at all. Mowgli is down the stream catching fish. Does the Sahib wish to see him? Come out, ye lacking manners. Come out of the bushes, and make your service to the Sahibs.'

Muller's eyes grew rounder and rounder. He swung himself off the plunging mare and dismounted, while the jungle gave up four wolves who fawned round Gisborne. The mother stood nursing her child and spurning them aside as they brushed against her bare feet.

'You were quite right about Mowgli,' said Gisborne. 'I meant to have told you, but I've got so used to these fellows in the last twelve months that it slipped my mind.'

'Oh, don't apologise,' said Muller. 'It's nothing. Gott in Himmel! "Und I work miracles — und dey come off too!"'

THE ONLY SON

She dropped the bar, she shot the bolt, she fed the fire anew,
For she heard a whimper under the sill and a great gray paw came through.
The fresh flame comforted the hut and shone on the roof-beam,
And the Only Son lay down again and dreamed that he dreamed a dream.
The last ash fell from the withered log with the click of a falling spark,
And the Only Son woke up again, and called across the dark: —
'Now was I born of womankind and laid in a mother's breast?
For I have dreamed of a shaggy hide whereon I went to rest.
And was I born of womankind and laid on a father's arm?
For I have dreamed of clashing teeth that guarded me from harm.
And was I born an Only Son and did I play alone?
For I have dreamed of comrades twain that bit me to the bone.
And did I break the barley-cake and steep it in the tyre?
For I have dreamed of a youngling kid new-riven from the byre:
For I have dreamed of a midnight sky and a midnight call to blood,
And red-mouthed shadows racing by, that thrust me from my food.
'Tis an hour yet and an hour yet to the rising of the moon,
But I can see the black roof-tree as plain as it were noon.
'Tis a league and a league to the Lena Falls where the trooping blackbuck
    go,
But I can hear the little fawn that bleats behind the doe.
'Tis a league and a league to the Lena Falls where the crop and the upland
    meet,
But I can smell the wet dawn-wind that wakes the sprouting wheat.
Unbar the door, I may not bide, but I must out and see
If those are wolves that wait outside or my own kin to me!'

. . . .

She loosed the bar, she slid the bolt, she opened the door anon,
And a gray bitch-wolf came out of the dark and fawned on the Only Son!